THE
SPIRIT HOLLOWS

THE
SPIRIT HOLLOWS

P.R. BREWER

First paperback edition 2021

Cover design by James T. Egan of Bookfly Design
Layout by Bodie D. Dykstra of BD Book Design
Map by LeslieAnn Khoury of Lizard Ink Maps

ISBN 978-1-7354440-0-0 (paperback)
ISBN 978-1-7354440-1-7 (ebook)

Published by Lockegee Books
Newark, Delaware

www.prbrewer.com

For Mom & Dad

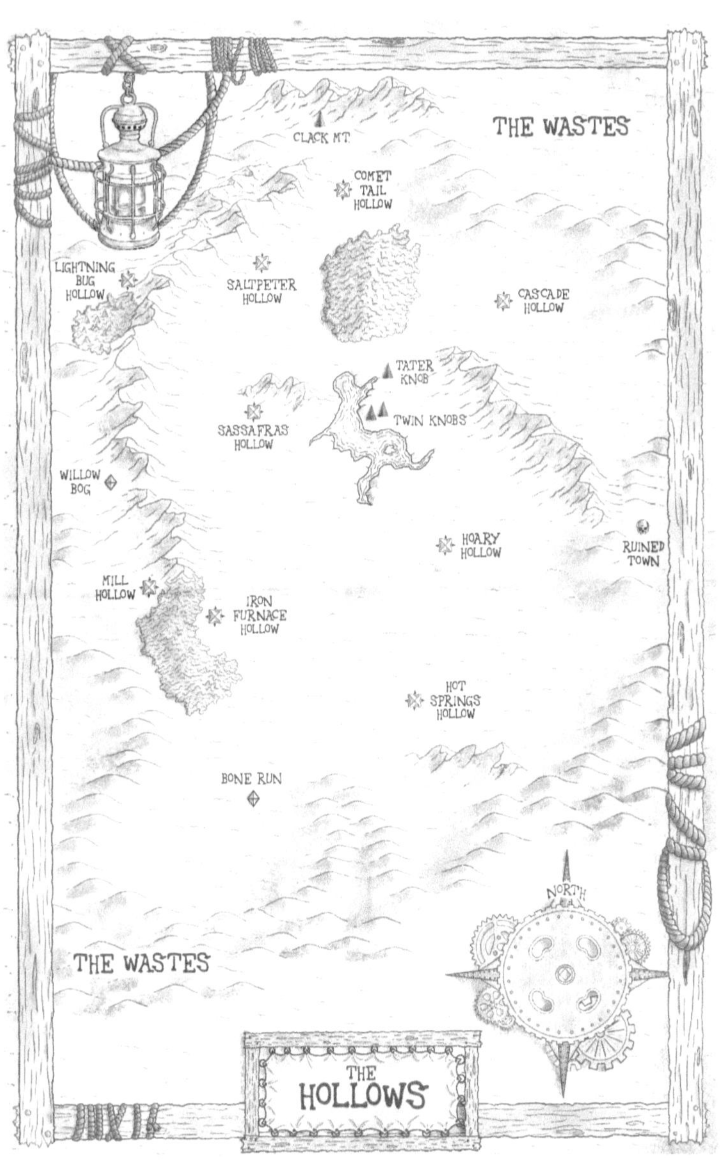

THE WASTES
CLACK MT.
COMET TAIL HOLLOW
LIGHTNING BUG HOLLOW
SALTPETER HOLLOW
CASCADE HOLLOW
TATER KNOB
TWIN KNOBS
SASSAFRAS HOLLOW
WILLOW BOG
HOARY HOLLOW
RUINED TOWN
MILL HOLLOW
IRON FURNACE HOLLOW
HOT SPRINGS HOLLOW
BONE RUN
THE WASTES
NORTH
THE HOLLOWS

PART ONE

THE ENGINEER'S DAUGHTER &
THE UNDERTAKER'S SON

1

QUINN SWITCHED OFF THE WAGON'S RADIO AND STARTED WATCHING for spirits in the pines. He didn't know what lay waiting down the road, or when he would find Lightning Bug Hollow. The sun had disappeared behind the hills and left him as easy pickings.

This Zora girl had better be real.

With a thump, the wheels jolted over a line of half buried railroad tracks. The headlamps blinked, as though signaling unseen presences to materialize all around him.

Quinn clucked at the horses to hurry. Ursula and Undine had warmed up to him right away, but the drive had taken longer than any of his trips on the seat of the Prosser family hearse, and his tailbone ached. Too bad he wasn't flying a zeppelin above the woods that stretched to the horizon. He would've jumped at an apprenticeship as a sky pilot—a chance to soar on wind currents and drift by cloudbanks, free from the stink of formaldehyde on his clothes—if only airships still existed and had places to go outside the Hollows.

Two yellow spots in his path startled him back to earth. A whitetail deer barred the way. The animal's eyes gleamed with reflected light, and early summer velvet coated its crown of antlers.

Before Quinn could pull on the reins, the whitetail dashed into the forest. He let out his breath. Spooked by a deer. At least the horses hadn't shied at it, or even broken stride.

The next bend brought the ruin of a shack into view. It sat a stone's throw from the road, ringed by bare ash. "Ho," he called out. Ursula and Undine halted short of a sign emblazoned with a skull in glowing paint.

It was a warning. A spirit had taken possession of this place—and not just any sort of spirit, but an elemental.

Quinn's hands trembled as he surveyed the shack's weathered siding. The holes in the roof. The jagged glass that rimmed the window frames. From the looks of it, the spirit had dwelled here since the Great Wakening.

The route forward led right past the thing.

Quinn braced his boots against the footboard. He'd skipped his chance yesterday at rushing back to Mom, and the funeral parlor, and the rest of his embalmed life. Anyhow, elementals were earthbound spirits. The one below the ruin shouldn't trouble him so long as he kept his distance.

"Walk on," he told the horses. To steady himself, he set to humming the song about the fiddler girl who'd beguiled a horde of wandering spirits away from the Hollows and into the Wastes. Of all the heroes from the old ballads, she was his favorite.

Midway through the second verse, a moth with eyespots on its wings flitted across the boundary of the blighted circle. Ursula pricked up her ears. A vibration rumbled in Quinn's molars, and the insides of his mouth turned cottony.

Traces of pale green foxfire crept in the gloom along the porch. As they spread across the lifeless ground, phosphorescent smoke rose to shroud the ruin. The moth flapped toward safety, but the vapors engulfed it, blackening its wings and crumbling it to dust.

Undine snorted. "Easy," Quinn managed to say, despite the dizziness sweeping over him.

The horses passed the skull sign, then the elemental itself. Quinn's vertigo faded, and the pulsing in his jaw slowed. From this angle, he could make out the remains of a tractor: an oil-powered one from long ago, abandoned to rust forever beside the shack.

He sagged in the seat as the adrenaline drained from his blood. The horses relaxed, and the wagon rolled onward.

HILDY'S INN, read the neon orange letters in the dusk ahead. They shone from the window of a low-slung building with solar panels patched on its tin roof. Beyond lay a narrow valley flanked by steep hillsides.

That must be Lightning Bug Hollow. Quinn parked the wagon and hopped down to hitch the horses to the rail.

"Howdy there, young man," called a scarf-headed woman in a rocking chair by the door. She stood and waved him into a room crammed with mismatched tables and stools. Checkered curtains and butter-colored walls gave it a cozy feel. "You look like you've come a ways."

"Three days to Sassafras Hollow, and two to here." He rubbed the scruff on his chin, which he hadn't shaved since setting out from home.

The wrinkles around the innkeeper's eyes deepened. "Are you kin to the tinkerer's daughter, by any chance?"

So his father had been telling the truth. "You mean Zora Coldiron?"

"She's the one."

Quinn nodded. "That's what I came to find out. Is it much farther to her house?"

"Thought I saw a family resemblance. Different hair, though." The innkeeper's lips twitched. "She's a bright kid, if a bit of a—never mind that, you'll meet her soon enough. The Coldirons live up the back of the hollow. Can I get you some food, or charge your wagon's battery?"

"A meal for the road sounds good." He swallowed the temptation to ask for gossip about his half-sister. If he didn't get a move on, Zora and her mother might be asleep when he arrived. And they might not take kindly to an unexpected stranger rousing them from their beds.

The innkeeper left through a pair of swinging doors, then came back with a slice of cornbread, a bottle of birch beer, and a paper bowl. Quinn salivated at the smell of smoked meat.

"My special burgoo," she said. "Grouse and rabbit. That's three bits. Sure you don't want to stay here and head on in the morning?"

"Thank you, but no. Not after coming this far already." Nor after spending seventeen years as an only child. He handed over the coins and went back out to the wagon.

Katydid chirps from the tall grass and bullfrog croaks from a dark pond accompanied the horses' hoofbeats during the ride through the hollow. The three-quarter moon cast soft light on vegetable gardens, rows of corn, and barns with hex signs painted on their fronts. Candles flickered from the windows of small, white houses.

A spirit like the one under the ruin could've snuffed the life from any of them.

The road ended at a one-story house. Antennae bristled from its roof, and wires ran from its eaves to a barn decorated with a network of lines connecting circles, squares, and triangles—a diagram of a circuit, rather than the usual star or rosette.

Quinn brought the horses to a stop and tied them to a post topped with a blue lamp. Probably one of those electrified bug-killers. Strips of reflective tape on a nearby mailbox spelled out FIONA COLDIRON—ENGINEER.

As he climbed the steps to the porch, his heartbeat sped up to match the clanking that emanated from the barn. He fidgeted with the bottom of his flannel shirt, pushed his hair from his eyes, and knocked.

Voices whispered inside the house, and then muffled footsteps approached the threshold. The door opened to reveal a short woman with copper-framed glasses and reddish-orange hair that showed gray streaks.

"Ms. Coldiron?" he asked.

"Yes?" She folded her arms across her chest.

"Pardon me for bothering you at this hour. My name's Quinn. Quinn Prosser, that is. Of Cascade Hollow." He hesitated. "I'm Vernon Moss's son."

The woman stared at him. "Vern's son?"

"That's right, ma'am. He sent me here with a message for Zora."

"Well, this is a surprise." After a long pause, she recovered herself. "A pleasant surprise."

Ms. Coldiron took Quinn's arm and ushered him to the living room. The wide-eyed girl in the floral print armchair didn't stand to greet him. She was in her mid-teens—maybe two years younger than him—with a freckled face and auburn hair pulled into pigtails. Her snub nose looked like the one he saw in the mirror every morning.

"Mom, is what he said . . ." she began, before trailing off with an air of bewilderment. He'd felt the same way when he'd learned about her, so that was another thing they had in common.

"Quinn, this is Zora." Ms. Coldiron patted the girl's shoulder. "Zora, your half-brother Quinn."

Zora gave him a tentative wave. He returned it with the widest smile he could muster.

"I didn't know," Ms. Coldiron murmured to her daughter. "I would've told you." She stroked the girl's pigtails. "Your father should've told me."

"I just found out the day before yesterday," said Quinn.

The mother filled a glass of water from a pitcher and brought it to him. "The last we heard from Vern was eight years ago this spring," she said. "He went off on one of his journeys and kept on going."

"That's right around when he stopped visiting or writing me." Back then, Quinn had hung on every word of his father's tales about seeing the Boiling Cauldron in Hot Springs Hollow, and the four-story library in Hoary Hollow, and the Grand Court where the Judges convened every fall for the All Hollows celebrations. "No explanation, nothing." He took a long drink and fumed.

"How is he?" Ms. Coldiron asked. "Still rambling from valley to valley and flirting with all the ladies?"

Quinn almost choked on his water. "He's called it quits as a peddler and gone back to the old Moss family farm."

"Now *that* doesn't sound like Vern," said Ms. Coldiron. "Did his ways finally catch up to him?"

"He told me he was fine." Quinn couldn't keep the sourness from his voice. "Just tired of living out of his wagon. Said it was time to gather some moss."

Zora frowned from her armchair. "Ha," she muttered.

Quinn decided he was going to like her.

"I'm sure he'd been saving that line for a long time," said Ms. Coldiron. "If that's what he wants, I hope it suits him. And your mother? I'm afraid I don't know her."

"Anne Prosser." He inspected his fingernails. They had dirt beneath them, like usual. "She's an undertaker." Folks sometimes got skittish when he told them that, as if he'd reminded them of their own mortality.

But Ms. Coldiron wasn't fazed. "I'd like to meet her someday and talk chemistry. Are you her assistant?"

"I've been helping around the parlor since I finished school this spring," Quinn said. "Beyond that, I haven't figured it out yet." All five of his classmates—including Paige Zhu—had already started their apprenticeships. Meanwhile, he'd been spending his time between funerals ignoring concerned looks from his mom and reading the latest batch of pulp novels he'd bought from the roving bookseller. *Addie the Urchin versus the Sorceress of Steam. Vampire Pirates of Red River Gorge. Voyage of the Mole-Ship to the Mastodon Caverns.* Stories about young adventurers who unearthed ancient enigmas or laid dark forces to rest, instead of digging graves and bearing palls.

"You don't want to be a mortician yourself?" said Ms. Coldiron. "I understand it's a steady trade."

He winced at the thought of going back to the hollow where everybody had him pegged as Pine-Box Prosser, successor to the family business. Mom had told him to take the summer off, though leaving home still felt like deserting her. "I'd like to see more sights besides the local cemeteries," he said.

The metallic drone from the barn filled the lull that followed.

"Though not as a peddler," he added.

"You mentioned you had a message for me," Zora said, in a firmer voice than before.

"Right. A few days after the solstice, I got a letter from our father asking me to call on him. When I showed up, he told me about his plan to retire. And about you." The electric lamplight picked out the dusting of acne across Zora's forehead and the grease stains on her brown overalls. "He said that since he didn't need his horses and wagon anymore, you and I could have them." She perked up at that. "Said he owed us as much."

"There's an understatement," put in Ms. Coldiron.

"So, I came here to meet y'all and talk over what to do," Quinn finished.

A look passed between mother and daughter. "What did you have in mind?" Ms. Coldiron asked.

"Undine and Ursula are good draft horses," he said. "Six and seven years old, even-tempered. The wagon is solid, too— it has two bunks, a stove, and a built-in battery. All told, they'd fetch a nice sum if we sold them."

Zora held up a finger. "How about we don't?"

"I'm open to that," said Quinn, "but what would you—or I—do with them?" Maybe she wanted to deliver widgets and whatnots for her mother.

"I'd like to demonstrate something to you." Zora sounded excited. "Outside. It's night now, so—"

"Quinn's traveled far to see us," interrupted Ms. Coldiron. "We should let him rest, and you can show him tomorrow."

"I don't mean to impose," he said. "I'm okay sleeping in the wagon."

Ms. Coldiron opened a trunk and pulled out a coverlet embroidered with lightning bolts and horseshoes. "You'll do no such thing. You're family, and you're staying in our home."

"That's kind of you." He rose to his feet. "Though I'm curious to see this demonstration, after I get Ursula and Undine settled. Mind if I put them up in your barn?"

"I'll go with you." Zora picked up two bronze-shafted forearm crutches from beside her chair. Gripping their handles, she stood and set off at a brisk pace.

As Quinn trailed her out the door, she glanced back and caught him gawking at her crutches. "Are you an engineer like your mom?" he asked.

"Wait and see," she said.

Once he'd unharnessed the horses, Zora led him to the barn and flipped a switch. A row of incandescent lights came to life in the rafters. Half a dozen goats bleated from a pen, and a sturdy-looking steam generator chugged away in one of the far corners.

He brushed the horses, watered them, gave them each a carrot for working so hard, and fed them some hay. When he was done, he followed Zora to a table cluttered with gears, wires, and all manner of doodads.

His half-sister grabbed a pair of blue-tinted goggles, put them on so that the lenses rested on her forehead, and then gave him another pair. "Wear these, but don't pull them over your eyes yet." She pointed at two oddly shaped devices. "Bring these, too."

One of the devices looked like a brass-plated crossbow with a flashlight mounted on its front and a panel of little bulbs on its top. The other resembled a shotgun, except that the barrel—a tube of thick glass—opened into a silver fan-like muzzle. "Be careful with my equipment," she called over her shoulder on her way back outside.

Quinn carried the crossbow-flashlight in one hand and the shotgun-fan in the other as she guided him into the woods behind the barn. The path was barely visible by the moonlight.

"So you're my big brother," Zora said. "This'll take some getting used to."

"I always wanted a sister." He tried to envision what it would've been like growing up with her. Less dreary, from what he'd seen so far. Less lonely, too.

"Better late than never, I hope."

Quinn stumbled into a clump of rhododendron. "Are you sure it's safe out here?" he asked.

"Worried we might run into a spirit?" She didn't slow down.

"Yes, now that you mention it." Particularly with the image of the elemental still lingering in his mind.

"You shouldn't be. Not while you're with me."

What in the Wastes did she mean? For all he knew, she was bringing him to the secret rites of the Spiritists.

Zora came to a fork and took the left-hand path. "Know how this hollow got its new name after the Great Wakening?"

"On account of the lightning bugs?"

She laughed. "We get those, but that's not why. Stop here."

Below them yawned a pit as wide across as a house. She sat with her legs dangling over the edge.

Quinn leaned forward. Nothing but darkness. "I reckon it's more impressive by day."

"We're not here for the sinkhole. We're here for what's in it. Keep watching." After a minute or so, a shimmering, yellowish-green point appeared. Then another, and another, as a faint buzzing came from the pit.

"It's started." Zora flipped down her goggles. "Give me the illuminator."

"The what?"

"The thing you have in your right hand."

He gave her the crossbow-flashlight.

"You'll need your goggles for this," she said.

He pulled them over his eyes, and Zora flicked a button on the device. It emitted a grainy pop as one of the bulbs on its panel turned orange. She pushed a second button, and a cone of blue light shone down into the sinkhole. Thousands of luminescent motes floated within the beam.

Quinn took a step backward. "Not insects, I take it."

"Correct. They're wisps."

"I don't believe I've heard of those before."

"Tiny earthbound spirits. The sinkhole is full of them. They come out at night when people are around."

Above the pit, miniature constellations formed, collapsed, and reformed in new shapes. "Can they hurt us?" Quinn asked.

"Nope. They're not strong enough to give you more than a mild tingle. All they do is fly around for a while and then settle back down. It's easy to mistake them for lightning bugs."

"So this illuminator helps find wisps?"

"Or any other spirits. It also dampens their power. Not as much as daylight would, but enough to weaken them."

Quinn shook his head. "Where in the Hollows did you get that thing?"

"I made it myself." She grinned. "But you haven't seen the best part. Take the device you're holding and aim it at the wisps."

"Like this?" He pointed the shotgun-fan toward the sinkhole.

"Exactly. Now fire it."

When he tapped the trigger, violet light crackled through the glass tube and out from the silver fan. The wisps touched by the ray disappeared in little puffs. The remaining spirits roiled with an angry whine and then streamed down into the pit.

"They're gone," he said in a hushed voice.

"I call that one the banisher."

"You made this, too? How do they work?"

"Both devices produce a form of energy, the kind that's in the spirits themselves. It's not electricity." She was talking faster and faster. "All the theories about the spirits being electromagnetic in nature are wrong."

What theories? He opened his mouth to speak, but she cut him off. "The illuminator creates a beam that resonates with the spirits to make them fluoresce if you're wearing these cobalt-filtered goggles. The banisher's argon tube generates a different wavelength of the same energy, one that does *something* to spirits, I'm still not sure what—maybe it destroys them, or maybe it sends them back to wherever they came from during the Wakenings."

"That seems"—he struggled for a word—"handy."

"Naturally. That's why I invented them." She gave him the illuminator. The orange bulb on its panel had turned dark again. "We're done here. Let's head back."

They retraced their steps until the treetops no longer hid the stars of the Big Dipper and the Northern Crown. "How strong is the, what did you call it, vanisher?" Quinn asked.

"Banisher. In principle, it should work on any of the common types of spirit."

"What sorts have you tried it on?"

Zora didn't reply right away. "So far, just the wisps, plus a boge that was hassling the neighbors' cows. You know boges, right—the pesky roamers?"

"I'm acquainted with them." He'd had a mortifying encounter with one last fall when Paige had talked him into sneaking away from the Harvest Festival to investigate stories of a pint-sized spirit in their hollow. She'd sold him on the idea that it would be more memorable than standing around the bonfire or dancing to the music—though he'd enjoyed the slow-dancing just fine—not to mention good practice for her upcoming apprenticeship as a Spotter. "Why'd you want to show me all this?" he asked Zora.

"How would you like to take that wagon on the road with me and hunt spirits?"

He stopped short. "*Hunt* them?" His half-sister seemed awfully young to be dabbling in such things.

"I could do the planning." She raised, and then lowered, one arm and crutch. "You could do the driving and the shooting. We'd be partners."

Quinn looked at her. He wasn't tall himself, but she only came up to his chin. "We'd be risking our hides tramping around at night. Just on the way here, I saw—"

"The elemental at the old station agent's house. But the Spotters marked that thing more than a hundred years ago, along with most the other big earthbounds in the Hollows. We can steer clear of those if we watch for the signs and stay on the beaten track."

"Maybe so, but what about the roamers?" His grandmother—Grandma Prosser, not the Grandma Moss who'd died before he was born—had given him childhood nightmares with her stories about how some of the giant ones could skeletonize a person in seconds.

"The deadlier types hardly ever leave the Wastes," said Zora. "Tall tales to the contrary. I'm sure my inventions can handle the rest."

Spirit-hunting. That might beat life as an assistant undertaker, or a traveling huckster. Or even an apprentice Spotter like Paige.

"Will you do it?" Zora leaned on her crutches and shuffled her feet. "Please say yes."

Quinn weighed the question. If he went along with her, they could start making up for the time together their father had cheated from them. And he could keep an eye out in case she got herself in trouble. Wasn't that what older siblings did?

On an impulse, he leveled the banisher at a tree.

"Go ahead," she told him. "It won't hurt anything that's not a spirit."

He squeezed the trigger and landed a hit at the center of the trunk. The sight galvanized him, as if the violet energy from the device had flowed through his own veins.

"I'll think on it," he said.

Ms. Coldiron was waiting for them when they came back into the house. "I assume Zora's tried to recruit you for her schemes," she said to Quinn.

"That she did."

"It's not like he's doing anything more important," said Zora. Then she turned to him, abashed. "Sorry, that came out—"

"Zora, could you shut down the generator?" asked Ms. Coldiron.

"But Mom—"

"I'd like to talk to Quinn alone."

Zora left without another word, her crutches and boots sounding out a double-time stomp.

Quinn held his peace. His half-sister might be brash, but she had a point.

"Zora and I have lived in Lightning Bug Hollow since she was born," Ms. Coldiron said, after the door clicked shut. "I've taught her everything I know by now—how to build corn-diesel generators, selenium photocells, clockwork engines, and just about anything else we can with the resources in the Hollows. She's a brilliant engineer."

"That's clear," Quinn said.

"She could have a comfortable life here, and one day take over my trade." Ms. Coldiron lit a pair of candles. "Instead, my daughter is dead set on fighting the spirits. She has been"— her voice faltered—"ever since she was seven. Many others have tried, of course. To my knowledge, none has ever succeeded."

The electric lamps in the living room winked out, but the blue one by the road stayed lit. Not a bug-killer at all, but some battery-powered spirit-ward of Zora's. More effective than a hex sign, he supposed.

"The wisps she's been experimenting on may be harmless," Ms. Coldiron said into the candlelight, "but they're nothing compared to what else is out there. I'm inclined to forbid her from launching this expedition of hers until she's older and has conducted more research under—let's say—controlled conditions."

By which time his summer away from home would be long over. Quinn took a deep breath. "What if I give you my word I'll try to look out for her?"

"I've heard promises like that before." Ms. Coldiron pushed her glasses up her nose. "How do I know I can trust yours?"

"I won't let Zora down," he said. Outside the window, his half-sister walked past the wagon. *Their* wagon. "I'm different from our father."

Ms. Coldiron sighed. "Stay with us a few days, and we'll see."

Quinn nodded and crossed the threshold to join Zora on the porch. The noise from the generator had stopped, leaving only the calls of the katydids.

"Well?" she said.

"Your mother didn't sound too keen on your plan."

"Let me deal with her," Zora said. "I can beg and bargain till she says yes. What do *you* want?"

An owl hooted from somewhere in the valley. "What I want," he said, "is to go on a genuine adventure with my long-lost sister."

She beamed at him. "Good answer, big brother."

Quinn rested his elbows beside Zora's on the front railing. Maybe this was his chance to follow in the footsteps of the fiddler girl from the legends, traveling the Hollows and protecting people from spirits.

Though come to think of it, that hadn't worked out so well for her in the end.

2

ZORA TAPPED HER FOOT ON THE GROUND. DAWN HAD BROKEN above the hump of Cloud Splitter Ridge, chasing the fog from the hollow below. She was ready to teach the spirits that they should be frightened of her, not the other way around.

"Remember our deal," lectured her mom. "Stick to—"

"The ones that can't hurt us," said Zora. "Write to you every chance I get. Visit you every half moon." She'd spent the past three days negotiating for permission to leave home. In her spare time, she'd overhauled the wagon by rewiring its headlamps and attaching solar panels to its roof. Quinn had pitched in by painting COLDIRON & PROSSER VENTURES over the lettering that read VERNON MOSS—HARDWARE—ELIXIRS—SUNDRIES.

"I loaded your trunks," her brother called out. He was standing by the wagon's doorway, all doe-eyed in his slate-gray shirt and dusty corduroys. "They're mighty heavy. What's in them— bars of lead you plan on turning into gold?"

"Scientific equipment," she said. "I'm not some storybook alchemist." She watched from a safe distance while he harnessed Ursula and Undine. He'd sworn the chestnut-colored mares were gentle as could be, but a kick from one of those hooves could split a cranium.

Zora's mom started polishing her glasses, a sure sign she was about to get grouchy. "Don't make me regret letting you do this."

"I can take care of myself." Zora went for a farewell hug to forestall any argument. Then she took hold of the handle she'd bolted to the side of the wagon, pulled herself onto the seat, and stowed her crutches behind her.

Quinn jumped up next to her. With his flowy dark hair and high cheekbones, he looked the part of a dashing junior mortician. That must come from the Prosser side of his family tree.

"And you," Zora's mom told him. "Don't let her talk you into anything reckless."

"I'll do my best, ma'am," he said, sounding bashful.

Zora's mom gave him a wicker basket. "I packed some hard-boiled eggs, sandwiches, and apples for you both." She grabbed Zora's hand. "Be careful. You're still my little fox kit." The two of them squeezed each other's fingers before letting go.

Quinn made a kissy noise at the horses. As they started their way down the hollow, Zora glanced back. Her mom had tears on her cheeks and was holding her fist to her mouth.

"Are you all right?" Quinn asked.

"Of course." Zora fought back a sniffle. She refused to embarrass herself by crying in front of him. "This is just the first time I've left my hollow without Mom."

His eyes widened. "Will you miss it here?"

"Not hardly." They drove on through the landscape Zora had seen almost every day for the past fifteen years. The same scarecrows guarding their cornfields, the same cows grazing in their pastures. "We've never fit in, though it doesn't seem to bother Mom. There are only a few people around my age, and every single one of them is boring. All they talk about is who's courting whom, or who's going to win what at All Hollows, or how to sneak moonshine."

"You don't care about any of those things?"

Zora could tell he felt sorry for her. She lifted her chin. "Do you?"

"Maybe the courting part, if it happens to involve me."

"Ha! Are you pining for some sweetheart back in Waterfall Hollow or wherever?" Most likely that apprentice Spotter he'd mentioned several times.

"It's Cascade Hollow, and no." A wistful note had entered his voice. "Not anymore." He didn't elaborate, and she didn't ask.

Quinn stopped the wagon at Hildy's Inn to mail a letter home. He returned with a jar of blackberry preserves and fresh biscuits wrapped in aluminum foil.

"What'll your mom think about you hunting spirits?" Zora asked, as they left Lightning Bug Hollow behind.

"I wrote that I'd met you and was helping you work on your inventions," he said. "But I didn't specify what they were for. Our funeral home's been in the family for generations, and I'm not ready to tell my mom that the line of Prosser undertakers may end with her." His expression darkened. "What do you make of our father's disappearing act?"

"I was just a little kid when he went away." She fussed with her pigtails. "Why didn't he tell us about each other?"

"I asked him that. Along with why he stayed gone for so long, and why he got back in touch out of the blue. He said it was too thick a thorn patch to untangle. His words, not mine."

Poor Quinn. "My mom's still angry about what happened back then," she said. Would hearing that lessen the sting for him?

"If mine missed him for her own sake, she never showed it. Said she'd been fine before he came along and was fine without him."

"And what about you?"

Quinn stared off toward the hills, then suddenly grinned. "I'm just glad to be doing this with you, little sis."

Zora felt a surge of warmth toward him as she patted his arm. "Me, too."

Ursula and Undine clamped down their tails and made little windsucking gulps when they came to the station agent's house. The place looked as desolate as ever.

"You've never tried the banisher on that thing?" Quinn asked.

"Not yet." She'd need to build a ray tube the length of their wagon to stop an elemental—even a small one like Old Smoky here.

As they neared the dead circle, a crow glided past the skull sign and landed on the rooftop. Lucky for the bird the sun was up, thought Zora. When she was five, Mom and Dad had brought her here with a rat they'd trapped to show her what happened to anything that came too close to an elemental after sunset. After a few desperate screeches from its cage, the creature had festered into a pile of scorched fur and red innards. Within seconds, nothing had remained of it but a chalky residue.

She'd sobbed all the way home—partly from terror at the spirit, partly out of pity for the rat.

The crow spread its wings and flew away into the woods.

The wagon clattered past the empty ruin and then past the railroad tracks that had led to the cities of the Bluegrass back in the days of Zora's great-great-great-great-grandparents. Before spirits a thousand times larger than Old Smoky had overrun the lands beyond the Hollows.

During the ride through the hemlock stands of Needles Gap, she tried to instruct Quinn as to how her inventions worked. She started with the basic principles of paraoptics, but she'd lost her brother by time she made it to the difference between ectospectral amplitude and etheric modulation. "All you need to do is to point the banisher in the right direction and fire away," she assured him.

When he asked about other kinds of spirit-tech, she couldn't help but scoff. "You mean auditory necrography and phantasmal thermometry? People have played with those for decades, and what have they found? Not a cup of steamed spit."

He consulted a sepia-toned road map with one star drawn on it to mark the wisps, another for Old Smoky, and a third off to the east. "What've you learned so far about this spirit we're hunting in Saltpeter Hollow?"

"The story on the radio said the locals had never seen it before, so it's a roamer of some sort. And it broke some things, so it must be stronger than, say, a boge."

"That doesn't exactly narrow it down," he said, in his low-key, deliberate way.

She waved her hands. "Do you know how many different varieties the Spotters have catalogued?"

"I bet it's a lot. Am I right?"

"More than three hundred! I've gone through all my books, but without more information it's impossible to find a match."

Once they'd busted a few spirits, he wouldn't sound so dubious. In the meantime, she should try not to yell at him. He could still change his mind about working with her.

"We ought to make sure we know what we're getting into," said Quinn. "Like Addie the Urchin. When she needs to defeat one of the Power Mages, she always finds out everything she can about their strengths and weaknesses."

"Who?" Zora had never heard of anyone named Addie.

He frowned. "I gather you haven't read any of the novels in that series."

Urchins fighting wizards, or whatever "Power Mages" were? Her brother's own weakness must be fairy tales. "I'm sure they're riveting," she said. "But don't worry. No matter what this spirit is, we'll chase it down with the illuminator and spank it with the banisher."

"If you say so."

The horses trotted by the mouth of Glowworm Hollow (even narrower and sleepier than her own hollow) and the turnoff for the Buzzard Knob Coal Mine (long forsaken except by bats and, allegedly, a ring of Spiritists). At the next crossroads, Quinn steered them onto the pike that followed the broad, willow-filled basin of Triplet Creek.

They parked for the night at a forlorn establishment billing itself as the Possum Lick Trading Post. After a supper of cornmeal-crusted bluegill, Quinn left to tend to the horses.

Zora went inside the wagon and turned on the lamp. The ribs of the ceiling were dark brown against a cream background. She plopped down on one of the bunks and let her crutches fall onto the paisley rug. Then she removed her boots, unstrapped her leather and steel ankle braces, and wiggled her toes.

Free for another night.

When Quinn came back, he sat on the other bed. "Since you know so much about the spirits," he said, "maybe you can explain to me why they came here in the first place."

Zora put on a sage tone to cover her elation at finally having someone—besides her mom, that is—who seemed receptive to her theories. "Most spiritologists think the things simply wandered here from their own dimension, looking for fresh prey. But *I* think an intelligent force sent them to clear the life from our world and let it lie fallow. Like how people used to slash and burn forests so they could farm the land afterward."

"I've heard those same notions from—from an old classmate of mine. Either way, why didn't the spirits finish off the Hollows?"

"Maybe they get a kick out of keeping us trapped here." A dog barked from behind the trading post. Zora listened for a few seconds, but no other sounds followed. "They won't like it so much when we show up to get rid of them. All of them."

"*All* of them? How do you intend to do that?"

She'd been waiting for that question. She'd never told anyone her full plan—not even Mom—but Quinn was her partner now, so he deserved to know. "First, we need to test my inventions on different types. None of the nasty ones yet, just the nuisances. Both devices work on wisps, which are earthbounds. And they work on boges, which are roamers. But those are small fry. The spirit in Saltpeter Hollow should be bigger."

He shifted on his bunk, as though he expected a nixie to jump out from the water jug.

"Though not by too much," she added.

"Let's hope. Your mother did say little ones only."

"While we're doing that, I can fine-tune my inventions till we're ready for a public demonstration."

"And then?"

Zora raised an index finger. "We help people with spirit troubles and make money doing it." She raised another finger and her voice. "We take that money and build an arsenal." She held out her thumb. "We wipe the spirits from the Hollows forever." She made a fist. "We cut through the Wastes, take back the lands beyond, and discover whether anyone else survived the Wakenings. Think of it—no more running and hiding from those monsters."

"That's an ambitious plan you have there," Quinn said, without as much fervor as she would've preferred. "Out of curiosity, have you ever seen the Wastes?"

"Not up close." Last winter, Zora had taken a trip with Mom to visit Grandma and Grandpa at their farm near the western edge of the Hollows. One evening they'd climbed a hill to watch the sun go down and the eerie green spirit-aurora appear above the Wastes. "How about you?"

"Me neither. I'll bet our father has, though, what with all his traveling."

She followed his gaze to the clock on the back wall of the wagon. Its face bore a twelve-petal rosette, one of the hex signs Sylvanian wayfarers had introduced to the Hollows after the Great Wakening. None of which had saved Sylvania itself during the Lesser Wakening.

What was the name of that design? Right, the Daddy Hex. How fitting. Good for nothing, just like her huckster father.

At least she and Quinn had each other now.

"We should get a good night's sleep," he said, "in case we find this spirit tomorrow."

Zora pulled a quilt over herself and snuggled into her pillow. "Then good night, big brother."

He switched off the lamp and fell asleep within minutes. She tossed and turned in bed long past midnight, thinking about the day ahead. Through the window, the forest outside looked like an endless, shadowy void.

Saltpeter Hollow was bustling when they arrived late the following morning. In a farmers' market, sellers chatted with buyers across tables stacked with cauliflower, cabbages, and lettuce. Children tossed beanbags at boards laid out on the village green, and a rakish-looking young man plucked out a tune on a banjo while he sang about shivering in the pines.

Quinn slowed the horses as they pulled up behind a crowd of people walking toward a brick hall. The flag flying from the building's rooftop depicted a valley between two hills, with the sun in the background. "Looks like a Court Day," he said. "The Judge for this circuit must be here."

On the opposite side of the street sat three wagons, each with a gaudy sign. One advertised clockwork-driven lawnmowers. Another hawked every type of pill known to the pharmaceutical arts, from antacids to antibiotics. The third, embellished with arcane symbols, proclaimed, FORTUNES TOLD BY MADAME MOONBOW—LEARN WHAT FATE AWAITS YOU.

Zora sniffed at that last sign. "What a load of cow poop."

"Your inventions use some kind of mysterious energy nobody's ever heard of," Quinn said. "I thought you'd have a more open mind."

"I'm a paraphysicist," she said. "Madame Moonbow here is just a hooey-monger."

"We could talk to her. Maybe she knows something about the spirit we're after."

"That's ridiculous. She doesn't know anything." Then she saw his smile and caught on that he was teasing her. "More data might be good," she conceded. "Just not from a two-bit pumpkin-seed-reader. An eyewitness would be ideal. That could help us pin down what type of spirit it is."

They passed a granite schoolhouse on the right and a clapboard junk shop on the left. "Are we going to tell anybody what we're up to?" he asked.

Zora hadn't decided about that. "What do you think?"

"Let's keep it to ourselves for now. That way we can avoid any awkward questions."

"Okay. Where do we find someone who can give us the latest news?" Between the two of them, her brother might be the expert at this sort of thing. After all that experience consoling mourners, he should have no trouble interviewing spirit-witnesses.

He gestured to a timbered building with an awning that shaded tables and chairs. "I'm hungry. How about we stable the horses at that tavern and get some food?"

Zora and Quinn sat at the bar, eating and trying to eavesdrop on the conversations around them. Her crutches had drawn a few stares as they'd entered, but no one had said anything to her. He'd asked for fried chicken and hush puppies, with a bottle of cider. She'd ordered the same, except with Earl's Electrified Ginger Ale instead.

The tavern-keeper came back to check on them. "Want another drink?" he asked Quinn. "Something stronger, maybe?"

"Not tonight. Say, is it true there's a new roamer in these parts?"

"Mm-hmm. I hear tell there's bad spirit weather all through the Hollows so far this summer." The man stroked his mutton-chops as he scrutinized Quinn. "Don't believe I've seen you before. Not from around here?"

"My sister and I are taking a trip, maybe as far as the Big Lake."

"Sounds dandy," said the tavern-keeper. "As for the roamer, it's gone blundering into the south end of the hollow. Nobody's quite sure what sort it is."

"Did it show up last night?" Zora asked. She didn't want to be left out of the discussion.

"Sure did. Got into a boneyard, made a mess of some flowers, and knocked a gravestone clean flat. According to that fellow over there." He indicated the customer sitting a few empty seats to her left, a fresh-faced young man wearing the olive uniform and cap of the Rangers.

Quinn turned the other way, as if to hide his face, and Zora wondered what skeletons her brother could possibly have in the closet of his funeral home. Maybe he'd bootlegged corn liquor in the family hearse or gambled with silver bits filched from long-dead corpses, but he seemed far too proper for anything like that.

"Just stay away from the south end come nighttime and you'll be safe," said the tavern-keeper, before leaving to serve a new customer.

Zora considered approaching the Ranger for more information. The man had a friendly appearance, despite the pneumatic pistol in his holster. Then again, the authorities in the Hollows—such as they were—might look sideways at two teenage spirit investigators.

Best not to risk it.

Instead, she leaned close to Quinn and spoke in a low voice. "The announcers on the Limestone Knob station said the first manifestation took place at a well. The spirit tore away the bucket and smashed it against a tree. The second appearance was at a nearby barn. It drove some sheep wild and scattered bales of hay everywhere. And now this graveyard."

"So that's where we look?" he whispered back.

"Exactly. We could scout it out this afternoon and come back later with the equipment."

He eyed his drumstick like he'd lost his appetite, but Zora ate her chicken to the bone. Then she scarfed down her last hush puppy and guzzled the rest of her caffeinated ginger ale.

Their first real spirit hunt was only a few hours away.

The two of them walked toward the south end of the hollow until they came to a stone well with a frayed rope hanging from its pulley. "This looks promising," Zora said.

Within shouting distance of the well, they found a cemetery on a hillside overlooking a small creek with high banks. She sat on a tabletop tomb and pointed a crutch at a tilted headstone.

"Hardly clean flat," she said. "But layfolk often exaggerate how strong spirits are."

Quinn paced the lichen-encrusted grave markers with a faraway look in his eyes. "Homesick for your old stomping grounds?" Zora asked.

He shook his head. "Just thinking of the ghost stories my grandma used to tell me. Seems like a good setting for an old-fashioned haunting."

"Ghosts?" Her brother was being silly again. "There's no scientific evidence for disembodied human souls."

"I never saw one in my family's line of work." He laughed, but then turned pensive. "If ghosts were real, they might make better company than spirits."

"I'm not scared of either." Not anymore, she added to herself. "Let's go look for the barn."

They sighted three different barns in quick succession, the last of which looked more ransacked than the others. "This has to be the right place," Zora said.

Quinn broke off from humming the song the young banjoist in the market had played. "Where should we set our lookout tonight?"

She nodded toward the slope above the graveyard. "We'd have a good view up there."

"We still don't know what sort of spirit it is."

"That shouldn't make a difference as long as you're fast enough on the trigger. This one's only done piddly stuff. It's not like we're talking about, say, a hount or a spire."

Back at the wagon, Zora calibrated the banisher and gave it to Quinn so he could practice his aim. Afterwards, he read a book with an absurd title—*Night of the Moonshine Wereskunks*, or some such nonsense—while she leafed through her battered copy of Nevan McBrain's *Field Guide to the Spirits of the Hollows* and jotted notes.

Clouds rolled in to blanket the hollow. By nightfall, it was so dark they could hardly see their way back to the hilltop above the graveyard. Halfway up, Quinn tripped and almost went sprawling.

"Be careful with my inventions," Zora said.

"You don't need to keep telling me that." Despite his genteel manners, he was evidently capable of getting snippy. "And let's talk quietly, in case that Ranger or somebody else comes around tonight."

"We're not doing anything wrong."

"No, but we are a mite suspicious-looking. How would you like a spray of buckshot in your backside from some jittery farmer?"

"Good point." She wouldn't put it past the local rubes to mistake them for poachers, or thieves, or even spirit-worshippers.

Zora perched herself on an anvil-shaped rock at the crest of the slope. The moon peeked through the clouds, and the headstones stood out below as dim, gray lumps. The creek at the bottom of the hill was a black ribbon on a slightly less black background.

Quinn handed her the illuminator, and she turned it on. The spirit sensors remained dark.

They waited on the hilltop in the warm night. The only excitement during the first hour came when a whip-poor-will called from a nearby tree, making them both jump. At the end of the second hour, Zora took a stick of candy from a pocket of her overalls and crunched on it. "Want some?" she asked.

"No thanks. Hold on. I see something." To the north, a globe of light was hovering along the road toward the well. Zora raised her device, and Quinn clutched the banisher. She could hear his rapid breathing over the chorus of insects.

Footsteps scuffed on the dirt below, and the light resolved into a lantern held by the young Ranger from the tavern. *Go away*, Zora mouthed, but the man took his time moseying from the well to the graveyard. He lifted his lantern to examine the headstones before starting back down the road.

Once he was gone, she looked at the illuminator again. "Still nothing."

As the night dragged by, she leaned her chin on her knees to rest. Sometime later, a shout from her brother broke through the fog in her head.

Zora jerked awake. One orange indicator dot was showing on her device's panel. She pulled on her goggles, and Quinn copied her. Sitting up straight on her rock, she swept the illuminator to the left. The orange light disappeared. She swept the illuminator back, and the light returned. The same thing happened when she turned the device to the right and back. "The spirit's coming this way," she said.

Off in the distance, a flash of green zigzagged across the hillside. The sensor panel went dark again, and Zora traced an arc with the illuminator's tip. When she'd completed a half circle, the orange dot reappeared. "Now it's behind us," she said. How had that happened? No spirit should be that fast, not even a whimpus. She bit back a vile word, one she'd learned from her classmates before Mom stopped making her go to school and let her work on engineering projects at home instead.

"I don't like this," said Quinn.

"It's fine. A single dot means it's not that powerful." A second bulb popped. "That just means it's getting closer." Blood rushed inside her ears. "Ready?"

He grunted, and she turned on her device's beam. The cone of blue was empty. "Must still be too far away," she said under her breath.

An echoing whistle came from in front of them, soft and low at first but then louder and higher. Three orange dots now. Zora peered ahead—

—and recoiled as a thin, glittering shape undulated through the illuminator's light. Quinn fired at it, but missed.

"It's out of sight," he said. "What was it?"

"No idea. Let me find it again." The whistling bounced around the slope like a ventriloquist's voice. Zora waved her device with hands that shook only a tiny bit. "There!"

The sinuous form writhed inside the beam. Her brother fired again, and this time the violet ray struck its target. The spirit spiraled in on itself with a bang, leaving behind a whiff of decay.

"Did I get it?" Quinn asked.

Zora checked the indicator panel. All clear. "We did it!" she crowed. Quinn smiled as she handed him the illuminator, slid to the ground, and started a victory dance.

A burst of pops broke the silence, and a glint of orange caught the corner of her eye. At that instant, one of her crutches flailed toward her brother and cracked him upside the forehead.

Then something yanked her backwards down the hill.

3

THE DARKNESS TOOK QUINN BACK TO WHEN HE AND HIS CLASS-mates had played at burying one another alive in one of the funeral home's cast-off coffins.

After a moment of disoriented panic, he realized he was looking at the starless sky. The ground beneath him pitched like a lake in a storm.

He stood too quickly and almost fell back down.

Both devices lay on the grass near his feet. He picked them up, then tucked the banisher under one arm and jabbed the buttons on the illuminator. The spirit was nowhere to be seen, and neither was Zora.

Quinn barreled downhill, using the beam to light his way. Had he already broken his promise to Ms. Coldiron? Had the roamer hurt—

Zora shouted his name from the graveyard.

"I'm here," he called back, as his gut unclenched. She was sitting among the headstones, holding her crutches. Her face was pale blue, with a dab of purple blood on her lips, and dirt caked the knees of her overalls.

"Stop shining that at me." She covered her eyes. "Are you okay?"

He touched his brow. "Just a knock upstairs. How about you?"

"I skinned myself in a dozen places, but I'm all right." Zora gave a rueful laugh. "Sorry about your head. That wasn't me— the spirit grabbed my crutch. Then it started pulling. I held on tight, and it dragged me down here. I was about to plow into an open grave, but it let go."

Quinn made a quick spin with the illuminator. "What happened back there? Did the banisher not work, or was there more than one spirit?"

"I'm not sure. Roamers are usually solitary, but a few types hunt in packs."

"We should go back to the wagon." He felt rattled, and not just by the blow to his skull. For all his sister's bold talk and fancy gizmos, that whatever-it-was had whooped their tails.

Zora stood and groaned. "I think you're right." She favored her left arm as they walked through the graveyard.

When they reached the creek, two of the illuminator's bulbs blinked orange. Zora sat on the edge of the bank, and Quinn handed her the device. She searched the night until a third dot appeared. "It's on the other side," she said.

A whistle reverberated from the far bank, then stopped abruptly. The knot on his forehead throbbed. "Behind you!" Zora barked. As he twisted around, the illuminator popped three times.

Green light coiled toward them, sending ripples through the air. He pulled the banisher's trigger. The glass tube flickered, and violet sparks fizzled from the metal fan.

Zora swore.

Quinn's vision distorted around its edges; a smell like rotting leaves filled his nose. With a shrill blast, the spirit slammed into his chest. A current of energy radiated along his nerves, up to his inner ears and down to his feet. He collided with Zora, and together they plunged into the creek.

Bedraggled and sore, they trudged back through Saltpeter Hollow, their boots squelching with each step. Quinn flicked mud from his sleeves and poked at the rip in his trousers. As adventures went, this one was off to a wretched start.

"Your inventions didn't fare so well against something that could fight back," he told Zora.

"You must've broken the banisher when you dropped it."

"After I got sucker-punched with *your* crutch by a spirit *you* said we'd already stopped."

"Well, I was wrong about that," she snapped.

The curved roof of their wagon came into sight. "I'm starting to think I made a mistake in agreeing to this," he said, climbing onto the seat. The fiddler girl had defeated a spire the size of a water tower in her first battle against the spirits. How had he ever imagined he could do anything like that?

"Wait," Zora said, more calmly. "I've figured out—"

Quinn held up his palm. "Sorry, but I'm done for."

"What do you mean?" she asked, as he went inside the wagon. "For the night, or—or—for good?" Her voice sounded small and uncertain. "This trip is my chance to prove what I can do. I thought we—I mean, without you . . ."

Guilt stirred inside his ribcage, but he didn't look back at Zora. "Let's talk about it in the morning," he said, taking off his soggy clothes and flumping onto his bed. Then he wrapped himself in his quilt, shivering despite the warmth as he tried to forget the sensation of the spirit's touch. She was right about one thing: it hadn't felt like a shock of electricity at all. More like brushing up against something so different—so *wrong*—that it didn't even belong in this world.

When Quinn awoke, the hour hand of his father's clock was pointing to the top petal of the rosette. That hex sign was supposed to be lucky, but it hadn't helped them so far.

Sunlight shone through one of the small, round windows onto Zora's empty bed. He prodded his bruised forehead, then fished fresh clothes from a drawer below his bunk and pulled them on.

He found his sister hunched over the wagon's seat, holding a book in her lap and scribbling on a scrap of paper. She had dark circles under her eyes. The banisher lay next to her, partly disassembled.

"Good morning—or maybe afternoon," she said. "Did you sleep well?"

Quinn nodded. "Did you sleep at all?"

"I had too much on my mind. Listen, I apologize about yesterday."

Last night's events seemed hazy and unreal to him. "I recall I was rather ornery myself."

"I mean about not being ready. You were right. We should've found out more about the spirit." Zora clapped her hands and smiled. "But I know what it is now, and how to stop it, too." Her face fell. "If you're still willing, that is."

"Go on." Quinn wasn't sure he was ready to slink home just yet. Paige would never quit so easily. In her letter, she'd even joked about the rash she'd picked up from stepping barefoot on a little waterbound spirit.

"I was stumped at first," said Zora, "because it didn't fit any of the profiles in the *Field Guide*. But when it came back the second time—right before it knocked us into the creek—I remembered something." She handed him a thin, dog-eared copy of *Notes on Unverified Rare Spirits*, by Nevan McBrain. "Look at page 77." He opened the book to a circled entry:

Three firsthand accounts (F, 43; F, 20; M, 22) on the 51st of Spring, 122 AW, at Sliding Rock testified to a spirit with unusual properties. Each witness described a lambent snake-shaped entity that produced a resonant whistle, moved at high velocity, and manipulated objects with substantial force. The first witness reported two such spirits, "like a pair of nightcrawlers." The second witness observed "a bendy thing that was neither here nor there, yet both at once." The third told of a spirit that "blinked to and fro as it moved." Triangulating the accounts suggests the presence of a single roaming spirit that manifests as two reflecting components.

Along the margin, someone—Zora, he assumed—had written THE TANGLE? in spidery letters.

"Two reflecting components," he repeated. "That does sound like our unknown spirit. I gather I didn't stop the thing by shooting just the half of it there on the hillside."

"Correct. We need to hit both parts. Otherwise it'll come right back, like it did by the creek."

Quinn skimmed the passage again. "How does it even do that?"

"Quantum entanglement of odic force, I'm guessing."

He gave her a mystified look. "Spooky physics," she said.

"A spirit that can be two places at once *is* a hair-raising prospect. Before I met you, I would've called it supernatural."

"Now that we know what we're up against, I have an idea." Zora pounded a fist against the seat. "I want a rematch with this spirit. It messed with me, and my crutches, and my inventions." Quinn raised his eyebrows. "And my big brother," she added. "Will you give it a second try? We'll be more prepared this time, I promise."

"All right." One more shot wouldn't kill them. Probably. "What's your idea?"

"First thing, I need you to buy some extra parts." She handed him a list. "It's all common stuff. The junk store we passed yesterday should have everything."

"Me? What are you going to do?"

"I'm going to take a nap. Can you wake me when you're done?"

The store had no sign and didn't need one; the old contraptions lining its porch served just as well. Quinn stopped by the doorway to look at a small steam-powered earth-drill. That might be useful for digging graves, if Zora's plan flopped.

The inside of the shop was dank and cobwebby. Tarnished bits of machinery lay in jumbles on tables and heaps on the floor. He followed a path to the counter, but nobody was there. He rang the bell, and a smoke-colored cat scurried to the top of a nearby bookcase.

On the wall behind the counter hung a painting with wild, thickly layered brushstrokes depicting the wreck of the *Sheltowee* on its doomed voyage to seek the far edge of the Wastes. A black gash cut across the zeppelin's envelope, and flames erupted from it in reds and oranges against the inky sky. On the ground, spirits rendered in sickly shades of green and yellow chased ant-sized humans among skeletal trees. The long, swirling form of a hount held one unfortunate person in its grasp. The victim's arms stretched helplessly toward the heavens.

"You like that?" A man with tangled hair and shabby clothes sidled behind the counter. "My prized possession. Not for sale, I'm afraid."

"It seems—vivid," Quinn said, to be polite.

The proprietor rubbed his hands together. "Looking for something in particular today?"

Quinn handed him the list. "All this."

"You a tinkerer or something?"

"Not me. My sister."

"You mean the kid with these?" The man pantomimed Zora's walk.

The gesture nettled Quinn. News travels fast in narrow hollows, he thought. "She uses crutches, yes."

"What's she need them for, anyhow?"

"The parts?" said Quinn, though he knew full well what the man had meant. "She's building a new invention."

They looked at one another across the counter until the proprietor averted his eyes. "Let me dig them up for you," he said, and bustled off into the maze of junk.

"I'm back," said Quinn. Zora was hugging a pillow with both arms, and her reddish-brown hair had fallen over her face. Like this, she looked even younger than fifteen.

His sister kept on sleeping, so he sat down and opened his copy of *Addie the Urchin versus the Clockwork Conjurer*. He got as far as the first line, then set the book aside and picked up Nevan McBrain's *Field Guide to the Spirits of the Hollows* instead. If he intended to make a real go at spirit hunting, he should start studying.

Near the front of the book, Quinn found the entry for BOGE (*Roamer, small, solitary, innocuous*), along with an illustration resembling the star-shaped spirit he'd tracked with Paige last year. The opposite page showed the meteoric form of a BOLIDE (*Airbound, large, swarming, burns its prey*). He'd never seen one of those things before. Or any other airbound spirit, for that matter.

He turned to the end of the guide, going past the funnel-shaped WENGO (*Roamer, medium, solitary, touch causes paralysis*) and the blurry WHIMPUS (*Roamer, medium, solitary, effusions trigger sensory fluidity*), until he arrived at WISP (*Earthbound, tiny, hiving, innocuous*). The caption for the picture read, *Colony observed in Lightning Bug Hollow*.

The memory of the painting in the junk shop sent him paging back to the Hs. Right after HERN (*Roamer, medium, travels in packs, dangerous in numbers*), he came to HOUNT (*Roamer, colossal, solitary, lethal*). *The closest I ever came to death while monitoring a spirit*, Nevan McBrain had written, *was during my encounter with a hount in the near reaches of the Wastes on the 15th of Winter, 123 AW.*

Quinn shut the book and gently shook Zora's shoulder. "Time to get up, sleepyhead."

She opened one eye. "Did you get everything?"

He held up a cardboard box full of parts. "Ten bits for all of it."

"Fantastic. Wait for me outside, and I'll be right there."

A minute later, Zora emerged in brown overalls that were clean but otherwise identical to the pair she'd worn for the past three days. She redid her pigtails and sifted through the box. "Let's start with this," she said, picking up a glass pipe and a spool of copper wire.

Quinn went into the wagon to start some grits on the stove, then came back to watch her work. "So, tell me," he said. "I know you're smart and all, but how did you learn about this spirit energy when nobody else could?"

"Eber since the sfirits came"—she removed a fuse from the corner of her mouth—"people have argued about how to go about warding them off. On one side are the types who tout some sort of hocus-pocus, be it hexes, charms, dowsing—you name it. Of those, most are frauds, and they generally try to swindle as much money from the chumps as they can before moving on to the next hollow. The rest of that crowd are true believers, and they tend to give up quickly or come to gruesome ends. On the other side—"

"Would be scientists such as yourself."

"Exactly. The early paraphysicists tried to account for the spirits as natural phenomena. They had the right idea, but every one of their attempts failed. See, they'd overlooked one thing." She stopped and waited for him to ask.

He played along. "What was that?"

"They'd assumed that the laws of the universe after the Great Wakening were the same as beforehand." She threaded the glass pipe through a clamp. "But the rules of our reality are different from the ones in the old textbooks. Not by much, but enough."

"Did the change open the way for the spirits to enter this

world?" A disquieting thought struck him. "Or did the spirits themselves cause the change?"

"I don't know." She lifted the device to her eye to test its line of sight. "For all our sakes, I'm rooting for the first option. Anyway, I came up with my hypothesis two years ago, and it helped me discover how to detect spirit energy. Along with how to disrupt it." She gave her handiwork to Quinn. "Think you can manage this?"

He balanced the reconfigured device and ran his fingertip along the trigger. "A little clumsy, but it should work."

At sundown, Quinn and Zora returned to the scene of their fight with the spirit. The uncloaked moon cast silver highlights on the banks of the creek and the monuments of the graveyard. "Are you sure it'll come back?" he asked.

"You've heard how the spirits are drawn to humans?" said Zora. "Some Spotters think they're especially attracted to people they've bumped into before. So our target may fancy you now."

A phantom prickle ran down his back. "I have to say, I'm not thrilled with that notion."

"It's fine." She showed her canines. "We're going to get even with this thing."

They took their places at the top of the hill, and Zora motioned for the illuminator. "How did you do all this before I came along?" he asked. "Did your mother help you?"

"No," said Zora. "Mom wanted no part of it. With the wisps, it was easy. I just lugged my inventions one at a time and put the illuminator on a tripod while I used the banisher. Same for the boge, but that required some patience—since it was a roamer, I had to stay in one place and wait for it to come to me. It took a few nights. When you showed up on my doorstep, I'd just started working on ways to streamline the illuminator." She gave him a sidelong glance. "I notice you haven't asked me about my crutches."

"I figured you'd tell me about that when—if—you wanted to."

"I use them because I have nerve damage through my legs and feet." Her demeanor was matter-of-fact.

My daughter is dead set on fighting the spirits, Ms. Coldiron had said. *She has been ever since* . . . Maybe Zora was out to avenge a childhood injury inflicted by a roamer straying through her hollow. "Did it happen when you were seven?" he asked.

"No, I was born with it." She glared at him. "Why did you say seven?"

Quinn cursed himself for a jackass. "Your mother told me that was the age you decided to become a spirit-hunter. I reckoned there might be a connection. Wrongly, I take it."

"That wasn't—never mind what that was. Mom shouldn't have said that." Zora mumbled something else to herself.

"Forget I mentioned it. And I'm—"

"When I was a baby," she broke in, "Mom built an etherscope so the doctors could scan my body. They found a little fiber of tissue tethered to the end of my spinal cord. As best as they could figure, that's the cause of my nerve damage. Which is permanent, by the way." One bulb on the illuminator's panel turned orange. "Looks like our spirit is back."

He adjusted his goggles and rested the banisher on his shoulder. The now-familiar whistle rolled across the hillside, rising in volume and pitch as it came.

"Closer," she said. "Closer—gone." She whipped her device

in the opposite direction. "Ha, there it is again. We're wise to your tricks now."

Quinn gritted his teeth. "When's it going to be in range?"

"Two dots—three—now!" The blue beam cut through the darkness to reveal the spirit as it wormed through the night. Its winding motion slowed, and its whistle dropped to a wobbling bass.

He took aim and fired. A pair of violet rays leaped from the banisher—one forward from the original barrel, one backward from the new barrel Zora had added. The spirit shrieked from two angles, and twin explosions lit the hillside.

"That felt plumb satisfying," Quinn said. He turned and caught the look of spite on Zora's moonlit face as she watched the last specks of the roamer fade away.

Did she harbor some secret grudge against the spirits, after all?

Then her expression cleared. "Gone," she said. "For real, this time. But we should keep checking on the way back, just in case." She saluted with her device. "Good shooting, big brother."

He took the illuminator. "Nice work rigging the extra barrel."

"Kid stuff," Zora said, as they started down the hillside. "The only drawback is that doubling the ray cuts its strength in half."

"You didn't mention that part before."

"I knew we'd have enough power." She looked away, then back. "Well, I was almost certain."

They swept for signs of spirits when they reached the graveyard, and again when they passed the creek, but found nothing either time.

"If I ever meet Nevan McBrain," she said, "I'll tell him we verified the existence of that spirit."

"He's still alive?" Chasing spirits with Zora's inventions seemed hazardous enough, yet the famous Spotter had managed to track all the ones listed in his book armed with nothing but his wits.

"Last I heard, though by all accounts he's been laying low for years. What do you think of calling it a 'tangle'? You know, because of the quantum entanglement." She sounded giddy. "Tradition says the person who discovers a new type of spirit gets to name it."

"That's a good handle for it." Quinn stifled a yawn as they passed the well. He couldn't wait to curl up in his bed.

"Pleasant evening for a stroll," a voice called out from behind them. "Ain't it?"

They stopped and turned. A man was standing in the middle of the road. One of his hands held an unlit lantern; the other hung near the holster on his belt.

Quinn tried to lower the illuminator as surreptitiously as he could. "Sure is, sir. Quite a pretty moon."

"Yes, but let's have a bit more light, shall we?" The man switched on his lantern. He was the Ranger they'd seen yesterday. "Emerson Tate, of Lost Hollow. And y'all might be?"

They gave their names and hollows, then fell silent.

Ranger Tate raised the lantern. "I could swear I recognize y'all. Maybe we've run across each other somewhere?"

"Hard to tell," Quinn said. "You know, with the uniform and all." An amateur spirit hunt didn't break any law as far as he knew, but he still felt uneasy around Rangers. During his last few years of school, Paige's talent for hatching shenanigans had almost landed them both in all sorts of trouble.

He smiled at the recollection before remembering to frown.

"Right," said the Ranger. He pointed to the illuminator in Quinn's hand. "What's that, if y'all don't mind me asking?"

While Quinn tripped over his words, Zora jumped in. "I built it for the All Hollows Science Fair. It's an experimental type of . . . um, flashlight." Quinn flicked on the beam to demonstrate. "Blue's my favorite color," she added. "Nifty, isn't it?"

Ranger Tate didn't bother replying to that.

"We don't mean to distract you from your patrol," said Quinn. "And it's past my sister's bedtime"—she gave him a stink-eye—"so we were fixing to call it a night."

"Is that your wagon parked by the tavern up the road?"

"Yes, sir."

"Good night to y'all, then," said the Ranger. Just as Quinn exhaled, the man spoke again. "But first, here's a thought. Seeing as how a spirit's been reported around here, perhaps a pair of young folks—much like yourselves—might get the notion in their heads to do a bit of investigating on their own." Steel lay under his mild tenor. "My thinking is that such things are best left to the Spotters—and even for them, it's mighty dangerous."

"Oh, I promise you we don't aspire to be *Spotters*," said Zora. Which was true, as far as it went.

"That's a relief to hear." Ranger Tate looked at her crutches. "Earlier today, I saw two distinctive sets of tracks around here. I'd sure regret it if the spirit plaguing this hollow harmed somebody who happened to cross its way."

"I wouldn't lose sleep over that." She did a poor job of disguising her smirk. "I've got a hunch your spirit won't be pestering anyone again." Quinn fought down the urge to kick her in the shin. He'd probably just jam his toes on her brace, anyhow.

"That may be," said the Ranger. "But if one were to go looking, I'm sure there's plenty of worse things waiting out there."

4

TWO MOONS LATER, ZORA SAT ON A SLAB OF LIMESTONE AT THE bottom of a ravine near Bone Run. Sweat dripped onto the bridge of her goggles as a trace of sulfur wafted in the humid air. She fanned herself with her left hand and studied the illuminator strapped to her right forearm. All at once, four orange dots appeared.

"Dead ahead," she called. "And closing in." Not far away, a beep from Quinn's banisher echoed her warning. Before they'd left for this place, she'd attached spirit sensors to his weapon's stock and fitted a small illuminator to its glass barrel.

Hints of yellow haze drifted through the wall of bamboo along the edge of the ravine. At Zora's signal, two cones of blue light converged on the cane. The leafy shafts shook and then parted to reveal a thick, glowing cloud that levitated above the ravine like a ball of swamp gas.

"So that's a nimbus?" Quinn whispered. As soon as the words left his mouth, the spirit made a phlegmy sound and surged toward Zora.

"Yes," she shouted. "Now would be a good time to—"

He blasted it with violet energy, and it liquified into a noxious puddle.

"Ew." Zora gagged. "Of all the spirits we've fought, this was undoubtedly the most disgusting." The two of them had kept busy since their success in Saltpeter Hollow. All told, they'd visited a dozen hollows and banished fifteen different types of spirits. Neither she nor Quinn had suffered any injuries other than a few scratches, thanks to her planning and his increasingly sharp aim. The whimpus had been the biggest challenge. Each time they'd cornered it, it had scrambled their senses with low-frequency kirlian waves and then sped away. After three nights of hearing colors and smelling noises, they'd finally blown it up like summer solstice pyrotechnics loaded with green-burning barium salts.

The morning after their nimbus-hunt, they set forth from the apple orchards of Bone Run to check out reports of a boge in Shallow Flats. While Quinn listened to a ballad on the radio (a mournful one about bidding farewell to Old Kentucky), Zora read a newspaper she'd picked up at a general store. Along with the Limestone Knob station, the three dailies printed in the Hollows provided most of their intelligence on spirit activity. The rest came from stops at inns, taverns, and other watering holes during their travels.

"Anything interesting?" Quinn asked.

"Not unless you like wedding announcements or obituaries. Hey, this service is taking place at your mom's. Have you told her yet how you've been spending your summer vacation?" Zora was curious to meet Ms. Prosser, but Quinn kept putting off their visit to his home.

"I figured I'd wait till All Hollows, when she expects me back at work. I just"—he shook his head. "I want to keep chasing spirits with you come fall, but I don't want to disappoint her. I'm still trying to sort out what to say."

"If she finds out before you tell her, it's your funeral," Zora said.

He stuck his tongue out at her.

She laughed and turned the pages of the newspaper. "Here's a column about the so-called wave of spirit weather. Says the Spotters and Rangers should work together to figure out what's going on and do something about it. Ha—good luck with that."

"Is it really getting worse?"

Zora shrugged. "These things ebb and flow. Like Nevan McBrain says, spirit weather's not the same as spirit climate." She read some more and then stopped at an ad on the last page:

BLAZE A TRAIL TO GLORY—AND CASH!!!

Local merchants' association seeks help in surveying night route between Mill and Iron Furnace Hollows through spirit-troubled forest. Experts & amateurs welcome. Reward of 50 bits for good faith attempts, 500 for successfully marking safe path. Bonus for driving away any spirits. Inquire at Mill Hollow Arcade on the 66th of summer.

"Look!" She pointed to the ad. "Forget the boge. How long would it take to get to here?"

Quinn counted out loud. "If we start now, we could make it smack dab on the 66th. Does this mean we're going to let the Hollows know about your inventions?"

"I'm tired of skulking around," she said. "And five hundred bits is a lot of money. Plus the bonus." They'd used up almost all their savings on parts for new devices, hay for the horses, and provisions for themselves.

"The Rangers might start poking their noses into our business once they get wind of what we're up to." Her brother hadn't stopped fretting about their run-in with that Tate fellow.

"If they can't do anything about the spirits except stand around holding their useless pop guns, they should just stay out of our way."

"And what if a bona fide Spotter shows up?"

"The most one of them can do is find and identify spirits." Zora couldn't resist a smug grin. "We can get rid of the things." The more she thought about it, the more eager she was to see everyone's surprised faces after she and Quinn conquered that spirit-infested forest.

True to her brother's calculations, it took them three days to reach Mill Hollow. Quinn pulled the wagon into a lot, and Zora waited there under the sweltering afternoon sun while he found a shady pasture where Ursula and Undine could rest. Then he rejoined her for the walk through the open-air shopping arcade. Along the way, she overheard the usual comments (*What happened to her? — Poor dear — But look how well she gets around*) from people who thought she was out of earshot, or who didn't care one way or the other.

Past stalls of cheese, soap, and candles stood a wooden pavilion festooned with banners for MACK-ANICAL WARES. Under its roof, a woman and a man—both middle-aged, with dressy clothes—sat behind a table. He was bald, while she had black curls beneath the brim of her garden hat.

"That must be the merchants' welcoming committee," Zora said.

Two other people were loitering beside the table. The man to the left, who looked twice Zora's age, wore white trousers and a sleeveless white shirt. Tattoos of hex signs covered his arms, from the sun wheels on his biceps to the triple stars on the backs of his hands. His eyes smoldered, and his whole body twitched with restless energy.

The young woman to the right of the table made for a striking contrast. She was dressed in a full-length skirt, a long-sleeved shirt, and gloves—all solid black. A fancy sort of umbrella—also black—shaded her pale face, and she squinted from behind thick blue lenses set in boxy frames. Although she appeared to be in her teens, her long hair was a snowy gold.

Zora strode up to the pair sitting behind the table. The straw-hatted merchant woman introduced herself as Viola Mack of Mill Hollow and her companion as Kirk Slocum of Iron Furnace Hollow.

"Coldiron and Prosser Ventures," said Zora. "Spirit hunters for hire."

"How *marvelous*," said Ms. Mack. She turned to Quinn. "Perhaps you'd like to meet your—ah—colleagues who came to help us with our problem." She indicated the tattooed man. "This is Mr. McKinley Crouch."

"Good to meet you," Quinn said, offering his hand.

Mr. Crouch responded with a hoarse mumble, then backed away and closed his eyes as though concentrating. Zora abandoned her own effort to greet him.

"And this," the merchant went on, "is Ms. Signe Janasdottir."

The bespectacled young woman raised one of her gloved

hands. "Enchanted," she said, in a placid voice. "Call me Signe." Zora nodded curtly, while her brother smiled at their would-be competitor.

"We're right pleased at the turnout from our ad," Mr. Slocum said. "Before y'all arrived, we'd been discussing with the others how to proceed. They'd agreed that Mr. Crouch would begin after sunset. And"—he cleared his throat—"if necessary, Ms. Janasdottir would start next. As our most recent arrival, Mr. Prosser, you—beg your pardon, you and Ms. Coldiron—would go after her. Is that agreeable?"

Quinn looked at Zora. "Fine by me," she said, feigning indifference. "How come you can't just go through this forest during the day, or take some other road if you need to travel at night?"

"That's what we've always done," said Ms. Mack. "But the pike around Saddleback Mountain goes a fair bit out of our way."

"It's prone to flooding, too," said Mr. Slocum. "With all the mud from that last storm, it took my team a whole day to deliver a shipment of my finest—"

"So, you want to build a new road?" Zora asked, before the man could bore her to sleep.

The interruption didn't perturb him. "Not just any road. A *rail*road."

Ms. Mack nodded. "The trade between my factory here and Mr. Slocum's ironworks over yonder has grown to such *bountiful* levels that we need a quicker way to deliver our goods to one another. Imagine—the first working rail line through these parts in almost a century and a half!"

"We could go back and forth between our hollows lickety-split," said Mr. Slocum. "We've already designed a locomotive that runs on hemp diesel, what with how coal and oil are so scarce nowadays. And supposing this project pans out—why, we can build an entire railroad system."

Not a bad idea, Zora thought. If these two gasbags pulled it off, maybe she'd hitch a ride on their train.

"But you need to route it through the forest," said Quinn.

"And therein lies the catch." Mr. Slocum deflated a little. "Deadfall Wood sits on flat, dry land, but we don't want to lay our tracks over top of some spirit. That'd throw a wrench into our plans for running the train at night. Then there's all the dirt we'd need to move. What if we dig up an earthbound? It might bust free and lodge itself under somebody's home, or even this here arcade."

Ms. Mack fluttered her hands. "The forest has been beset with spirits ever since the Great Wakening. We've tried sending our own workers to investigate, but those *horrible* things are just too thick on the ground. Nobody has made it across without fleeing like their britches were on fire. Why, one poor man even" —she stopped at the look from her fellow merchant.

Mr. Slocum took over for her. "There's several different sorts, judging by the tales of those who've gone into the forest. All earthbound, we assume, since they never wander into our hollows." The merchant wiped his head with a handkerchief. "The only good news is that none of the spirits lurking in there seems to be an elemental. Our workers described the worst as large, round ones rising up from the ground like hot air balloons."

"Orbs," said Signe. Zora revised her estimation of the young woman up a notch.

"That's what our research suggested," Ms. Mack agreed.

"Not deadly, but a truly *loathsome* type of spirit nonetheless. Or so we hear."

"The rest are smaller," said Mr. Slocum. "Some like fire running along the ground, others like steam rising up from holes."

Those sounded like flambs and gizes, thought Zora. No challenge there, but the orbs would be a good test for her inventions. "Got it. What's the bonus for clearing them out?"

The merchants exchanged glances, and Signe's eyes narrowed behind her blue lenses. The tattooed man, who had pressed his palms together in front of his face, seemed oblivious to the conversation.

"To be honest," said Mr. Slocum, "we hadn't arrived at a specific figure for that. Of course, y'all can rest assured that we'd compensate anybody quite generously if they accomplished such a feat." Zora laughed inwardly. These two saps were in for a shock.

Ms. Mack changed the subject by offering to treat them to a chili supper while they waited. Zora seated herself at a nearby picnic table to talk strategy with Quinn, but he confounded her by inviting their two rivals to join them. The tattooed man declined and went off by himself to meditate. Signe accepted and sat at the other side of the table.

"I'm concerned about Mr. Crouch," the young woman said. "I have the distinct impression he doesn't know what he's doing."

"You'd prefer to go first?" asked Zora.

"I volunteered to." Signe gave a small sigh. "But he arrived before me and insisted on his prerogative."

"How thoughtful of you." Zora made no effort to hide her sarcasm.

The two of them locked eyes. Then Quinn asked Signe whether she'd been a Spotter for long.

"Oh, I'm not a Spotter. I have my own approach to the spirits I've been developing since I was a child, though I've never done something like this before. And you?"

"We've only been at it a couple of moons," he said. "But I think we're getting the hang of it."

Signe leaned forward. "What's your technique for finding spirits?"

Before Quinn could speak, Zora mashed his toes with one of her crutches. "Trade secrets," she said. Her brother flashed an apologetic look across the table.

"Perhaps you'll enlighten me later," Signe told him. "Did you say you're from Cascade Hollow? I've always wanted to see the caverns there."

The pair of them chatted away about stalagmites and stalactites while Zora listened sullenly. When Quinn asked Signe about her family, she blathered on about how she was the youngest of seven siblings and the black sheep of the flock. "My brothers and sisters all work in the family printing business or as teachers," she explained. "But with my nearsightedness, setting type or grading papers all day would be one big headache—even wearing these glasses. So, once I graduated this spring, I decided to strike out on my own."

"I just finished school, too," said Quinn. "Speaking of your glasses, I've got a pair of blue goggles myself" —Zora glowered at him—"but I'm not sure how well I carry off the style."

Signe ducked her head and smiled. "I had mine specially made. Truth be told, my choice of lenses is more practical than aesthetic. For one thing, I'm rather light-sensitive." She dipped the umbrella. "That's why I carry this wherever I go." From there, she and Quinn turned to talking about some novel in which a pair of hormone-drunk teenagers—one a mechanic, the other a witch—fell in love, broke an ancient curse, and ended a feud between their hollows.

After Zora finished eating, she left by herself to explore the stalls in the arcade. She returned at twilight to find a crowd gathering by the pavilion.

The tattooed man stood from his cross-legged pose and flexed his arms. "I shall now proceed with my appointed charge," he declared in his raspy voice. Then he removed his shirt. Letters in black ink covered his chest:

I

NIR

SANCTUS SPIRITUS

I

NIR

I

"What does that mean?" Quinn whispered to Zora.

"Just some superstitious gibberish," she said, in a voice loud enough for everyone at the table to hear.

The tattooed man recaptured their attention by gesticulating theatrically. "I forbid you my house and my yard, my stable and barn," he chanted as he marched away from the arcade and toward the woods.

Zora cringed at the man's antics. She hoped he didn't get himself injured. Or worse.

"Come not into my house," he continued. "Begone into another, or climb every knob in the Hollows, count every cornstalk, ford every creek, before you return." When he reached the end of his litany, he started over at the beginning. Soon he reached the edge of the forest and disappeared within it.

The spell of silence over the arcade broke as everyone talked at once. A trio of musicians took that as their cue to mount a nearby stage and commence playing in a minor key. The henna-haired woman on the mandolin sang in a husky alto about a kid whose magic violin bewitched a pack of spirits into devouring the high priest of the Spiritists. Quinn seemed enthralled, but Zora was unimpressed. Her own experiments with sonic weaponry had yielded nothing worthwhile.

Meanwhile, Signe stole occasional glances across the table.

Just as the musicians completed their set, a distant scream echoed through the hollow. A hush fell across the arcade, and everyone craned their necks toward the murky woods.

"Oh, dear," said Ms. Mack.

The screaming came again, louder this time. Then the tattooed man sprinted out of the forest with a wild look in his bulging eyes. Grime streaked his once-white trousers, and red lines crisscrossed the letters on his bare chest.

That hadn't taken long, thought Zora.

"Say, now," called out Mr. Slocum. "Slow down there—"

The tattooed man ran right past the merchants and on through the arcade. When Quinn jumped up to chase after him, the musicians joined the pursuit. Together, they caught the man and held him until he regained a measure of lucidity.

The merchants made their way over, with Zora, Signe, and a gaggle of spectators following close behind.

Ms. Mack put her hand on the tattooed man's shoulder. "There, there, Mr. Crouch. Are you wounded?"

"Just cuts from tree branches." He gasped for breath. "From running into them."

"We're right happy to see you in one piece," said Mr. Slocum. The merchants led the tattooed man to a table, and one draped a quilt around him while the other poured him a shot of moonshine. He gulped it and coughed.

"Now, then," said Ms. Mack. "Do you feel up to telling us about your—ah—visitation in the forest?"

Zora jostled closer to make sure she heard the next part.

"I began my charm," the tattooed man croaked, "and wended among the trees. It was dark, but I trusted the words to keep me safe. I stumbled over roots and through thorns, but I pressed onward."

"*Wonderfully* brave of you," said Ms. Mack. "What happened next?"

"I passed the spirits that burned below my feet, and no harm came to me. I passed the spirits that breathed on me from the ground, and no harm came to me. But then"—he closed his eyes—"the great, glaring bubbles of the earth—for the earth has bubbles, as the water does—they foamed up, and the words did not stop them." The man's voice quavered. "They loomed before me, and I felt—I felt—I can say no more about it."

Despite herself, Zora shuddered. According to the *Field Guide*, the slightest brush with an orb's aura could send any earthly creature—animal or human—into a frenzy.

"After all that, you deserve your compensation," said Mr. Slocum. "A pity your method didn't work, but it was gutsy of you to try."

The tattooed man hung his head. "I trusted the words to keep me safe, but they failed. Nay, *I* failed. This night has brought me low. Now I must seek out a stronger charm so that I may fulfill my vow."

"No doubt you will, my good sir." Mr. Slocum thumped him on the back. "But tonight you should rest. Recuperate, so you can get back on the horse. Figuratively speaking, of course, since I recollect you arriving here on foot."

Once he'd steered the tattooed man toward an inn, the merchant conferred with his associate in urgent whispers. "Well, darling," Ms. Mack told Signe, "looks like it's your turn."

"Indeed," said the young woman, with a serenity that annoyed Zora.

"Are you sure you want to do this?" Quinn asked Signe.

She picked up a backpack and started poking through its contents. "If I don't, are you and your sister still going to try?"

Quinn shot Zora an inquiring look. She nodded vigorously. "I suppose we will," he said.

"That's what I thought. It's sweet of you to worry, but I'll be fine." Signe strapped on her backpack and then offered her umbrella to Quinn. "Could you hold on to this for me?"

He accepted it, looking confused but flattered. As he ran his fingers along its ruffled trim, Zora gave the umbrella a furtive look-over. No sign of any spirit-faking mechanisms, or camouflaged recording devices, or booby traps.

After a parting bow, Signe walked toward the boundary of the same forest the tattooed man had entered—and exited—not long before. Her black clothes swiftly blended into the shadows.

"At least she's not trying to cast some incantation," Zora said. "That's smart—she'll have more breath for running."

"Do you think she'll be okay?" asked Quinn.

"Mr. McMumble Chant came back alive, so I expect your

new story-time friend will too." She wondered what Signe's brand of hooey might be. Not that it mattered. "Why do you care so much?"

"I thought she seemed—well, nice, didn't she?"

"Of course you would think that. She paid plenty of attention to you, just like those merchants did." Zora squirmed at the whiny edge in her voice but kept on going. "Just like the people we meet in the taverns and inns and stores we visit. They talk to you. Not me."

Quinn took so long to reply she began to doubt he would. "I'm sorry," he said, when he finally spoke. "I hadn't noticed that."

The lamps lining the arcade blurred in her vision. "I appreciate having you around, big brother. But people take you more seriously than me, even though I'm the brains of our operation."

He rubbed his knuckles on the top of her head. "You're right—you *are* the brains. What does that make me?"

She leaned against him. "Would you settle for the bumbling assistant?"

The two of them stayed in the arcade for a while to see whether Signe returned as quickly as the tattooed man had. When she didn't, Zora suggested they turn in for the night. "Look at it this way," she said. "At least Ms. Spooky Jack-o-lantern doesn't need to worry about the spirits scaring her hair white. She's already got that covered."

Quinn looked at her reproachfully.

"I know," she said, tugging on his arm. "That was mean." He let her pull him away, and together they headed to the wagon.

At the first light of dawn, Zora and Quinn revisited the arcade. She brought her expedition log, while he carried Signe's umbrella.

The two merchants were still sitting at their table, with glassy eyes. Everyone else was gone, including the tattooed man. "Ms. Janasdottir's not back yet," said Mr. Slocum.

"I hope nothing's happened to her in that *ghastly* place," added Ms. Mack.

The sun rose, and the air grew muggy. Zora opened her log to a page of notes on flambs, gizes, and orbs.

"Should we search for her?" asked Quinn.

Zora read back over the words she'd copied from the *Field Guide* last night: *An orb's power to stampede its victims draws from the fear in their own minds.* "Let's go find—"

"I see her!" shouted Ms. Mack.

They watched as Signe emerged from the forest. Her glasses were foggy, and wet spots had formed in the armpits of her shirt. No one spoke as she approached the table.

The pale young woman pushed a strand of damp hair from her face and shaded her eyes with one hand. "Fate favors us," she said. "It's all taken care of."

5

QUINN HELD OUT SIGNE'S PARASOL. "YOU MADE IT PAST THE ORBS?" he asked. "You found a safe route?"

She took the parasol and opened it, then smiled at him. "Not only that, I located every spirit in the forest."

Next to him, Zora made a strangled squawk, like an outraged banty rooster. The merchants looked just as surprised as her, but much more pleased. "Well, I'll be," said Mr. Slocum.

Pride showed on Signe's elfin features. "I've staked flags to mark them. Keep away from those places, and you shouldn't have any problems building your railroad."

"That's *magnificent* news," said Ms. Mack. "How ever did you do it?"

"Being the seventh child of a seventh child, I possess the gift of perceiving spirits even when they're invisible to others. And I've chosen to use this second sight to bring harmony to the Hollows." Signe wiped her glasses with her shirt. "Though the reward would be nice, too."

Quinn goggled at her. *Seventh child of a seventh child?* She'd said she wasn't a Spotter, apprentice or otherwise, but she hadn't mentioned anything about possessing mystical powers.

Though in fairness, it was Zora—not Signe—who'd nixed the conversation about spirit-hunting methods.

His sister scowled. "No doubt you'll want to corroborate her story," she told the merchants.

"That does sound advisable," said Ms. Mack, as Mr. Slocum mopped his scalp. The task obviously didn't appeal to either of them.

Zora stepped forward. "My brother and I can do it for you. Tonight. Once we've seen for ourselves, we'll vouch for her reward. Provided she's earned it."

"If that's what you prefer"—irritation seeped into Signe's tranquil manner—"I have no objection."

"All right, then," said Mr. Slocum. "I'm glad that's settled."

Quinn hustled Zora to the edge of the arcade. "We should find out more about this second sight before you go calling her a liar," he whispered.

"The one with the tattoos was clueless." Zora had that know-it-all air she got whenever he challenged her on anything to do with the spirits. "Spooky here, on the other hand, quacks like a fraud."

Over at the table, the merchants were drawing on a map and peppering Signe with questions. "She *did* spend a night in a forest full of spirits," Quinn said.

Zora snorted. "I bet she went a few steps into the woods and then sat on her butt the whole time without ever leaving sight of here."

"Why are you so suspicious of her?"

"Because of that claptrap she pitched!" Zora imitated Signe's languid tone. "Seventh child, sixth sense, third eye, my backside. Don't tell me you fell for that."

He bristled. "You're being kind of a—let's talk about this later." Signe was walking their way with her parasol balanced on her shoulder.

"So, you're really going into that forest," she said to him.

"Seems to be the plan."

She came closer and touched his arm with her gloved fingers. "I could go with you. The spirits in there are powerful. I can protect you."

Zora spoke first. "Your concern is appreciated, but we work alone."

Signe pulled away from him, then put one hand on her hip and turned to Zora. "I hope you know as much about spirits as you think you do."

Quinn wanted to tell Signe to never mind his sister, that she could join them. "Maybe another time," he said.

She blinked at him from behind her thick lenses. "I'll come to see you off at sunset."

It would be a shame if she turned out to be a charlatan, he thought as he watched her go. She'd read the entire *Witch Hollow, Forge Hollow* series—including the disappointing final book ghostwritten by the original author's son—and knew all the songs about the fiddler girl.

"We'll see who's right," Zora said.

When Quinn and Zora arrived at the arcade that evening, they drew curious glances from everybody they passed. The banisher rested over his shoulder in a makeshift holster, and six brass canisters honeycombed with amethyst tiles hung from a bandolier across his chest. Zora wore an illuminator strapped to each arm.

The merchants sat up with speculative expressions. "Those are some *remarkable* doohickeys y'all have there," said Ms. Mack.

Signe stood nearby, solemn as a graveyard statue. Her new outfit—a black dress with purple frills and matching purple gloves—looked spiffier than the one she'd worn yesterday. Quinn brushed his own faded shirt and patched trousers before waving to her. She nodded, then looked askance at his weapons and chewed her lip.

"Thanks for coming out tonight," Zora announced to the crowd milling around them. "My brother and I are going to use our new spirit-detecting technology to verify this young woman's claims."

Signe tilted her nose upward.

"If all's as she says," Zora went on, "we'll be the first to congratulate her. If not—why, we'll do the job ourselves."

"Great performance," Quinn said, so that only his sister could hear. "Can we go now?"

"See y'all tomorrow!" Zora shouted, basking in the attention. He started toward the forest, and she hurried to catch up. When he looked over his shoulder, Signe was twisting her whitish hair into loops.

Was she worried for their sake, or her own?

A few steps into the woods, and the bright arcade seemed far away. The canopy of leaves blocked out the moon; neither beast nor insect intruded upon the silence. He switched on the banisher's sensors and the flashlight piggybacked to its barrel. Some of the trees reached higher than any he'd ever seen, while others stood dead where they'd grown.

As Quinn helped Zora over a fallen log coated with fungus, his device beeped. He traded looks with his sister, and they advanced cautiously until they found a small flag staked in the ground. He stooped closer to read the letter inked on the white cloth.

It was an F.

The banisher beeped again. Beyond the flag, yellow-green tendrils of fire crawled along the forest floor. Quinn held out his hand, but the spirits gave off no trace of heat.

"Flambs," Zora said. "Just like I figured. Don't touch them, or you'll feel pins and needles for days."

He pointed at the flag. "F for flamb. Signe must've put it there."

Zora blew out her breath. "I suppose."

"Should we look for more flags?"

"Not yet." She knelt, then pulled on her blue-tinted goggles and activated an illuminator. The spirits sputtered within the beam.

"You can shoot them now," she said, but he watched, mesmerized, as the flambs danced in ever-changing patterns across pyres of twigs and pinecones.

"Quit lollygagging." Zora waggled a crutch at him. "Remember what happened to that tattooed buffoon in here. And remember . . ." She turned off the beam. "I want to do this one."

He handed her the banisher, and she leveled it at the spirits. One sweep of its ray extinguished them all, throwing ghostly embers toward the treetops. A smell like burnt fur permeated the air.

"Let's go." Zora gave him back the device and stalked onward past the flag.

Quinn followed her toward the heart of the forest. Why *did* his sister hate the spirits with such ferocity? She'd deflected all his questions on the subject. "No orbs yet," he said. "We must've taken a different route than Mr. Crouch."

As they hunted through the pits and mounds that dotted the forest, they came across another flag. This one bore the letter G.

A jet of chartreuse steam erupted from the ground beyond the flag, spraying the leaves with beads of iridescent goo. Zora shone an illuminator at the spirit. "Gize," she said. "Zap it."

Quinn fired the banisher, and the spirit evaporated with a gurgle. "So Signe was telling the truth," he said.

"I don't get it." Zora plucked the flag from the dirt. "How could—Ha! Her eyes must be sensitive to spirit energy. And her blue glasses must work the same as our cobalt goggles."

That sounded outlandish to him, but no more than half of what Zora said about spirit-y doings. *Paraphysics*, he reminded himself. "In other words, she does have a gift."

"An ability. But not because she's the seventh niece of a seventh aunt, or any hokum like that. It must be a mutation of some sort." Zora dropped the flag and picked her way across a snarl of exposed roots. "I'd love to see how those eyeballs of hers work. Did your mom ever teach you how to do dissections?"

"That's uncharitable of you, little sis."

"I'm joking. Mostly."

"Maybe we should ask Signe to work with us. That talent of hers could be useful." He pictured himself promenading through the woods with her as she used a charmed parasol to shield them from a downpour of raindrop-sized airbound spirits.

"We don't need her help," said Zora. "My inventions can do everything she can, plus more." She halted without warning, and Quinn bumped into her.

A row of flags stretched across their path. The circles on them looked like blank eyes staring back from the darkness.

"O for orbs." He glanced at the banisher's battery gauge. Still almost full.

"These things are stronger than any spirit we've faced yet," said Zora. "So watch out."

"You're sure we can handle them?"

"Just be ready with those grenades."

A tremor shook his bones, and a dull thudding started from under the ground. Moments later, a second beat joined it. Then two more. Zora sat back on her heels, and a clutch of orange bulbs came to life on her devices.

The drumming beneath Quinn's feet grew louder. His ears popped as he lifted the banisher.

Something huge and globular rose from the earth to bathe the woods in green light.

The orb stopped when it was eye level with him. Zora pointed one of her illuminators at it, and the spirit's halo reflected the beam like a soap bubble. Three more orbs surfaced behind it.

The first spirit reached toward him with its aura. "Shoot!" Zora called out, her voice tight.

Quinn pierced the orb with violet, and its halo dimmed. He held the trigger, but the spirit kept on coming.

"It's not enough." His mouth had gone dry. "Take this and keep it up!" He thrust the banisher into her hands. As she fumbled with it, the first orb's halo expanded again.

The other spirits floated closer. If he failed now, he'd end up lost in the dark forest, trying to find his way back to Zora.

Quinn pulled a grenade from his bandolier and pushed a button on it, then threw it at the nearest orb. A flash of violet dazzled him, and a wet boom followed a split second later. Once his vision returned, the spirit was gone.

In the meantime, Zora had shifted her aim toward another orb drawing within range. While she held it off, Quinn flung another grenade. He shut his eyes just before the explosion.

Two orbs—and two pulsing beats—remained. Zora alternated her fire between them in a futile effort to keep both at bay.

He grabbed a pair of grenades, used his thumbs to activate them, and lobbed them at the spirits. One landed a direct hit. The other went wide, but enough of the blast caught its target to shear away the thing's aura.

Zora focused the ray on the last of the orbs, and the spirit ruptured into fragments that vanished before they reached the ground.

Quinn felt as if he'd just carried a corpse down three flights of stairs. He sat on the forest floor next to his sister. Everything was so still he could scarcely credit what had just happened.

"Four points for us," she said. "Zero for them. Though it's a good thing the new grenades worked."

"How long do they take to recharge?" He could make out mauve glows where the devices had landed. "We'll need them again if we run into more of those things."

"About ten minutes."

"I'll collect them in a bit," he said. "For now, I just want to stay here."

She had no argument with that.

Quinn and Zora spent the rest of the night combing the woods for spirits. Aided by Signe's flags, they found and banished five more orbs—including a solitary giant that took three grenades to finish off—along with eleven patches of flambs and a score of gizes.

As the sky lightened in the east, they turned back toward Mill Hollow. Partway there, Zora called for a break and pulled up the cuffs of her overalls to knead her calves. "Your myopic clairvoyant really did mark all the spirits in this forest," she said. "Maybe we could use another set of eyes."

"I think you're right." Quinn didn't point out that his sister had been wrong about Signe earlier. "And she seemed interested in helping us."

Zora gave him a sly look. "I think she just wants to bat her squinty eyes at you some more."

"Really?" he asked, before he could check himself.

"You're soft on her." She snickered. "I'll leave the accounting for taste to the biologists. Just don't expect me to buy her rigmarole about being a magical fairy girl or whatever."

Let the two of them debate that, he told himself.

When they arrived at the pavilion, the merchants were dozing in their chairs. Signe peered at them from a bench with her folded-up parasol on her lap. The arcade lay quiet and empty except for a lone dog scrounging through the stalls.

Zora woke the merchants by knocking on their table.

Mr. Slocum rubbed his eyes. "How'd it go?"

Quinn made sure to speak first this time. "Everything was as Ms. Janasdottir said. She deserves your reward for marking a route past the spirits." Signe puffed up on hearing that.

"My apologies for doubting you," added Zora.

"That's *exceptional*," said Ms. Mack. "Now let's see about your reward—"

"One other thing," said Zora. "You don't need to worry about following any flags. We cleared out all the spirits."

The merchants regarded her with thunderstruck faces. "You did *what*?" Signe squeaked, jumping to her feet.

Zora extended one arm to show off an illuminator. "We used these to light them up, and the inventions my brother has to get rid of them."

"But how?" asked Mr. Slocum, still incredulous.

"As a merchant," Zora said, "I'm sure you'll understand our keeping that information to ourselves. But feel free to confirm our claims." She pointed toward the forest. "We'll wait for our bonus."

Signe frowned. "That wasn't necessary. I'd already blazed a trail."

"The orbs were dangerous," said Quinn, who'd envisioned a reaction more along the lines of starry-eyed wonderment. "You said so yourself, and we all saw what they did to poor Mr. Crouch." He steeled himself. "Actually, we were hoping you would—"

She didn't wait for him to finish. "Yes, meddling with spirits is perilous. Which is why I'm so appalled by your rash actions."

That left Quinn speechless, his fancies of mixing romance and spirit-chasing abruptly dispelled.

"The people of the Hollows have spent generations living in the shadow of those monsters." Zora's cheeks reddened beneath her freckles. "Now that I've given us the power to fight back, we ought to use it."

Signe's face remained calm, but she'd set to tapping her palm with her parasol. "What makes you think they'll let you attack them, without finding a way to strike back?"

Zora's voice rose. "*They* brought this war to *us*. What would you do—teach them songs? Draw rainbows with them?"

"We're surrounded by beings that could kill us all, if they chose to," said Signe. "I came up with a solution that would've preserved the balance between spirits and humans in this place. Then you went and jeopardized everyone. Especially yourself, you arrogant brat."

"Hey, now." Quinn stepped between them. He wouldn't stand for anyone talking to his sister that way. "No call for that."

"And you." Signe pointed the tip of her parasol at him. "She's just a kid, but I thought you'd be more sensible. I see I misjudged you."

He stiffened. "I reckon I was wrong about you, too."

They stared at one another for the space of a few breaths. Signe lowered her parasol, and her jaw moved as though she were about to reply. Instead, she turned toward the merchants, who'd watched the exchange with dazed looks. "I'll be in my wagon," she said, and strode away through the arcade.

Quinn started after her, but caught himself before he'd gone three paces.

"So much for adding her as a partner," said Zora.

His sister spent the rest of the day gloating while he drove the wagon. "This trip was just what we needed," she said, for what must've been the tenth time. "We whomped those orbs and made out like river bandits doing it. When we get back to my lab, I can finish the new prototype."

All true. Yet Quinn found himself in a dour mood as they rode through the sticky evening air.

"I think she's a Spiritist," Zora said, without preamble.

"Who's a Spiritist?"

"You know. Ms. Smarty Jinxbottom."

"You're kidding."

"Nope. Think about what she said. Arguing we should surrender to the spirits instead of fighting them." She patted his head. "You're too good for her."

The wheels squished in their tracks. Mushrooms lined the sides of the road, and ferns carpeted the ground beyond them. He and Zora had come to Willow Bog.

Quinn held back a sigh. "All she said was that it's unwise to disturb them."

"Of course," Zora said. "You'd hardly expect a spirit-lover to come right out and call for bowing down and offering sacrifices to those things. So instead we get plausible-sounding bilge about living in peace with the spirits."

Ursula and Undine swished their tails at a cloud of gnats. "What makes you think the Spiritists are even real?" Quinn asked, slapping a mosquito on his arm. Every tale he'd ever heard about the cult had involved the teller's friend-of-a-cousin or cousin-of-a-friend from some unnamed hollow.

Zora harrumphed. "Human nature. The misguided and the gullible will sink to any depths in the face of a danger they don't comprehend."

Ahead of them, the road curved past a shanty balanced on wooden stilts. Quinn glimpsed long, white hair in the window—but grayish white, not goldish white. "Maybe Signe had a point," he said. "We're only a pair of teenagers, against all the spirits in the Hollows and beyond."

"We can't quit," Zora insisted. "We've just started the next part of the plan, and now—"

"Hold up there," a voice shouted from the roadside.

Quinn stopped the wagon. An elderly woman was standing on the shanty's porch. "Are y'all those spirit-hunters?" she asked.

Zora's eyes bugged. "You've heard of us?"

The woman nodded. "My nephew came by earlier today, bursting to tell me about a pair of young folks who could drive out spirits. A dark-haired boy, and a redheaded girl with"— she thwacked a cane against the porch—"two of these. If you're them, I sure could use your help."

Quinn vaulted down from the wagon. "We're the spirit-hunters, all right. What's troubling you?"

"A kelpie," the woman said. "It's dwelled hereabouts since the Lesser Wakening, but it's acting up something awful this summer. My grandkids can't even sleep at night anymore. If the floods come again, I'm afraid it may break loose and hurt them. It took one of our kittens during the last big rain."

"We'll pay a call on this waterbound for you." Zora strapped on her illuminators. "Show us where it is."

The first stars of the night had appeared in the sky. Quinn and his sister were sitting on milk crates by an oxbow lake fringed with cattails and smothered with lily pads. Whirligigs spun on its surface, stirring up tiny whirlpools in the black water.

When a splash came from the opposite bank, he raised his banisher to scan the oxbow.

"Just a snapping turtle," Zora said.

Quinn ate another bite of the fried catfish they'd received as their fee for this job. "Word gets around fast in the Hollows," he said. "After we swing by your home, I need to hurry on over to mine and talk with Mom about my future." He was still nervous about how that would go, but he'd finally decided what he wanted to say.

Their devices lit up, and dragonflies scattered into the bulrushes. An algae-hued shape welled up from among the lily pads to burble vacantly. Its weed-like limbs gave off a dull sheen as they unfurled.

Quinn plugged the kelpie on the first try, and it blew up in a spout of fetid water. Ripples spread across the lake before settling.

Forget the reward from the merchants, he thought. Keeping the old woman's grandchildren safe from a spirit that could flow right under their house topped beating the orbs.

Zora pumped an arm in the air. "We just bagged ourselves a waterbound. And when"—she broke off in mid-boast.

A sound murmured in the back of Quinn's brain, almost like a voice. He imagined he heard garbled words, but they were gone before he could make sense of them.

Zora gazed off into the cattails.

"What was that?" he asked.

"Nothing," she said. "Just a rogue wave of spirit energy."

He shook his head to clear away a muzzy feeling. "Are you sure?" He'd never experienced anything like that, not even when the tangle had struck him in Saltpeter Hollow. And none of Zora's books had mentioned a whispering spirit, either.

"Of course." She took off her goggles and smiled at him. "So how do you like being a living legend, big brother?"

PART TWO

THE MANSION ON THE MOUNTAIN &
THE HOUSE IN THE HOLLOW

6

Zora slumped on the Prosser funeral home's porch swing and waited for her stomach to stop churning. Ducking away by herself to explore the house had seemed like a good way to give Quinn and his mom some time alone to talk—that is, until she'd come across a puffy-cheeked cadaver laid out on a table. One sight of it and she'd bolted outside for some fresh air.

Voices carried to her through the open window. Quinn had just confessed that he'd spent the past two moons hunting spirits, and the liquid nitrogen in Ms. Prosser's tone boded trouble. Still, it could've been worse. At least she'd found out straight from her son, instead of the increasingly extravagant tales winding their way through the Hollows.

Zora strained to hear the quiet conversation inside. When she'd told *her* mom about the orbs, their argument had rattled the walls of the Coldiron house, but this side of the family did things differently.

"I could tell from your letters you were hiding something," Ms. Prosser was saying. "You'd never shown an interest in tinkering before, and then you write me about some vague scheme to test gadgets with your sister. Are you doing this on account of Paige going off to be a Spotter?"

"No." Quinn had gone all huffy. "Well, maybe that was part of it at first. But not anymore. She has her calling, you have yours, and now I have mine."

Ms. Prosser sighed. "At first, I was just relieved you weren't moping around the parlor. I told myself you were trying to be a good brother, whatever you were up to."

"I have been," Quinn said. "I promised Ms. Coldiron I'd try to keep her daughter safe."

That was news to Zora. She wasn't sure whether to be touched or insulted.

"Chasing after spirits is not what I call safe," said Ms. Prosser. "This isn't one of your make-believe stories. I've a mind to set you polishing caskets and repainting the hearse till you come to your senses."

A pair of bumblebees flew past Zora, buzzing like miniature gyroscopes. She tried to slow her heartbeat by concentrating on the hanging pots of fuchsia. The neatly trimmed yard. The water tumbling over the small cliff at the head of the valley. Minus Quinn as a partner, she'd be stuck back in Lightning Bug Hollow with her mom and a barn full of goats.

"That girl's too smart to be gambling your lives on such recklessness," Ms. Prosser went on. "Plus, she's so small and—and delicate. She belongs in her lab, not gallivanting through the woods after dark."

Zora ground her teeth until her jaws hurt. She was nobody's fragile little flower. Sooner or later, everyone would know that.

"I daresay my sister belongs where she sets her mind to be," said Quinn.

A clock struck inside the funeral home, and a squirrel scampered down one of the white porch columns. Four more chimes sounded, then died away.

"You know, your father used to go on about the mysteries of the spirits," said Ms. Prosser, after what felt like an eon. "Why they first appeared. Where they came from. Why they spared the Hollows. And so on."

It was Quinn's turn to sound surprised. "You never mentioned that."

Zora leaned closer to the window.

"Vernon told me stories about seeing them on his trips," said Ms. Prosser. "In spite of the danger, he took to traveling after nightfall. Said he could save time and make more money that way. I always suspected him of embellishing some details and neglecting to mention others."

"What kind of stories?" asked Quinn.

"Being stalked by a pack of herns and barely escaping with his life, for one." She paused. "Working with some wild-eyed Spotter on a hush-hush project that came to naught. Taking shortcuts through the Border Hollows by the spirit-shine from the Ruined Town. Beyond that, you'd have to ask him." Another pause, longer this time. "You should check on your sister while I think about what you've told me."

Zora kicked her feet to start the swing rocking just as Quinn stepped through the doorway. He didn't seem to notice the open window. "You look like you've seen an elemental in broad daylight," he said. "Or one of Cascade Hollow's famous ghosts."

"I still don't believe in those." She glanced at the six-bulb spirit detector strapped to her wrist. She'd built it the night after their stop at Willow Bog, on the odd chance she'd been wrong about that aftershock of spirit-energy from the kelpie. Since then, she'd taken to wearing the device—her wrist-watcher, she'd named it—all the time, even to bed.

Hoofbeats echoed through the valley as a man on horseback rounded the turnoff for the funeral home. His red and gold uniform marked him as a courier.

Ms. Prosser came outside to the porch, wearing a leather smock over her house dress. She was a slender woman who shared Quinn's fine features, though hers showed lines from age. Her dark braid hung past her shoulder blades.

"Hi, Ms. Prosser," said Zora, more meekly than she'd meant to. Something about Quinn's mom intimidated her. Maybe it was her watchful, reserved manner. Or maybe it was the fact that she kept dead bodies lying around her house.

"That's Aunt Anne to you, young lady." Ms. Prosser's voice was stern, but she smiled as she spoke.

The rider brought his horse to a stop, dismounted, and delivered a stack of letters to Ms. Prosser. She flipped through them and then held up a cucumber-colored envelope. "To Coldiron and Prosser Ventures," she said.

Quinn took it. "From Evelyn Fontaine of Clack Mountain. Do you know her?"

Zora shook her head.

"I've never met her," said Ms. Prosser. "But rumor has it she's the richest person in the North Hollows."

Quinn opened the envelope and read aloud:

Dear Ms. Coldiron & Mr. Prosser,

If this letter reaches you, I hope it finds you well. My sources tell me you've developed technology for finding and eliminating spirits. Allow me to congratulate you on your ingenuity.

At the risk of being presumptuous, I'd like to hire you to investigate a spirit trespassing on my property. Knowing something of these beings myself, I've gleaned that it's a dahoo. *If the reports I've heard are true, dealing with such a minor spirit should be well within your capabilities.*

No doubt you're busy, but I'm prepared to pay a 100-bit consultation fee and all your expenses if you visit my home on Clack Mountain at your earliest convenience to discuss this issue—along with other potential opportunities. I'm confident we can reach a satisfactory arrangement. Directions are enclosed.

Respectfully yours,
Evelyn Fontaine

"Our first commission!" shouted Zora. Her brother grinned, and even Ms. Prosser looked impressed.

"What do you suppose 'other potential opportunities' means?" Quinn asked.

"I'd like to know," said Zora. "Inventing's not cheap."

"See," Quinn told his mom, "here's another chance for us to help somebody and make money doing it. The dahoo is"—he wrinkled his forehead—"a rare but innocuous type of roaming spirit." Zora had to give him credit for how much he'd learned from reading her guides at bedtime. He might be ready for some fundamentals of paraphysics, or even a primer on the debate over the celestial and terrestrial theories of spirigenesis.

"It's your decision." Ms. Prosser said, with a hint of sadness. "I can't tell you what to do anymore, Quinn."

"I believe in what we're doing." He nodded at Zora. "And I believe we're the ones to do it." She resisted the impulse to hug him. As partners, the two of them could take on anything. Well, anything except an elemental.

"I've seen firsthand what spirits can do to careless folks," Ms. Prosser said. "I've helped bury their bodies. Just keep that in mind." She gave them each a somber look. "Both of you."

Zora and Quinn set out for the North Hollows the next morning. Two and a half days later, they caught their first glimpse of Clack Mountain. The massive limestone formations on its slopes resembled ancient forts and towers.

Perspiration trickled under Zora's starched white shirt and brown plaid skirt. Not exactly practical clothes for spirit-hunting, but this house call might be the key to making her—their—plans come true. She'd even let her hair down to make herself look more grown-up. Beside her, Quinn was sweating through his best funeral suit.

When they reached the base of the mountain, they followed the letter's directions onto a narrow road that spiraled upward. By the time they arrived at the peak, the horses were tired, and Zora was hungry for dinner.

A three-story mansion of greenish stone spread its wings across the flat summit. Dormer windows along the top floor reflected the late afternoon sun, and a weathervane in the shape of a crescent moon rose above the cupola on the roof.

She eyed the walls. "I've never seen rock like that before."

"It's called serpentine." Quinn steered the wagon toward a

stable. "Not local stuff. They must've shipped it from Sylvania before the spirits blocked the route."

"Just you wait," said Zora. "We'll reopen the Pass one of these days." No radio signal had reached the Hollows from the outside world for sixty-six years, but maybe someone in Sylvania had escaped the Lesser Wakening. "How do you know so much about geology, anyway?"

"Grave digging and headstones, remember?"

"Oh. Right."

Quinn unharnessed the horses and got them settled while Zora approached the mansion. The front steps led to oak double doors with relief carvings of deer on the right-hand side and goats on the left.

Her brother rejoined her. "How do I look?" he asked, as he tucked in his shirt.

Zora reached up with one hand to smooth his hair. "A little shaggy, but still respectable. You even shaved."

He rapped an iron knocker in the shape of a woman's head with antlers. Nobody came out to greet them. "Try again," she said.

The doors opened, so silently Zora almost started. A tall woman looked out at them from the mansion's front hallway. Her salt and pepper hair fell to the collar of her emerald dress.

She smiled. "You must be Ms. Coldiron and Mr. Prosser."

"That's us," said Zora. "Are you . . ."

"Evelyn Fontaine." The woman beckoned them into a foyer lit by electric lamps with frosted shades. "Come, come. I'm so pleased you accepted my invitation."

A thick rug deadened the thumping of Zora's crutches. She

listened in vain for the hum of a generator big enough to power a house this size.

The foyer opened into a cavernous study. Four velvet couches formed a square in its center beneath an ornate chandelier that hung from the high ceiling. Rays of gold and green streamed through a stained glass window depicting another antlered woman. Must be the family motif, Zora decided.

"Have a seat," their host said. Quinn eased himself onto one of the couches and glanced at the gilded spines on the bookshelves. Zora sat next to him, so closely her knee almost touched his. She felt self-conscious surrounded by such unfamiliar elegance.

"You must be parched." Ms. Fontaine pulled the stopper from an amber-colored bottle. "Bourbon?"

Zora stared at the whiskey, which was probably worth more than their wagon. "Just water." Quinn seemed to think about the offer, but then seconded her request.

Ms. Fontaine brought them crystal tumblers of water and poured bourbon over ice for herself. "So, you're the famed prodigies who are launching a new age in the Hollows."

"Thank you," Zora stammered, as the blood rose to her cheeks. "We've only started exploring the potential of my inventions."

"Though we hope we can help you with your problem, ma'am," Quinn added.

Ms. Fontaine raised her glass. "Then to you, my guests." She sipped the bourbon and set it aside. "Before we talk business, allow me to show you something I think will interest you." She guided them through an arched doorway into a long corridor. Recessed bulbs filled it with soft light, and picture frames lined the wood-paneled walls.

Their host held out her arms as if to encompass the corridor. "My collection of spirit photographs. The largest of its kind in the Hollows."

The picture closest to Zora captured a fuzzy circle trailing dozens of slender threads. "A medusa?" she asked.

The woman gave her an approving look. "Just so, my young friend." She pointed to the next photograph. "Do you know what this one is?"

Zora let out a gasp when she saw the snakelike form. "The spirit from Saltpeter Hollow!" Then she lowered her voice an octave to its normal register. "I named it the tangle."

"I imagined you'd recognize it," said Ms. Fontaine. "As you can tell, I've done my homework on the pair of you."

Quinn inspected a close-up portrait of a boge. "Did you take these pictures yourself?"

"Dear me, no. I'm hardly a brave adventurer like you. I prefer to craft the plans and let others do the rest." She wrapped her arm around Zora's shoulder. "And now, pardon me while I make some preparations. My helpers are away for the night, so I'll be serving dinner myself. In the meantime, perhaps you'd like to examine the rest of my gallery."

"Absolutely," Zora said. She'd never seen anything that compared to this collection.

Ms. Fontaine rolled up her sleeves as she left through the arched doorway. "What do you think?" Quinn asked, when her footsteps had faded away.

"All minor spirits. Her photographers must not have the guts to try for anything bigger."

"I meant about her."

"She knows her stuff." Zora spun the end of one crutch in

a circle. "Plus, the woman has money to spare. This could be a great opportunity for us."

Quinn walked to the door at the other end of the gallery. "I wonder whether there's more back here." He turned the handle, but the door was locked. "I reckon not."

They browsed the collection until Ms. Fontaine returned and conducted them to a dining room every bit as fancy as the other rooms they'd visited. Paintings of deer—including a reproduction, or possibly the original, of *The Monarch of the Hollow*—decorated three of the walls. The bay window in the fourth wall overlooked the hills to the west. Two gold candelabras cast a gentle glow onto a table large enough to seat a dozen.

Ms. Fontaine took the place at the head of the table and waved them to chairs on either side of her. Then she ladled food from silver dishes onto their plates. Crawdads in tomato sauce. Thin slices of pink steak. A medley of gold carrots, red potatoes, and some vegetable that smelled of licorice. Dewberry pie.

Zora dug into her steak, while her brother sampled each dish. "Everything's delicious," he said.

Their host inclined her head. "And now to the reasons behind my invitation. For starters, I'm curious whether you'd be willing to explain how your inventions work."

Zora swallowed the food in her mouth. "Sorry, but no. We're not ready to share that information with anyone."

"I could make it worth your while," said Ms. Fontaine.

"Not at any price," said Zora. "At least not yet."

Ms. Fontaine laughed softly. "I can't say I'm surprised. But would you be open to having an investor?"

"Sure!" Zora could scarcely contain her excitement. "We could do so much more if we had the resources."

"I'd like to pursue that subject, after the immediate issue has been resolved. Speaking of which—have you ever dealt with a dahoo?"

"Not yet," said Quinn.

"But your spirit should be no match for us," added Zora.

"Excellent." Ms. Fontaine took a small leather case from a buffet. "I'm willing to pay your going rate for a cluster of orbs—yes, I know all about that, too—if you can attend to this one spirit. Double if you bring back a photograph of it. Perhaps you noticed my collection doesn't include a dahoo." She opened the case to reveal a camera. "Do you know how to use one of these?"

"My mom taught me how," Quinn said. "Hers isn't so shiny, mind you."

Ms. Fontaine handed him the camera. With its graceful lines and brass trim, the thing was a work of art.

"We'll take your picture," Zora said. "And then we'll get the spirit out of your hair permanently."

Ms. Fontaine smiled. "That's what I'd hoped to hear."

Night had fallen over Clack Mountain. While Quinn fed the horses, Zora went inside the wagon, changed into her overalls, and fastened the illuminators to her arms.

"Everything's fully charged," she said, when her brother came back.

He holstered the banisher and hooked the spirit-grenades to his bandolier. Then he picked up her latest prototype, a brass disk with vents along its sides and a quartz window on its top. "Should we bring this, just in case?"

She nodded and pocketed a remote control.

Their new client was waiting for them on the mansion's veranda. "That's where the spirit appeared." She directed them toward the north face of the mountain. "Three times in the past five evenings." Beyond a black row of hills, the spirit-aurora scintillated on the horizon.

Quinn slipped the camera into a backpack with the prototype. "This could take a while, so we may not see you till the morning."

"Farewell, then," Ms. Fontaine said. "And happy hunting."

Zora tied up her pigtails, and Quinn turned on the banisher's flashlight attachment. He took point as they navigated down the mountainside. Every few minutes, she checked her devices for evidence of the spirit.

Her brother pointed to a streak of light in the sky. "Shooting star. Want to make a wish?"

"We're on the doorstep of the Wastes," she said. "So it could be a bolide or some other type of airbound. Like the ones that brought down the airship *Sheltowee*." A zeppelin full of hydrogen gas and a spark of spirit-energy must've made for an explosive combination.

"Bubble-burster," he muttered.

They wound their way toward one of the limestone monoliths. "Sedimentary rock," she said.

"I know. Once upon a time, the Hollows and all the rest of Old Appalachia lay at the bottom of a great sea." He tapped his forehead. "Remember, I'm the geology expert here."

As they passed the hulking shape, a rustling came from the other side of it. "Did you hear that?" Quinn whispered.

"Yes." Zora looked at her wrist-watcher. "It's not the spirit."

"It sounded big. Stay here, but be ready." He switched

off the flashlight and started creeping around the limestone formation.

Before he'd taken more than a few steps, a dark figure ran away into the trees. Within seconds, it was out of earshot.

Quinn made his way back to Zora, no longer bothering with stealth. "What was it?" she asked. "A deer? A bear?"

"A person. Following us."

Her chest tightened. "Who?"

"I couldn't see."

"I bet it's a Spiritist." Like that snotty Signe person, Zora thought but didn't say. "I'm sure they'd like to get back at us for what we've been doing."

"Maybe," said Quinn. "Or maybe it's a copycat. You heard our client—folks might pay a lot to get their hands on your devices."

That did make a lot of sense. "What should we do?"

"Our mystery friend seems shy—too shy, I'm guessing, to try anything direct. How about we go ahead, but stay on guard for spirits *and* people?"

She relaxed a little. "If anyone did spy on us, they'd never be able to duplicate my inventions just from watching."

"I've been using them all summer," he said, "and I still couldn't do it."

They continued down the mountainside for the better part of an hour until a series of beeps and pops brought them to a stop. One orange bulb showed on the stock of the banisher and each of Zora's devices. "I think we've found our dahoo," she said.

They snuck behind a nearby boulder, and Quinn scrambled to the top. "I've got a bead on it," he said.

"Let me see." Using her hands and knees, she worked her

way next to him. A ring of light was weaving toward them through the trees. As it moved, its color shifted back and forth between yellow and dark green. It was a dahoo, all right; everything about it matched the description in the *Field Guide*.

Quinn gave Zora the banisher to hold while he removed the prototype from his pack. "Cover me," he said. Then he slid down and ran partway toward the spirit. Once he'd set the brass disk on the ground, he dashed back to the boulder.

"Great job, big brother," Zora said. "Right in its path." She took the remote control from her pocket.

The ring-shaped spirit neared their trap, keening as it came. Quinn held the camera to his eye, and she poised her thumb over the detonator. "Hold on till it's a bit closer," he said.

The dahoo stopped in the middle of the clearing. Its aura lightened, and its cry went ultrasonic.

Quinn snapped four pictures. A flash of deep crimson accompanied each click of the shutter, creating an illusion that his face was soaked in blood. Zora wondered whether the camera captured infrared rays along with visible light. She'd never paid much thought to spirit-photography, but maybe it warranted a closer look.

"Got it," Quinn said.

The spirit turned dark green again and made a beeline toward them. The instant it passed over the trap, Zora pressed the detonator. A half-sphere of violet light radiated from the brass disk, enveloping the dahoo. Its wailing ceased as it dissolved.

"Overkill for such a dinky spirit," said Zora. "But now we know it works." While Quinn retrieved the disk, she peeked at the camera. She was tempted to take it apart, but that probably wouldn't please its owner. After a final going-over, she gave it back to her brother for safekeeping.

They started back up the mountainside, using the constellations of the Swan and the Lyre to guide their way. Zora's mood soared as she tallied up figures in her head. With the money from this job, she could take a crack at building a full-blown elemental-buster. And if Ms. Fontaine decided to invest some of her wealth into developing new spirit-tech, the possibilities would be limitless.

Three noises—one from her right arm, one from her left, and another from her wrist-watcher—interrupted her thoughts.

"Another dahoo?" asked Quinn.

"Unlikely. Nevan McBrain says they're solitary." She pointed toward the closest limestone formation, a four-story giant with trees growing on its top. "We can hide over there while we figure this out." She set out toward it, and Quinn followed her with the banisher at the ready.

Halfway to the monolith, Zora heard a barrage of sounds that turned her insides to ice, from esophagus to intestines. Every light on her devices had turned orange. All six bulbs on her wrist. All *twenty* bulbs on each arm.

Quinn stared past her. With panic rising in her heart, she wheeled around. A spirit was racing toward them from below. Not another harmless dahoo, but a rippling monstrosity that stretched the length of a steamboat.

It was a hount—and if it caught them, it would undoubtedly kill them.

7

QUINN FROZE, TRANSFIXED BY THE SIGHT OF THE SPIRIT RUSHING toward them like a river of boiling green light. His mind flashed back to the junkshop in Saltpeter Hollow. The thing streaming up the mountainside was the spitting image of the worst nightmare in the painting. Zora's inventions couldn't save them, not against this.

And it knew they were here.

"Go!" He pushed his sister toward the limestone formation. She took off as fast as her feet and crutches could carry her.

Not fast enough. The hount was gaining on them. Even if they made it to the rock, what then?

Quinn stopped to face the spirit. "Don't slow down," he called out. Zora passed him, gulping for air.

As the hount bore down upon them, eddies from its aura stripped leaves and bark from the trees. Quinn ripped a spirit-grenade from the bandolier on his chest. A roar like a waterfall hammered in his skull.

He hurled the grenade as hard as he could, straight at the spirit. In the same motion, he grabbed another grenade and threw it after the first one. Without waiting to see the results, he started running again. Two explosions thundered behind him, followed by an ear-splitting scream. When he caught up with Zora, he chanced a look back. The hount was flowing away toward the other side of the rock formation.

"You wounded it," she said, between pants for breath, "but it'll take more than that to stop it." Her eyes were huge.

Quinn scanned the rock face for any sign of shelter. After a few frantic seconds, he spotted a crack running from the top of the formation almost to the bottom. He pointed, and Zora hurried toward it with him right on her heels.

Dangling her crutches by their cuffs from her elbows, she used her hands to pull herself up toward the crevice. Quinn gave her a shove on the rear to push her the rest of the way, and she landed on her stomach with a grunt.

He hoisted himself after her. In the meantime, she'd risen to her feet and squeezed herself deeper into the crevice. "Maybe it won't be able to reach us here," she said.

Quinn backed away from the mouth of their hiding spot. "If the hount's still out there, we're trapped."

She looked up, and he followed her gaze to a sliver of star-filled sky. A pit formed in his stomach as he realized what he had to do. If he climbed to the top, he'd be able to see whether the spirit was searching for them.

Quinn gave Zora the banisher and two of the remaining grenades. Her lip quivered, but then she clenched her jaw. "If it shows up," she said, "I'll give it a good, hard sting."

He wiped his hands on his shirt and wedged himself between the two sides of the cleft. Before his courage could fail him, he began levering his way up. It was easy at first, but the gap grew wider as he went. Each time he raised a hand or foot, the strain grew worse. By the time he made it to the top, his forehead was slick and his arms were shaking.

Quinn peered down into the crevice. Zora waved the banisher at him, its lights throwing orange streaks across her pale face. He waved back, then followed the crack to the near edge of the rock formation. Far below, the mountainside sloped away into darkness. The spirit wasn't there. So far, so good.

No time to spare. He darted through scraggly pines to the other side. As soon as he had a clear view of the forest floor, he saw the seething glow of the hount. It was circling the rock, probing behind boulders and trees with foxfire tentacles. With every passing second, its aura grew brighter and its call grew louder. Next to it, an orb would've been like a tadpole to a rattlesnake.

Meddling with spirits is perilous, Signe had said. *What makes you think they'll let you attack them, without finding some way to strike back?*

Quinn returned to the crevice and started the descent back to Zora. This direction was even worse, seeing as how he had to look down to find his footholds. After a few nerve-rending minutes, he reached the narrower part and clambered as quickly as he dared. With a little ways to go, he slipped and fell backwards to the bottom. His pack cushioned his landing with a dull crunch.

Zora helped him into a sitting position, a worried expression on her face. "I'm fine," he said. He wasn't so sure about her prototype or Ms. Fontaine's camera. The bonus for photographing the dahoo was the least of their worries, anyhow. "It's coming."

"I'm sorry I got you into this." Zora's voice was raw. Even in the gloom of the cleft, he could see her tears.

All of a sudden, she cocked her head. Gesturing over her shoulder with her hand, she mouthed a word to him. Quinn gave her a blank look. She did it again, and this time he understood.

He slid off his pack and set it down. Through its fabric, a red light was flashing in a steady rhythm.

Keeping a grenade in one hand, he used the other to dig out the camera case and open it. Dents from the fall had twisted the elegant brass trim. The lens hung from the front, exposing a blinking, helix-shaped bulb inside the camera's metal guts.

Quinn placed the camera on the ground, and Zora removed the bulb. After a moment's scrutiny, she rotated it to show him the small black device attached to it. The next pulse of red revealed a toggle. She flipped it, and the flashes stopped. What in the Wastes—

The approaching roar of the hount scattered his thoughts. Chunks of his supper surged up his gullet, but he swallowed them back down.

Radiance the color of tarnished copper gathered at the mouth of the crevice. As Quinn watched with mounting dread, a tentacle slithered through the opening. He focused his entire will on not moving, not breathing. Zora sat motionless, betrayed only by the wobbling of the banisher's snout.

The tentacle lashed along the rock walls, seeking its prey. Now it was barely an arm's length away. Zora closed her eyes, then opened them again and took aim. Quinn lowered his thumb to the grenade's switch. It seemed as though all of reality had collapsed into this one crevice—a cramped world inhabited only by him, his sister, and the spirit at the threshold.

Before he or Zora could act, the tentacle withdrew as abruptly as it had come. The green light dwindled away, and the sounds from the hount receded into the night.

Still holding the banisher with one arm, Zora hugged him with the other. He held her tight, keeping his thumb suspended above the grenade all the while. They sat in silence for a long time.

"I'll check on it," Quinn whispered, at last. She let go, and he tiptoed toward the cleft's opening. Near the edge, he lowered himself onto his hands and knees to peek over the rim. Down the mountainside, the hount was thrashing through the trees. From the looks of it, it was trying to retrace their steps.

Zora crawled up beside him and blanched at the sight of the hount. Together, the two of them retreated into the crevice. "If it keeps hunting for us," she said, "it'll find us long before sunrise. And then we'll be done for."

"Was that flashing thing in the camera what I think it was?"

"A spirit-lure, you mean?" Her voice rang hollow within the crevice. "It doesn't look like any normal camera part, that's for sure. And I doubt it's a coincidence we ran across a hount straying outside the Wastes."

"Can you figure out how the device works?"

She shook her head. "If I had time to disassemble it, and the equipment from my lab back home. Right now? Not a chance."

Quinn pictured Ms. Fontaine reclining in her mansion, drinking a glass of bourbon beneath her stained glass window. "You know what this means, don't you?"

"Yes." Zora sounded beaten down. "But we have a more urgent problem."

Casting about for any sort of strategy, he reached into his backpack and pulled out the prototype they'd used on the dahoo. "Did I break this, too?"

She turned it over in her hands and touched a button on the side. "Nope." She hesitated. "I have a plan, but it's risky. For both of us, but you especially."

"Riskier than just waiting around for the hount to find us?"

Zora cracked the shadow of a grin and explained her idea. It seemed reasonable to him, as much as any plan could when it involved going *toward* the hount. "At least this way, we'll have a fighting chance," she said. "And we'll know for sure whether our client"—she was snarling now—"tried to trick us out here to our deaths."

Quinn stuffed the prototype and the device from the camera into his pack, patted the spirit-grenades strapped to his chest, and picked up the banisher. Then he dropped from the crevice's mouth onto the ground. The sound of pebbles shifting under his feet made him flinch. As lightly as he could, he stole down the mountainside in the direction of the hount.

A loud crash brought him to a halt. The spirit must've knocked down a rotten tree. Blasts of noise from the thing— Quinn couldn't help but think of them as frustrated groans— made the branches tremble overhead.

This spot would have to do; to go any closer would be court- ing certain death. He placed the prototype in the undergrowth. Next, he took the device with the helix-shaped bulb, set it on the disk, and flipped the toggle.

At the first flash of red, Quinn sprinted toward the crevice. Partway there, he slipped on a bed of pine needles and went down on one knee. Behind him, the clamor from the hount rose to a crescendo. His heart pounding, he got back up and kept go- ing until he reached the crevice.

Zora grasped his hand and tugged him up. In the back of his

mind, he marked how strong all those years of using crutches had made her arms.

"It took the bait," she whispered. Sure enough, the hount was coursing up the slope—toward the blinking red light if they were right, or past it and toward them if they were wrong.

Zora held up the remote.

As the spirit closed in on their trap, it slowed and reared so high in the air that its foremost tentacles cleared the tops of the surrounding pines.

When a pinpoint of red appeared, the hount thrust itself down at the light. Zora pushed the button on the remote. The mountainside turned violet, and a raging cry shook the walls of the crevice.

The stars in Quinn's eyes faded. The tattered form of the hount was careening northward.

"That's right!" His sister spat in its direction. "Run off to the Wastes, you worm, and stay there till we track you down and destroy you!" She punctuated her threat with a torrent of swear words.

Quinn placed a hand on her shoulder, and the tension in her muscles ebbed beneath his fingers.

"I'm calm now," she said. "I just get a bit—you know—carried away about the spirits sometimes."

Yes, he thought. And he meant to find out why, if they made it away from here alive.

"Let's stay in this hidey-hole till the morning," Zora went on. "The hount should take a long time to recover, but other spirits may be out on the mountain tonight."

Quinn surveyed the nightscape below them. The red pulses had stopped. The spirit must've crushed the device from the camera. "So, it really was a lure."

She nodded. "Turns out I wasn't the only person busy designing spirit-tech. No wonder she wanted to know how my devices worked."

"But why would Ms. Fontaine try to have us"—the word stuck in his throat.

"One logical hypothesis is that she wants to corner the market," said Zora. "I bet she planned on sending someone to find my inventions along with whatever was left of us."

"She's already rich. Why go to all this trouble?"

"Maybe she's greedy. But there's another explanation, too."

"Let me guess. You think she's a Spiritist, right? And she's out to serve us up as blood offerings to the things she worships." Since their trip to Mill Hollow, his sister had made the cult her new pet bugbear.

Zora frowned. "She does have her own shrine of spirit photographs."

"Which I recollect you admired at the time."

"Before I knew she was a slimy, lying murderer. We should go back to her house and teach her a lesson—"

"We're going there to get the horses, and then we're leaving." He gave Zora a warning look. "Without raising a fuss."

She leaned back against one wall of the crevice and wrapped her arms around her knees. "Fine."

Quinn felt a tickle from a caterpillar making its way down his sleeve. Measuring him for his coffin, his grandmother would've said, though she'd seen omens of death everywhere: in a clump of feathers, or a broken picture frame, or a blackbird on a windowsill.

"Can you do me a favor?" he asked.

"Of course, big brother."

"How about we don't tell my mother all the details of this particular expedition."

"I promise." Zora smiled. "By the way, I'm proud of you for owning up to her about being a spirit-hunter."

"That reminds me," he said. "She told me our father used to take an interest in the spirits. He even worked with a Spotter for a while, though Mom didn't know any details. Did you ever hear about that?"

An odd look crossed her face. "My mom never brought it up."

"We should pay him a call and see if we can learn more." The thought of it made Quinn's stomach twist. But if he and his sister could face down a hount together, they could wring a few straight answers out of their father.

"If that's what you want," she said. "Though I wouldn't expect much from him."

He sat down, resting his back against the other wall of the crevice so that he faced Zora, and shut his eyes. "Let me know if any other spirits show up."

When the first tinges of gray appeared in the thin fragment of night overhead, Quinn stood and stretched limbs gone stiff from a night of sitting on solid rock. With a yawn, Zora pushed herself to her feet.

He looked out over the fog-covered mountainside. All quiet. After helping his sister to the ground, he went to fetch the prototype. While he was at it, he collected the remains of the spirit-lure. Maybe Zora could reverse-engineer the pieces into something useful.

As they trekked up the mountain, the mist lifted to unveil

giant blocks of limestone protruding from the slope. Goaded by his anxiety about the horses, Quinn set a harsh pace. He could tell that Zora was struggling to keep up, but she didn't complain.

From behind them came the click of a pneumatic pistol being cocked.

"Mr. Prosser of Cascade Hollow and Ms. Coldiron of Lightning Bug Hollow," said a familiar voice. "Fancy meeting y'all here. The two of you turn up in the most interesting places." The speaker's tone went frosty. "Turn around slowly. And lower that whatchamacallit in your hands, Mr. Prosser."

Quinn put on his friendliest air. "Good to see you, Ranger Tate of—of—"

"Lost Hollow. Y'all are out and about awfully early."

"More like awfully late," put in Zora.

"I take it you're headed back to the Fontaine mansion this fine morning," said the Ranger. "Figured I'd come along."

"No need to trouble on our account," Quinn said, with an edge of desperation.

"I really must insist." The man made a causal-looking gesture with his pistol.

Quinn and his sister walked side by side as their escort trailed them. "You were quieter sneaking up on us this time than you were yesterday evening," Zora called back to the Ranger.

He didn't seem ruffled by her dig. "You're every bit as charming as I remember you, Ms. Coldiron. Your friend with the white hair and blue glasses isn't with you, is she?"

"Oh, her?" Zora said. "More of an acquaintance than a friend. You've met her?"

"No, but I'd like to someday. Maybe you can introduce me."

Quinn kept his mouth shut. What was the Ranger's part

in all this? The man had mentioned Signe, which meant he'd heard the story about them and the orbs. And Ms. Fontaine had boasted about knowing how much they'd been paid for that job. Come to think of it, how had *she* learned about them and the tangle? He decided to go fishing. "I imagine your boss will be surprised to see us back at her place."

"My boss?" The Ranger sounded caught off guard for the first time. "Captain Flores is at the Twin Knobs Headquarters. We're visiting *your* boss, not mine."

"That evil woman's not our boss!" shouted Zora. "As a rule, I don't work for people who try to get me killed."

"Stop there." Ranger Tate gave them a penetrating stare. "What in the Hollows are you talking about?"

Quinn glanced at his sister. "I suppose it can't hurt to tell him," she said. "Either he's helping Ms. Fontaine, in which case he already knows, or he isn't, in which case he should know."

As the Ranger listened with a stony face, Quinn told him about the summons to Clack Mountain, their mission to photograph and eliminate the dahoo, the appearance of the hount, and their discovery of the spirit-lure inside the camera.

"Antler Lady owes us a lot of money," added Zora.

Ranger Tate lifted his cap and scratched his head. "That puts a different light on things. Here I was thinking y'all were in cahoots with Ms. Fontaine. I'd already seen you lurking around Saltpeter Hollow and heard tales about your dealings with those spirits out by Mill Hollow."

"You make it sound as though we were hobnobbing with them or something," complained Zora. "We were *getting rid* of them."

"That's certainly what you've gone around bragging to

everybody," the man said. "But we Rangers suspected y'all had some tricks up your sleeves. We also wondered whether Ms. Janasdottir was part of the scam—her playing one side and y'all the other, with the whole gang splitting the money later."

Despite the gravity of the situation, Quinn had to stifle a laugh. The notion of his sister plotting with Signe was the funniest part. "What brings you this way?" he asked.

"I came here last night"—the man stopped, as if deciding how much to say. "I came to investigate Ms. Fontaine. When y'all arrived, that made me powerfully suspicious. So at nightfall, I followed the two of you to see what I could learn." His expression turned peevish. "I botched that one, but afterwards I managed to spot your light show. The next thing I know, here comes a monster-sized roamer." He looked down at Zora. "Did y'all really stop it?"

She stuck out her chin. "We sure did."

"Incredible. Anyhow, I got one look at the hount and reckoned it was time to take cover. Found myself a likely tree and nested in it for the night. Another big spirit wandered through the woods a while later—I'm not sure what it was, but it looked like a carpet of shiny moss scuttling along the ground."

"Could've been a lichender," Zora said.

The Ranger repeated the name to himself before continuing. "Then the sun poked up, I heard y'all walking under my tree, and here we are."

"Why were you investigating Ms. Fontaine?" Quinn asked.

"Let's just say she's not a good sort." His tone discouraged any further questions. "It's time we had a chat with her."

The full light of day had filtered through the leaves by the time they reached the summit. The wagon was still there, with its sign spelling out COLDIRON & PROSSER VENTURES in bold blue letters. The interior of the stable lay in shadows.

Quinn took a step forward, but the Ranger caught his arm. The man raised his pistol and signaled for the siblings to stay behind him. Moving in single file, they approached the stable. Ursula whinnied from within it, while Undine stuck her head through a window to gaze at them with her enormous black eyes.

Zora hissed and pointed at the wagon's open door. Somebody had forced the lock, leaving scratches in the paint around the frame. Quinn jumped onto the seat to look inside. Books, clothes, and spare parts for his sister's inventions lay strewn about the floor and bunks.

Ranger Tate was already strolling toward the front porch of the mansion. Quinn followed him, with Zora bringing up the rear. Still holding his pistol, the Ranger thumped the knocker once, then again. The three of them stood waiting for the doors to open.

They didn't open.

The Ranger banged harder, this time with his fist. "Ms. Fontaine!" he called out. "I'd like a word with you."

"Come on, you copperhead!" hollered Zora.

The mansion remained silent. Quinn looked down at the knocker, and the iron smile of the antlered woman seemed to mock him.

8

ZORA SMACKED THE THICK WOODEN DOORS WITH ONE OF HER crutches. First things first, she wanted to shove that Fontaine woman's face through her own stained-glass window. Afterwards, they could search for whatever lay hidden within the mansion—a secret workshop, perhaps, or proof of a Spiritist conspiracy.

"Easy," Ranger Tate drawled. "You'd need an ax to get through that. Let's see if there's another way inside."

When they searched along the stone walls, they found iron grilles with antler designs blocking all the first-story windows. Quinn pried at the nearest set of bars, but they didn't budge.

"Stay where you are," the Ranger said, as he circled toward the back of the mansion.

"Do you suppose she's in there, watching us?" asked Quinn.

Zora made a rude gesture toward the windows, just in case. Her brother put his palm to his forehead.

Ranger Tate appeared around the opposite side of the mansion, vexation on his soft features. "This place is like a fortress," he said. "The owner must've bargained on some sort of ruckus."

Zora stamped a foot. "What now?"

"Now, I go to the station at Tower Hill, shoot a message to the Judge for this circuit, and come back with reinforcements. Along with a battering ram for those doors."

Quinn raised a hand, as if he were in a classroom. "What about us?"

"Free to go. I'd rather y'all scoot on home and stay out of trouble." The Ranger smoothed his baggy uniform. "But I doubt you'll listen to my advice, sound though it may be."

"So," Zora said, "what are the chances Ms. Fontaine is mixed up with Spiritists?"

Ranger Tate gave her a crooked smile. "I'd call that an excellent question."

"That's not what *I'd* call an informative answer."

"You're a perceptive young woman, Ms. Coldiron." The Ranger's smile faded. "Steer clear of her. I can't say more, but there's lowdown doings afoot in the Hollows. And if y'all wind up in a jam again—as I halfway expect—then send word to me."

During the ride back down the mountain, Zora bickered with Quinn about their next step. He was for pressing on to Sassafras Hollow to visit their father and demand some answers, while she favored going back to her lab to reconstruct the spirit-lure. "If that rich snake tries to pull one over on us again," she said, "a defense against her technology could save our skins."

"All right, you win." Quinn stopped the wagon and grinned at her. "You can drive us there."

She shrank back on the seat. "But I don't know how."

"Then it's my turn to teach you something." He made way for Zora to slide over, and she took the reins.

"Hold them here," he said. "Good. Now give the horses the go-ahead."

"Walk on," she told Ursula and Undine in what she hoped was a suitably authoritative tone. The animals hesitated, as if sensing her uncertainty, but then resumed their steady gait.

"You're doing fine," Quinn said. "Better than me when I first tried."

Once she'd settled into driving the wagon (which turned out to be unexpectedly enjoyable), her brother switched on the radio. The Limestone Knob station was playing a song about a wandering fiddler girl who cast a spell with her music to seal the borders of the Hollows against the worst of the spirits—elementals strong enough to lay waste to entire valleys, hounts that stretched as far as the eye could see, spires taller than the hills themselves.

When the song ended, Zora's mind started buzzing with a new idea for an invention.

Around noontime, Zora and Quinn reached a village in Comet Tail Hollow. After buying turkey sandwiches at a stand painted with astronomically suspect celestial objects, they decided they were far enough away from Clack Mountain to catch up on their sleep. Neither of them made any move to clean the mess left behind last night by their would-be-murderer. Or, more likely, by her underlings. Zora had a hard time imagining Evelyn Fontaine rummaging through an old wagon that smelled of unwashed sheets and dirty socks.

"Nobody on our tails," said Quinn, as he looked out the window toward the northern hills. "Yet."

The air inside the wagon was stifling, so Zora undid her overalls and added them to the clutter. Before resting her head on her pillow, she made sure her wrist-watcher was charged. She fell asleep almost as soon as she closed her eyes.

She dreamed of stumbling through a snow-covered forest while an army of spirits chased her. Strings of flashing red winter solstice lights entangled her scrawny legs.

Soon, whispered a voice in her head.

The next thing she knew, the wrist-watcher was beeping in her ear.

Zora sat upright and blinked groggily at the orange dots on the device. A few feet away, Quinn was scrabbling on the floor in his undershirt and trousers.

Something like lightning cut through the darkness outside her window and then vanished.

She reached down to grab her overalls. By the time she'd wriggled into them, her brother had found the banisher.

A scream came from nearby—the cry of a frightened child, or a spirit that could mimic one.

Quinn shoved open the door. Zora followed him onto the seat of the wagon, leaving her boots and braces behind.

All along the street, people were shouting from windows and pointing at the sky. At the ground. At one another. On the roof of a tavern, a yellow spirit crackled up and down an antenna. A varc, like the one Zora had seen eight years ago in her own hollow. Across the street, a door slammed shut against a glowing whirlwind of dust and leaves. That must be a vorx. Farther away, a pack of translucent green lumps caromed down an alley to the sound of inhuman cackles. She had no clue what those things were.

In the middle of the street, a tall man wearing a leather duster pointed a spyglass at the varc and spoke to a young woman standing next to him. Zora couldn't make out his words over the hubbub.

Violet light bisected the spirit flickering along the antenna. When the varc winked out of existence, the tall man gave a startled yawp. Quinn shifted his aim, and the vorx exploded in a cloud of debris. Several onlookers cheered from the windows of the surrounding buildings.

Zora ducked into the wagon. A hasty search yielded three of the remaining spirit-grenades, which she stuffed into the pockets of her overalls, and one of her illuminators, which she slid through a belt loop.

Quinn leaped to the ground and ran after the green lumps.

"Over there!" yelled the woman in the street. A new spirit was oozing toward Zora, effervescence bubbling on its wide, flat surface. She tossed one grenade at it. Not hard enough—the mauve blast splashed harmlessly on the dirt. She threw a second grenade and scored a hit that left spatters of effluvium across the road.

"Nicely done," called the tall man, as his companion pumped her fist.

Quinn came back into view, holding the banisher high. "Are there more?"

Zora brushed her loose hair from her eyes and scanned the village with her illuminator. "I don't see any."

Her brother ran over to the wagon, and she lowered herself from the seat to stand beside him. The ruts of wheel tracks dug into the soles of her bare feet.

The two people in the street were approaching, with the

woman in the lead. She had black, pixieish hair and looked seventeen or so. Her shirt was sleeveless, her trousers snug. When she saw Quinn, her jaw dropped.

Then she tackled him. "Look at you," she shouted, after she'd released him. "I'd heard the rumors, but who would've thunk? Pine-Box Prosser, wandering the Hollows and kicking spirit butt!"

Zora's own jaw dropped at that.

"It's good to see you," Quinn said, in a more subdued tone. "By the way, this is my sister, Zora."

"Your *sister*?" The young woman pounced on Zora and hugged her, too. "Pine-Box and I go way back," she said. "I can tell you some stories about him."

Quinn looked skyward. "Zora, this is Paige Zhu of Cascade Hollow. An old friend of mine."

The tall man cleared his throat. Judging by the creases on his face and the grizzle that showed against his dark brown skin, he had at least three decades on Zora. His round-rimmed glasses made him look like some kind of owl. Maybe a barred owl.

"Sorry, boss," said Paige, not sounding especially contrite. "Forgot my manners there."

The man doffed his rumpled top hat. "Darius Epps of Three Mounds. I gather you two are the renowned spirit-hunting siblings."

"Everybody who's anybody in our racket knows who y'all are by now," Paige said. Her companion looked at her reprovingly, and she sucked her lips into her mouth.

Zora suppressed a squeal. "You're the Spotter who wrote *A Taxonomy of Waterbound Spirits*?"

"That would be me." The man's deep voice carried a hint of amusement.

"I have a copy of your book," she said. "You know, we ran into this kelpie the other day—at first I thought it was one of your lesser stagnant subtypes, but then I noticed its aura"—she realized she was babbling and stopped.

"I would like nothing more than to hear your anecdote," he said. "Sadly, it must wait until we've learned more about the situation in this village."

"What in the Hollows *is* going on here, sir?" asked Quinn.

Mr. Epps put a thumb to his chin. "I can tell you this much. Yesterday, I received tidings of some unusual spirit activity. Along with my indomitable apprentice"—Paige performed a mock curtsey—"I came here to see for myself. When we arrived this afternoon, we spoke to every witness we could find. Not long after sunset, the spirits came. A veritable storm of them."

"Four different types of roamers ganging up," added Paige. "Bizarre, isn't it?"

"Indeed," said Mr. Epps. "A most ominous development, particularly in conjunction with the wave of spirit weather across the Hollows this summer."

Quinn made his fretful face. "So it is getting worse."

The Spotter nodded. "I would even say it's reached the highest level in my lifetime, let alone yours."

"Did your witnesses report any other sorts of spirits around here?" asked Zora.

Mr. Epps ticked off his fingers one by one. "Varc, vorx, mive, geists. All accounted for." He reflected for a moment. "Though one of the locals we interviewed also mentioned seeing a strange sort of spirit last night, like an oversized pinwheel."

"What"—Zora bit her tongue. First that fluke wave of energy with the kelpie, now this.

"The description didn't match any variety familiar to me," the man continued. "I presume that it was merely the varc or the vorx. Misperceptions and faulty memories often distort untrained observations of spirits."

He's probably right, Zora told herself. After all, this village was a long way off from the oxbow at Willow Bog.

"I should do a quick patrol, to be safe," said Quinn.

"That would wise." The Spotter inspected the banisher with unabashed curiosity. "Do you mind if I accompany you? I confess to being fascinated by this apparatus of yours."

Zora looked at Quinn, and he looked back at her. Given how Ms. Fontaine had bamboozled them, she was hesitant to trust a stranger again. Then again, Mr. Epps was an eminent Spotter, and Paige was Quinn's friend. She gave her brother a subtle nod.

"By all means," Quinn said. "Though let me put on some shoes first."

Paige sniffed. "Good idea."

"You should remain in the vicinity," the Spotter told his apprentice. "Keep watch for other manifestations and record your account of tonight's events." She pouted but didn't argue.

"I'll stay here, too," Zora said. "I'm still worn out from our last spirit hunt."

"I can't wait to hear about that," said Paige. "How about we swap tales while they're gone?"

Quinn shook his head as he walked past them toward the wagon. Then Zora caught him glancing over his shoulder at Paige.

The apprentice Spotter chose a window seat in the village tavern as their sentry post. She wrote several pages of notes in a journal, stopping every so often to consult a damp-stained copy of the *Field Guide to the Spirits of the Hollows*.

Zora had just finished updating her own expedition log when a ferret-faced young woman came over from the bar and looked down her nose at them. The carbide lamps hanging from the ceiling gave her complexion a ruddy tint. She waited for their order with her thumbs hooked in the folds of her denim apron.

Paige smiled. "How about that spirit weather we're having."

"Uh-huh." The bartender gave her the once-over. "Say, where're your people from?"

"Cascade Hollow."

"I meant before that," Ferret-Face said, in a nasal monotone.

"Well, now, my great-grandma *did* move there all the way from Chimney Rock Hollow."

"Before the Wakenings," the bartender persisted.

"There were Zhus in the Hollows back then, too." Paige's smile was tight this time. "Otherwise, I wouldn't be here, would I? Anyhow, I'd like a shot of your best moonshine."

"We don't have any."

"Check under the counter," Paige said. "My Spotter's intuition tells me you'll find some there." She eyed Zora. "Make that two."

As Ferret-Face stalked away, Zora pinned her hair back into pigtails. "I'm a few seasons shy of drinking age," she said in an undertone.

Paige laughed. "If you're old enough to fight spirits, I say you're old enough to try a little booze."

Zora couldn't deny that logic. "So you went to school with Quinn?"

"Sure enough. Back then, he was always hanging around his mom's funeral parlor with his nose buried—hah, buried, I didn't even plan that—in some old-timey book." The apprentice grinned. "Did he ever tell you about the time we went spirit-chasing together?"

"Go on," said Zora.

Paige spread her fingers in the air. "There we are, at the Harvest Festival. Pine-Box is in undertaker black, and I'm wearing this poofy blue dress my mom sewed herself. Hardly the best clothes for spirit-spotting, mind you." She looked Zora up and down. "Not like your overalls. Say, ever try wearing them without the undershirt? I bet you'd turn a few heads."

Zora's skin went warm, from her cheeks to the top of her chest. The mounted head of a buck deer gazed down at her indifferently.

The bartender came back and plunked two shot glasses on the table. "Here," she said. "This batch of stump hole whiskey is all we've got."

Paige clinked her glass against Zora's before gulping down its contents. Zora sipped from hers and fought the urge to spit out the moonshine. Clearly an acquired taste. She took another sip. Still revolting.

"After an hour at the dance," Paige went on, "I'm bored out of my skull, so I talk him into helping me track down a boge."

"He mentioned he'd seen one of those," said Zora, between pecks at her drink.

"Oh, did he?" Paige waved her empty glass at the bar. "I take lead, with him right behind me, when this little green light starts twinkling. I can see Pine-Box is scared, so I tell him to hang back while I get a closer look." She paused for dramatic effect. "Meanwhile, the boge has looped behind us. A minute later, I hear this high-pitched screech, and your brother hot-foots it toward me like all the roamers in the Wastes are after him. But then"—she chortled—"then he trips over a root and goes splat in this perfectly situated mud puddle. All over his dressy clothes."

The bartender brought a second round without saying a word. Once she'd left, Paige tossed her head back and drained her shot. Zora took the opportunity to peer through the window. Everything seemed peaceful in the darkness outside the tavern.

"I have to admit," Paige said, "that I busted out laughing. He was pretty sore about it, but he let it slide." She scrutinized the bottom of her glass. Her mood had veered from jovial to melancholy. "He always was a good sport. I'm not sure why he put up with me."

Zora studied the apprentice's suntanned face and arms. It wasn't that difficult to figure out a likely reason. "My brother wouldn't run from a boge anymore," she said. "We use those things for target practice. A hount, on the other hand . . ." She took a fair-sized drink from her glass—it was easier this time—and told the story of their night on Clack Mountain, making sure to dwell on Quinn's heroics.

Paige let out a low whistle. "That tops the yarn I'd heard about the orbs."

"So how do you like training to be a Spotter?" Zora asked,

as the room revolved like a slow-motion centrifuge. The last time she'd felt this lightheaded was when she'd inhaled a lungful of helium for an ill-conceived experiment in vocal parasonics. Could that be the moonshine already? She'd had only one drink, plus change, but her mass *was* on the small side for an adult. Or even a near-adult.

"It's the raccoon's whiskers," said Paige. "I've already seen two dozen types of spirits this summer. Mostly waterbounds, since my boss is working on a second edition of his book." She held up her journal. "The cramming and note-taking aren't my favorite parts, but if I keep slogging away I should get to do some solo outings by winter."

Zora raised her half-filled glass to her eye. "Spotted any major spirits?"

"Just small ones. This past moon, we went to the Big Lake to follow up on some legends about a jumbo-sized waterbound, but we didn't find so much as a shoal of welkies. Word of advice, by the way: those things may be teensy, but they're worse to touch than poison ivy."

"And how's working with Mr. Epps?"

Paige's expression turned proud. "Give or take Old Man McBrain—wherever he's vamoosed to—my boss knows his spirits as well as anybody in the Hollows. I'll allow he may come across as highfalutin. Fact is, he's always after me to mind my words. Says when he was an apprentice, he learned that speaking careful made people take him more serious. I get his point." She nodded toward the snooty bartender. "You know how folks in the Hollows can be."

"I do," said Zora, who was getting drowsy from watching the blades of the tavern's rickety fan.

"Figured as much. Speaking of my boss, here he comes with your big brother." Paige grabbed Zora's glass from across the table, slurped the rest of its contents, and set it down again. Then she waved through the window.

Quinn and Mr. Epps entered the tavern with a pair of strangers in tow: a disheveled woman wearing a calico robe, and a little girl with red-rimmed eyes and salt tracks on her cheeks. The child clung to the woman's robe with one hand and a sock bunny with the other.

"What's up, boss?" asked Paige.

"We located another witness for our unidentified spirit," said the Spotter. "Meet Cora and Samantha Stegall."

Zora knocked over her empty glass. "You saw it?"

Ms. Stegall shook her head. "Not me." She ran her fingers through the girl's hair. "Sammie did."

The bartender returned, sporting a put-upon expression. "Would y'all like to order something?" she asked the newcomers.

"My daughter and I need a room," said Ms. Stegall. "We can't go home tonight. It ain't safe there."

"That'll be ten bits."

The woman reached for her pockets, only to find her robe didn't have any. "I didn't have a chance to get my money."

"We don't do credit here," said Ferret-Face, in her flat voice.

Mr. Epps took some coins from a pouch and counted them. "Ten bits for their room." He added another coin. "And one bit for your inimitable service." The bartender took the money and stood there, perplexed.

"You can skedaddle for now," Paige told her. After casting one last glare, Ferret-Face slunk back to the bar.

Zora stood and immediately felt dizzy. "Take my seat," she said to Sammie. When the girl didn't move, Ms. Stegall sat down and lifted her daughter onto her lap.

"Can you tell me exactly what you saw?" Zora asked, doing her best to keep her voice level.

Sammie looked up at her mom, then at the rest of them. "It's okay," Quinn said, in a comforting tone he must've learned from working funerals. "We're here to help you."

"Why do you have those?" the girl asked, staring at Zora's crutches as Ms. Stegall tried to shush her. "What's wrong with you?"

"I built them to help me walk." Zora held up one of her illuminators. "And I built this to hunt down spirits that go picking on kids."

"I saw a big, scary roamer," the girl blurted. "Right outside my bedroom window."

"What did it look like?" Don't push too hard, Zora reminded herself.

"Green, like a glowworm. And always moving."

"Moving how?"

Sammie frowned in concentration. "This one time, Ms. Judd—she's my teacher—she brought a toy to show the class how the earth goes around the sun."

"Orbital rotation?" Zora's head spun. She wished she hadn't drunk the moonshine. Not now.

The girl's face brightened. "That's what Ms. Judd called it." She drew a spiral in the air with her finger. "The spirit went around, and around, and around. I couldn't stop watching it. Then my mom came."

Zora opened her expedition log to a blank page. Holding her

pen in a white-knuckle grip, she sketched a picture and showed it to Sammie.

The girl snuggled closer against her mom. "That's it."

"Looks like an atom," said Quinn, surprising Zora with his physics knowledge.

"It doesn't resemble any spirit I've ever observed," said Mr. Epps. "Do you recognize it, Ms. Coldiron?"

Zora pretended she hadn't heard the Spotter. "Sammie, what did it do?"

"Nothing. It just kept spinning and making a weird sound like this." The girl hummed a few low notes.

"Did you get any"—Zora stumbled over her next question—"impressions from it?"

"What does that mean?" Sammie asked.

"Just a feeling in your head about what it might've been doing."

The girl thought it over. "Yes."

"What was it?" Stay calm, Zora told herself. She imagined floating on the pond near her home in Lightning Bug Hollow. No gravity to pull on her arms and legs. Nothing to fear in the dark.

Sammie's voice was scarcely audible. "The spirit was watching me. It was watching me, and it knew I was scared." She began to weep. "It liked that."

Everyone was staring at the girl, even the bartender. Except for Quinn, who was staring at Zora.

"Sammie, we're going to find that spirit," she said. "And we're going to make it sorry it ever bothered you."

9

QUINN RUBBED HIS EYES AND SNUCK A PEEK ACROSS THE TABLE at Paige. By the tavern's dim light, he could make out flakes of sunburnt skin on her arms and the tip of her nose. When she turned his way, he looked down at his glass of water.

Four people sat squeezed into their booth. Ms. Stegall had long since shepherded her sleepy daughter upstairs for the night, but Quinn and his sister had stayed to talk with Paige and Mr. Epps. The Spotter hadn't offered any conjectures as to why the spirits were so restless across the Hollows, or why so many different sorts had attacked this village at once. Meanwhile, Zora kept whispering back and forth with Paige—a turn of events that disconcerted Quinn almost as much as all the spirit commotion. What had those two talked about during his absence, anyhow?

"Are you quite certain," Mr. Epps asked, with an unreadable expression, "that you don't know more about the spirit the child witnessed?"

Zora pinched her lips and shook her head. Quinn could tell she was stonewalling. He suspected the Spotter had picked up on her shiftiness as well, but the man was either too polite or too shrewd to say anything more. Paige, on the other hand, was apparently too tipsy from the moonshine she'd knocked back to catch the undercurrent in the conversation. From across the room, the weaselly-looking bartender scowled at them as she washed and dried shot glasses.

"Are *you* sure you don't want to come with us tomorrow?" Zora asked, glancing toward Paige. Quinn said nothing, choosing instead to watch through the window for anything still roaming in the darkness.

"It pains me to sacrifice an opportunity to reconnoiter an unknown variety of spirit," said Mr. Epps. "Regrettably, Ms. Zhu and I must leave at dawn to summon as many of my fellow Spotters as possible to our athenaeum in Three Mounds for a colloquy. The time has come to compare our data regarding this inundation of spirits and deliberate on a course of action."

"It's just an extra day," Paige pleaded. "Or I could go with them and catch up with you at the big gabfest."

Mr. Epps collected his hat and duster. "The safety of the entire Hollows may be at stake. As my apprentice, your place is with the Spotters." He smiled down at Paige. "But you may linger here tonight with your young compatriots."

Once the Spotter was gone, Zora announced that she was turning in as well. "I hope we cross paths again soon," she told Paige.

"I'll come with you." Quinn rose to his feet. "I may be settling into our nocturnal way of life, but the past two nights have tuckered me out."

Paige grabbed his wrist. "It's been moons since we talked. Stick around and have a drink with me." The slight slur in her voice and the smell on her breath called back memories of their clandestine visit to Old Woman Caudill's still—along with the pranks they'd played afterward using fake spirits made from fishing line and glow-in-the-dark paint.

"I would," he said, "but we have a job to do tomorrow." The words came out colder than he'd intended.

Paige let go of him, looking downcast. "You've gone all responsible on me, Quinn." She stood and bear-hugged Zora. "Lick the tar out of that spirit for me, Foxtails." Then she clasped his hands. "I'm glad you're doing so well," she whispered to him. "I hope you don't think ill of me."

"Nope," he said. "Not now, nor ever."

He meant it, but seeing her again still stung.

The next morning, Quinn stepped through the wagon's doorway into the shadow of a looming thunderhead. Ms. Stegall and Sammie were sitting on the tavern porch, eating scrambled eggs and grits. The mother gave him a hangdog look and stayed put, but the daughter bounded his way.

"Are you really going to get rid of that awful spirit?" she asked.

"We aim to try." The girl seemed to accept this with wide-eyed faith.

"I can't afford to pay you much," Ms. Stegall said, in a glum twang.

"No charge for y'all, ma'am." He'd rather do this sort of job for free than have any more dealings with the likes of Evelyn Fontaine.

Sammie bounced on her heels. "Where's your friend with the red hair and the crutches?"

"My sister's still working up to waking up." Quinn gestured

toward the wagon's interior, where he'd just seen Zora lying on her stomach with a pillow over her head. "Could you show me the way to your house?" he asked Ms. Stegall.

She pointed down the alley where he and Mr. Epps had run into her yesterday. "Go yonder a piece and you'll come to a yellow house. You can't miss it—it's the one that looks like it's falling apart." She shuddered. "Ain't sure I ever want to go back there. Maybe I should move in with my folks, like they keep telling me."

"Want us to get anything for you?"

"I'd be mighty grateful if you could fetch our clothes, and the quilts, and the bag on the dining room table." Ms. Stegall chewed a fingernail. "Besides those, there's not much worth bringing."

Sammie tugged her mother's robe. "Don't forget my other animals."

"Oh, right," said Ms. Stegall. "She means the stuffed ones in her bedroom."

"Consider it done," Quinn told them.

Zora came outside as Quinn finished hitching Ursula and Undine to the wagon. She was wearing her blue-tinted goggles down over her eyes. Her left pigtail hung lower than the right one, and stray auburn hairs dangled past her forehead.

Quinn covered his mouth with his hand to hide his smile. "Good afternoon, *Foxtails*," he said. "Ready to search for our mystery spirit?"

She responded with an inarticulate grumble. Taking that as confirmation, he climbed onto the seat and clucked at the horses.

"I liked your friend," Zora said.

Quinn felt the atmospheric pressure drop. Unless that was just his imagination. "Paige is a barrel of fun," he allowed.

"Why didn't you stay with her when I left? I was trying to give the two of you some time together."

"That's sweet of you, little sis, but I don't need another matchmaker in the family." For two whole years, his mom had kept up a stream of hints that he should court Paige. The friendship between their families went back three generations, which had made the situation all the more awkward.

Zora gave him a jab on the arm. "I just think you'd make a good pair."

A rising breeze rustled the leaves. "Why do you think that?" he asked.

"You fight spirits. She's training to be a Spotter. And she's prettier than prissy Ms. What's-Her-Face you got all flirty with back in Mill Hollow."

Quinn fixed his eyes on the road ahead of them. "I used to favor the notion of me and Paige together," he admitted. "But she wanted to set off by herself and see the Hollows."

"Oh." Zora got that same look as when she'd put one of her crutches down in Undine's poop. "Maybe she'll revise her opinion now that you're a legendary spirit-hunter."

"I don't reckon so." Quinn smelled ozone in the air. Would they reach the house ahead of the rain? "Before Paige went away this spring, she told me I ought to leave home, too. Find my own way, meet new folks. And she was right. I get that now." Bruised feelings or not, he should've had that drink with her; they did have a lot of catching up to do. "Anyhow, I seem to recollect you not being interested in who was courting whom. Or in sneaking moonshine, for that matter." His sister gave a guilty twitch, and he couldn't help but laugh. "Next thing, you'll be raring to go to All Hollows and take in the festivities."

"Ha," said Zora. "Not likely."

"While we're at it," he went on, "let's take a moment to talk about your own prospects for sparking. Hasn't anybody caught your eye during our travels through the Hollows?"

"There's nothing to discuss." She turned up her nose. "I'm too busy to go all googly-eyed over anyone. While the other young folks in my hollow were wasting their time at barn dances and hayrides, *I* was inventing the technology that's going to defeat the spirits once and for all someday."

"So there's no genius out there worthy of helping the brilliant Professor Coldiron scientifically test the—what do you call it—thermal energy of her kisses?"

"I guess not." Zora's tone had turned sulky, and Quinn regretted teasing her. "Besides"—she began, before stopping to look down at her boots.

"Besides what?" he asked, now serious.

"Besides nothing!"

After a short ride during which neither of them spoke, he sighted a yellow house up ahead. It sat by the road, surrounded by a weed-filled yard. As they neared it, thunder rolled through the hills.

"Sounds like we made it here just in time," said Zora.

Quinn parked the wagon by a small barn and saw to the horses. Then he and Zora approached the front walkway through a garden of tomato plants and watermelon vines. Ms. Stegall hadn't overstated the extent of her home's dilapidation:

the walls listed on their foundations, and patches of bare wood showed where the yellow paint had peeled away.

He took a seat on the porch. "Let's hold up here. I want to talk before we go inside."

"About what?" Zora didn't make eye contact with him.

"Whatever it is you haven't told me yet about why we're here." He raised a hand to ward off her protest. "You may be the brains, but I can put together some things by myself. Like how you've been keeping a secret from me. One to do with you and the spirits."

His sister sat beside him. "All right," she said. On the horizon, lightning struck the crown of a hill. Quinn counted to ten before the thunder came.

Once it had died away, Zora spoke again. "It goes back to when I was seven, like Mom said." She kept her face turned toward the storm. "Dad had just come back from one of his trips, and he'd brought me some new tools as a present. I'd already started building things like transformer circuits by myself." Another bolt of lightning flashed. "I remember being so thrilled he was home. Dad always spent more time on the road than with us. He and Mom usually wound up arguing when he visited, but that day they both seemed happy. They even decided to walk to Hildy's Inn for a special dinner. You remember the place?"

"Right," said Quinn, thinking back to the night he'd met Zora.

"Maybe they had things to discuss. Or maybe they were feeling"—she coughed—"romantic. I was disappointed about not getting to go along, but excited to play with my new tools. Not to mention proud of being left in charge of the house and the new puppy. See, some neighbors had given us one from their dog's litter. I named it Static."

Quinn had an unpleasant inkling as to where this tale was headed.

"I took the responsibility oh-so-seriously," Zora said. "I was anxious to prove I deserved to be treated like a grown-up. Even then, I could already out-tinker almost any apprentice engineer. And I was afraid Mom would change her mind about letting me have a pet. I wanted something living and breathing to play with, too." Her voice caught. "The other kids in my hollow left me out of their games more often than not. It was hard for me to keep up when they played tag or ran races. I was better at hide-and-seek or capture-the-flag, but they didn't always want to play those."

She stopped to regain her composure. Quinn pictured her as a little girl, all by herself with her gears and wires, not knowing she had a brother who would've rushed to visit her and play whatever games she liked. Who'd spent so many hours of his own childhood alone, listening to scratchy old phonograph records and keeping watch over the dead.

The two of them should've had the chance to grow up together.

"That's not important," she said, more evenly. "What matters is that not long after Mom and Dad had left for the evening, I heard a noise outside. A low drone. Static started barking fit to burst my eardrums. I went to the window, but I didn't see anything."

In the distance, a wall of rain advanced across the hollow. Quinn moved under the shelter of the porch, and his sister followed him. Seconds later, the downpour pounded on the tin roof, sending tiny waterfalls spilling from holes in the gutter.

"I went back to my project," Zora said, "and the puppy

calmed down. I figured it must've been a catamount or something like that, till the noise came back, louder and closer. Static started growling at the door. I crept up next to him and peeked through the keyhole. By this time, Static had gone nigh berserk. Then the sound stopped again. I still couldn't see anything, so I opened the door a crack."

"That was brave," Quinn said.

She shook her head. "It was a bad idea. Static squeezed past me and tore off into the woods. At that point, I was scared, truly scared. But I knew if something happened to him, it would be my fault. I put on a miner's lamp and went after him, which was mistake number two." She tapped her crutches against one another. "At that age, I hadn't built up much stamina. Within a few minutes, I was too tired to keep going. So I sat on the ground and broke down crying."

The trees beyond the yard swayed in the wind.

"After I got a grip on myself," Zora said, "I called for Static. That's when the humming started back up a third time. Everything around me was dark at first, but then I saw something green through the trees. By now, I was full and well terrified. Enough that"—she flipped her goggles onto her forehead and looked straight at Quinn. "I wet myself. I'd fancied myself such a big kid, but there I was in a puddle of my own pee." She pulled up her knees and buried her face in them.

He put an arm around her shaking shoulders. His eyes were watery now, too.

She raised her chin. "The spirit came toward me, and I got a clear view of it. I'm sure you can guess what it was."

"The kind Sammie told us about."

"For all I know, it was the exact same one. Since then,

I've read every description of spirits I could track down. Handwritten journals from the early years after the Great Wakening. Self-published pamphlets by wildcat spirit-chasers. Hoaxes printed by the *South Hollows Sun*. None of them mentions anything like this spirit. You heard Mr. Epps—even he didn't recognize a description of it."

"What happened next?"

"It floated nearer, spinning the whole time. It had some sort of hypnotic effect, I think. I watched it till a voice whispered in my mind. *Be afraid*, it said. *Be afraid of me.*"

"Stop right there," Quinn said. "You're telling me this thing can *talk* to humans?"

"Not talk, exactly. It must be able to generate ectospectral frequencies that resonate with the electrical impulses in the human brain. Maybe it's akin to how Signe—I mean, Ms. Spooky Jack-o-lantern—can see spirits."

The sky went bright, and a boom rattled the timbers of the house, but Zora didn't blink. "That's not the worst of it," she said. "The spirit changed the pitch of its sound, so low I could barely hear it. Then more spirits started coming through the woods. A few boges. A varc like the one from yesterday. A wengo, and one I've never managed to identify. Do you get it? That thing *summoned* the other ones."

Quinn stared at a rivulet flowing from a downspout into the black mouth of a cistern. Back in fourth grade, he'd toured Pipe Organ Cavern with his classmates and stood at the edge of the bottomless pit, the one folks called the Gateway of the Spirits. It *did* have a bottom, of course—Paige had proved that by tossing a rock over the rim—and the glow along its sides came from nothing more than cave fungus. Yet when he'd gazed into the pit, he'd been overcome by the fear that the spirits would pull him down to a world where they ruled in endless night.

The notion had haunted his dreams for moons afterward.

"That's what we're hunting," said Zora. "A roamer that can control other spirits."

"Did they do anything to you?" Quinn asked. "Did they hurt you?"

"They hovered around me in a half circle, with the spinning spirit in the middle, while I curled up in a petrified little ball till it whispered in my head again. *Run*, it told me. *Run for your life.*" Anger twisted her face. "I took off fast as I could, all the way home, and that night I made a decision. Someday, somehow, I'd find a way to fight the spirits—all of them, and this one in particular."

She slammed a fist against the porch, and then her fury seemed to dissipate. "When Mom and Dad came home an hour later, I told them the whole story. Mom tried to act calm, but I could tell how frightened she was. Dad was more agitated than I'd ever seen him. He asked a bunch of questions and made me swear to keep inside after dark from then on."

Quinn took a measure of bleak satisfaction at how thoroughly she'd broken *that* promise.

"One other thing," Zora said. "Dad set out in a hurry the next day, never mind that he was supposed to stay with us till the Spring Fair. He kissed me goodbye, and told me he loved me, and that's the last I ever saw of him." A slight waver undercut her attempt to sound impassive. "I always wondered whether he left because of me. Whether I was too much for him to deal with."

Low, dark clouds had obscured the faraway hills. Quinn

stood and walked to the edge of the porch, just out of reach from the rain. Once Zora was back in her lab, he could drive straight to their father's hollow to confront the man.

She pointed her thumb toward the house. "Forget about him. Let's face this thing together."

Quinn took his sister's hand and pulled her to her feet. "What about the puppy?" he asked.

Zora gave a half-hearted laugh. "Already home, safe and sound, by the time I got there. Mom let me keep him. After all that, how could she not?"

When Quinn tried the front door, it opened with a creak. Ms. Stegall evidently hadn't taken the time to lock it while fleeing with her daughter the previous evening. He and Zora stepped into the gloom-filled parlor and began exploring the first floor. In the living room, a couch with discolored upholstery faced a jury-rigged radio set. Half-melted candles jutted up like wax mushrooms from the mantle, and the fragments of a glass pitcher lay on the rug.

Quinn led the way to the kitchen, where they discovered a brown leather bag on the table. Further inspection revealed a half-eaten pie on the counter and food-encrusted plates in the bottom of a tub sink, but no evidence of the spirit's visitation.

The kitchen opened onto a staircase. Quinn climbed it, taking his time so Zora could use the railing and one crutch to keep pace with him.

"This is why my mom bought us a one-story house," she said.

At the top of the stairs, they found two bedrooms. Quinn searched the larger one first. A quilt embroidered with hex signs covered the pinewood bed along the far wall. The frame on the side-table held a photograph of a grinning, curly-haired man and a happier, more youthful Ms. Stegall. She was holding a baby.

The only sound in the house came from the rain pinging on the roof.

"Here's where the kid must've seen the thing," Zora called from the other bedroom. Quinn joined her, ducking to keep from banging his head on the slanted ceiling. Pastel drawings of cows and butterflies, or maybe unicorns and fairies, decorated the walls, and a small bed with a starflower-patterned quilt sat flush against the window. Neatly arranged stuffed animals—a hedgehog, a raccoon, a squonk, and a skunk—lined the headboard.

"It doesn't seem like the spirit caused any damage," Zora said.

Quinn retrieved the quilts, along with all the clothes he could find. Then he foraged through the closets until he located two trunks large enough to hold everything. He packed the photograph from the bedside table between Sammie's stuffed animals and Ms. Stegall's leather bag. "Did the spirit ever come back to your hollow?" he asked Zora.

"Not as far as I know. But I hope it pays another visit here tonight."

Quinn hauled the trunks to the wagon, fed the horses, and returned to the house with the spirit-hunting equipment. He rested on the couch in his freshly drenched clothes while Zora fiddled with the radio set. "Shoddy work," she said. "Not worth salvaging."

Night came early under the cover of the storm. They

conducted an initial sweep with their devices but found no trace of any spirit near the house. Their raid of the cupboards met with greater success, turning up one jar of shuck beans, another of apple butter, and a pan of slightly stale cornbread.

Quinn and Zora ate in the kitchen by candlelight, with the banisher on the table between them. As she lifted the last piece of cornbread to her mouth, a melody of beeps and pops rang out from her inventions. The empty jars reflected a solitary orange light on the banisher's stock.

Zora tilted her arm to show Quinn her wrist-watcher: one orange light. She held up the illuminators strapped to her arms: one orange light apiece.

He snatched the banisher from the table and stood so quickly his chair fell backward onto the floor.

"Slow down, big brother," said Zora. "I've waited eight years for this, so let's do it right." She extended her arms like wings, and the lights on the illuminators vanished. She brought them together so that they pointed toward the parlor, and the orange dots reappeared. "Making its way to the front door. Nice manners, for an abomination."

Quinn donned his goggles and approached the parlor with the banisher in firing position. He held his breath to listen for the humming Zora and Sammie had described, but all he heard was rain. No, wait. He could also make out a padding sound.

"Still only one light," said Zora, at his elbow. "Odd—I would've pegged it as a four-lighter, at minimum."

Quinn edged up to the door. "You illuminate it, and I'll banish it?"

She nodded. "Ready when you are."

"On the count of three."

"One," said Zora.

He put his hand on the knob.

"Two." She aimed an arm toward the door.

Was that a footstep on the porch?

"Three!"

Quinn pulled open the door, and Zora shone a sapphire beam into the darkness outside. As he raised the banisher, an agonized shriek froze his finger on the trigger.

A person lay in the mud at the bottom of the steps—a young woman dressed all in black, with whitish-yellow hair, holding up two gloved hands to shield her face from the blue light.

10

"COULD YOU KINDLY STOP THAT?" ASKED SIGNE JANASDOTTIR, from behind her outstretched fingers. "It's burning my eyes."

Zora cursed to herself and switched off the beam. Peculiar. The illuminators had never bothered her own eyes, nor her brother's, more than an ordinary flashlight would.

In the meantime, Quinn had rushed down the steps. After helping Signe up the porch, he fetched her umbrella from the puddle where she'd dropped it. How considerate of him.

Zora suddenly remembered the spirit sensors and swore, aloud this time. A single orange light still glowed on her wrist-watcher, matched by a bulb on each illuminator. "Quinn!" she shouted. "Look out!"

He thrust the umbrella into Signe's hands and waved the banisher at nothing in particular. "Where?"

Zora had been wondering about that herself. She didn't hear any humming. She didn't see any fluorescing. The only thing out here was a human interloper with a dreary wardrobe, a dearth of pigment, and bad timing. On a hunch, she whipped one illuminator toward the house. The light on the device went dark.

Signe regarded her through rain-flecked glasses. "May I ask what you're doing?"

Zora didn't answer. Instead, she slowly turned the illuminator toward Signe. The orange light winked back to life.

When comprehension dawned on Quinn's face, he redirected his aim.

"Hey, don't go pointing your—your thingamabob at me!" Signe said, her voice rising in alarm.

"Sorry," he told her. "I promise I won't shoot." He checked the sensors on the banisher's stock. "You're right, sis."

Signe glanced back and forth between them. "Do please tell me what's happening, if it's not too much trouble."

"Maybe you should explain," Quinn said to Zora.

She huffed, torn as to whether the spirit's absence or Signe's presence irked her more. "Ms. Janasdottir—if that is your real name—our devices show that you radiate the same form of energy as the spirits do."

"And?"

"And that's something we've never encountered in a human." Zora wished she had her ectospectrometer so she could collect some readings.

"Ah." Signe sounded gratified. "That must reflect my gift."

"Congratulations on having something in common with the spirits," Zora said. "For a minute there, we mistook you for one of them."

Her brother held open the door. "How about we all go inside and talk?"

"Why, thank you," said Signe. "And it's wonderful to see you again." She swept into the living room and made herself at home on the couch. Her waterlogged clothes clung tightly to her, which probably accounted for Quinn's distracted air.

"You need a new umbrella," Zora said. "That one didn't seem to do much good."

"It's not an umbrella." Signe pulled off her gloves. "It's a parasol."

Zora decided to dispense with the pussyfooting. "Why in the Wastes are you here?"

"I was looking for the two of you. What else?"

Quinn's eyebrows shot up. "You tracked us all the way to this house?"

"Not quite." Signe made a sound partway between a laugh and a sigh. "I was headed to the Big Lake when I heard a story on the radio about an extraordinary outburst of spirit weather in this hollow. One short detour later, I met a rather surly bartender who told me what had happened in her village the previous night. Along with where I could find the pair of spirit-chasers responsible."

"You mean the spirit-chasers who rescued that village," said Zora. Just how much had Ferret-Face overheard in the tavern, and how much had she told Signe?

"As you prefer." Signe's expression was bland. "I took the news as a sign I ought to speak with you, given how my current errand relates to your recent . . . escapades." She wrung her hair. "But first, I want to apologize for my remarks back in Mill Hollow. I chose my words poorly."

"I reckon we all lost our tempers a bit there," Quinn said. "I hope you'll forgive us, too."

Signe smiled at him. "No hard feelings."

Zora folded her arms and stewed. "Fine," she said, at last.

"Now how about you leave off being cryptic and tell us what this is about, before the spirit we're after shows up for real?"

"Gladly. I'm guessing you're aware of the surge in spirit activity this summer?"

Quinn nodded.

"I have a theory about that." Signe drew herself up. "So, exactly when did you start traveling around and using these weapons of yours to fight spirits?"

"Early summer," said Quinn.

Zora caught Signe's drift and wagged a finger at her. "You can't have the gall to blame *us* for spirit weather across the entire Hollows!"

"I'm not suggesting you meant to cause any problem," Signe said in a soothing tone. "I gather you mean well. Yet it's a fact that the spirits grew restive right around the time you began attacking them. You're a scientist—what does the evidence suggest to you?"

"Correlation doesn't equal causation," said Zora.

"Do you have another explanation?"

Quinn shot Zora a troubled look. "No," she admitted. "But you're making a big leap." Into a steaming mound of cow manure, she added to herself.

"For generations, humans and spirits have lived, if not in peace, at least in equilibrium," said Signe. "Not anymore. I hate to say I told you so, but I did warn you about the potential consequences of tampering with that balance."

"For your theory to be right, the spirits would need"—Zora choked back her next words. A guiding force, she'd almost said.

Quinn cradled the banisher and started wandering around the room.

"Some way of coordinating their actions?" finished Signe. "Perhaps. What do you think?"

"I never claimed to be an expert on their behavior," said Zora. She had no desire to tell anyone besides Quinn about her childhood run-in with the spirit they were hunting. "I'm more interested in their physical properties. Especially their vulnerabilities."

"My spirit vision doesn't give me any special insight into their ways, either." Signe looked thoughtful. "But someone who's spent a lifetime observing them might understand why they're in such a frenzy—and how to settle them down again."

"We just talked to one of the most experienced Spotters in the Hollows," said Quinn. "He didn't seem to know much more than we did."

"Ah, but you didn't speak with the legendary Nevan McBrain, did you? Wouldn't you like to hear what *he* thinks about this?"

"Possibly," said Zora. "Too bad he dropped out of sight years ago."

Signe's thick blue lenses magnified the knowing gleam in her eyes. "What if I told you I've learned where he is? And that I was on my way to visit him when I took this side trip to find you?" She held out her hands. "If you come with me, we can all go see him together."

Zora smelled a trap. "How'd you discover his whereabouts?"

"Oh, I've picked up a few secrets in my journeys through the Hollows. You know, there *are* methods besides going around shooting at everything."

Pretentious bat, thought Zora. She exchanged looks with her brother. "We'll talk it over once we've smoked out the spirit that showed up here last night."

"What kind is it, anyway? The bartender didn't seem to know."

"We have our little mysteries, too."

"Suit yourself. In the meantime, could you point me to the bathroom?"

"The outhouse is that way." Zora tilted her head toward the backyard.

Signe walked to the window and frowned. "Fantastic."

"Be careful," Quinn told her. "I'm not getting any signs—except from you—but this is no ordinary spirit."

"I'll keep my eyes open." She readied her umbrella—no, her *parasol*—and went out the back door.

"I don't trust her," Zora said, as soon as Signe was gone.

Quinn shook his head. "I have a hard time believing she's part of some grand Spiritist plot."

"Yet here she is, popping up like some nosy mole and accusing *us* of riling up the spirits, when we already know who else has figured out a way to do that."

"You aren't the least bit curious to meet Nevan McBrain?"

"If she's even telling the truth about that." Zora kept one eye on her illuminators and the other on the door. "We've already been hoodwinked once. What if she's in league with the money-bags who tried to kill us? Speaking of whom, we still need to get back to my lab so I can analyze what's left of her lure."

"Is there a chance Signe's right?"

Zora exhaled. "It's possible. But she's just guessing. Remember, your snow-headed honey-pie never liked what we were doing in the first place."

The sound of the back door opening cut short Quinn's reply. "The rain seems to be letting up," said Signe, brushing spots of crud from her skirt as she entered the living room. "A pity there's no indoor plumbing here. A hot bath would be lovely about now."

"Tracking down spirits can be a dirty business," Zora said.

"What do you intend to do if you find this one?"

Zora nodded at the banisher in her brother's hand. "The usual."

"Are you certain that's wise?"

"It went prowling after a kid," said Quinn. "We've got to stop it."

"Just make sure to stay out of our way," added Zora.

Signe kicked off her shoes and curled up on one end of the couch. "I'll take it easy here, then."

"I'm going to check the bedrooms." Quinn set off toward the stairs. "Y'all stay here and give a holler if anything happens."

Once Zora had scanned the first floor again, she hiked her overalls to her knees and adjusted the straps on her ankle braces. All the tromping around on Clack Mountain had rubbed her shins raw. When she looked up, Signe was watching her with a contemplative expression.

"Got something to say?" Zora asked.

"I hope I didn't offend you with my theory." Signe removed her glasses and cleaned them on her sleeve. "I'd like to be friends with you."

"With me, or my brother?"

"Both of you, though he does seem more open to the idea. I suppose when I was your age, I—"

"You may talk to me like I'm a kid," said Zora—an *arrogant brat*, Signe had called her back in Mill Hollow—"but you're only two years older than me. Even if you have hair like my grandma's." As soon as she'd said the words, she wished she could take them back.

Signe's eyebrows lowered, but her voice stayed neutral. "Zora, you're obviously an exceptional young woman. I have my doubts about how you're using your talents, but I'm sure you can put them to constructive ends. After we work out a plan to pacify the spirits, I could help you with that."

Zora inspected the floorboards, uncertain what to say. Was Signe being sincere, or just flimflamming her?

To Zora's relief, Quinn chose that moment to thump his way down the stairs.

"Please consider it," said Signe.

"Still clear," Quinn called from the kitchen. "Should we search outside, or wait here?"

"Let's stay put." Zora blew out the candles in the living room.

As they waited, she passed the time by mentally sketching the schematics for her next invention. Her brother settled onto the couch next to Signe, and the pair of them prattled about books they'd read, occasionally laughing or making animated gestures. Quinn described some of those implausible tales he favored, the ones with intrepid spelunkers searching through whispering caverns for lost silver mines or enigmatic steamboat captains battling lake serpents inside raging maelstroms. Signe went on about historical romances involving young women who commandeered airships to rescue their sweethearts from spirit-sieges, or who led forays into the Ruined Town to find lost artifacts from pre-Wakening times.

Hours later, Zora glowered for the hundredth time at the unlit bulbs on her illuminators. She and Quinn should've hustled here last night instead of dawdling at the tavern. If the spirit didn't come back to this house, they might never sniff it out again.

Everything was quiet except for a duet of snores from the couch—one in baritone, the other soprano. Quinn sat slumped against the cushions, his eyes closed but one hand on the banisher. Signe's stockinged feet covered his lap like two ink stains; the hair spilling over her face almost glowed in the darkness. Zora left them alone. No way she'd fall asleep with nerves as taut as hers.

And then she heard it.

At first, Zora thought the faint humming might be a trick of her worn-out mind. As it grew in volume, she went rigid.

Four orange lights, just like she'd thought.

Her voice failed her the first time she tried to wake her brother. She remembered to breathe. "Quinn!"

He stirred and opened his eyes. An instant later, he was on his feet with the banisher in both hands.

She pulled down her goggles, and Quinn grabbed his from the arm of the couch.

Signe sat up. "I thought I was dreaming that sound," she murmured. "People were dancing to it around a maypole decked out in green garlands."

Zora searched with her illuminators until she pinpointed the direction of the spirit. "It's coming from behind the house." She cast a suspicious look at Signe, who didn't seem to notice.

The humming intensified. Zora stuck close to Quinn as he made his way to the back door and peered outside. "I can't see anything," he said.

"I'm still showing four lights."

The noise ceased, and Zora's illuminators went dark save for one light apiece. Then a shuffling beside her made her jump.

It was only Signe. "You've run across this spirit before?" she asked.

Zora ignored the question. She was busy trying to figure out what to do next.

"Your call," said Quinn. "Should we try to follow it?"

She dithered. Give chase, and it might lead them into a trap. Sit tight, and it might slip away forever.

The spirit took the choice from her. The sound came again, and she quickly located its position. It had circled to the front of the house.

"What's it doing?" Signe's eyes were wide behind her blue glasses.

"This one likes to play games," Zora said.

Quinn pulled open the front door hard enough to make it slam against the wall. The banisher's beam floated across the road. The garden. The weed-filled yard. Nothing was out there.

Frightened neighs came from the barn.

Quinn crossed the threshold to the porch and spun his device to the left. Zora joined him and aimed an illuminator to the right. Still nothing.

Signe poked her head around the doorframe, muttering to herself. The humming stopped, and Quinn started down the porch steps.

"No," Zora said. "I think it wants us to leave the house." Next to her, Signe ran a finger along the handle of her parasol. Maybe she has something hidden inside it, thought Zora.

All three of them drew back inside the parlor, and the door groaned on its hinges as Quinn pushed it shut.

The humming returned before any of them had a chance to speak. Now the spirit was above them. Quinn charged up the staircase, while Zora followed one step at a time.

When she caught up with him in the small bedroom, he was standing motionless by the window. The pane shivered in time with the low droning. On the other side of the glass, a band of green light spun like a snake chasing its tail.

The spirit was larger than the one she'd seen eight years ago. Or perhaps it had grown. As Zora stared at it, her head went woozy and her pulse turned sluggish. The banisher hung loosely in Quinn's hands, with the muzzle pointed toward the floor. Behind them, another set of footsteps—lighter than her brother's, stockinged soles on wood—approached and then halted.

A new undertone emerged in the humming, one that gave Zora a crawling sensation along her spine.

Again.

The word echoed in her mind, and her stomach lurched. This *was* the same spirit that had taunted and terrorized her seven-year-old self. Quinn stood spellbound at her side; Signe was a shadow on the wall.

Fear me, again.

Not this time, Zora thought. She might be scared, but she was far from helpless.

You have grown stronger, little one.

Rage welled up inside Zora's chest. She released her hold on her left crutch, letting it hang by its cuff from her elbow, and used her hand to activate the illuminator strapped to her right arm.

So have I.

The hum dropped to a lower pitch, and then to an even lower one, and then to one that was less a sound in Zora's eardrums than an oscillation in her jawbone. She grasped her left crutch again and raised her right arm. Some invisible force resisted her, as though she were at the bottom of a pond of maple syrup, but she pushed until the illuminator pointed toward the spirit outside the window.

A distant rumble cut through the humming. Thunder, she told herself through the haze in her brain. But the storm had passed. Where else had she heard that noise?

Pits appeared in the windowpane.

Her thoughts fluttered. A barren ring of earth, and a sign with a skull on it. A rat in a cage. The ruin outside Lightning Bug Hollow.

Pop.

"No," she whispered. Not an elemental, of all the things the spirit could've summoned.

The pits in the window became webs, to the sound of cracking glass.

Run, said the voice in her head. *Run.* She sensed the spirit's triumph and, beneath that, its cold amusement at her despair.

The pane broke into shards.

Zora prodded Quinn in the side with one crutch. "Snap out of it!" she screamed. "We need to go!"

Pop, pop.

The glaze lifted from his eyes as he blinked at her. They both rushed for the doorway, with Zora in the lead. On her way, she shouldered the stunned-looking Signe toward the stairs.

Run, run, run.

Signe glanced back at the window, bleated in terror at

whatever she'd seen, and fled down the stairs. With a half-dozen steps left to go, she leaped the rest of the way and kept on running.

Another rumble filled the air, louder than the first. Willing her limbs not to shake, Zora gripped the railing to the staircase. If she didn't get out of here before the elemental breached the earth, she'd end up as a pile of dust.

But she was blocking Quinn's path. She moved aside to let him pass.

Instead, he scooped her up in his arms and staggered down the stairs. The banisher jabbed her back with each step, its constant beeps blurring with the noises from her own devices. They reached the bottom, and she squeezed out of his hold.

"Hurry!" Signe shouted from up ahead.

Zora rounded the corner to the living room and made for the parlor. Hints of luminescent energy glimmered along the radio's antenna as a rending sound rose from below. The insides of her teeth prickled, and a wave of nausea almost made her fall.

The front door stood ajar. Ten paces more and Zora was on the porch. When Quinn held out an arm to help her down the steps, she barked at him to keep going.

A second later, they plunged into the yard. Zora didn't dare look back at the house. She didn't know how powerful this elemental was, how far they needed to go to escape its sway.

Signe was watching them from beside the barn, her mouth open. Zora's lungs burned, but Quinn urged her onward. By the time she made it to the garden, the impulse to turn her head had grown too strong to resist. She caught a glimpse of green smoke wreathing blackened, crumbling weeds.

"Don't stop!" Signe waved her parasol at them.

Zora reached the barn just as her crutches began to wobble in her hands. She collapsed on the ground next to her brother and stared at the house. It sat encircled by powder that had been ragwort, burdock, and wild onions only moments ago. The elemental's glow washed over the warped siding and cascaded from the shattered windows.

Signe placed the balls of her hands on her forehead, hiding her face with her arms. Quinn put his fingers behind his ears and grimaced. Pain throbbed behind Zora's eye sockets.

Then the sensation vanished, along with every trace of phosphorescence around the house. The rumble was gone, and so was the humming.

Zora looked to the east. The top of the sun had cleared the hills. She and Quinn were safe, for now.

But how much of this was her fault?

PART THREE

THE SEER & THE SAGE

11

TORN LEAVES AND BROKEN BRANCHES LAY SCATTERED ALONG THE road back to the village. Ahead of Quinn, the horses kicked up mud with each step. He coaxed them past the blighted yard and set their pace at a trot.

Not that he was champing to tell Sammie and her mother what had happened to their home.

"Thank you for the ride," said Signe. "You spared me a walk through this muck." She unfolded her parasol and propped her heels on the passenger side of the wagon's dashboard. The toe of her left stocking had a hole in it where there hadn't been one last night. "Daylight or no, I wouldn't set foot in that house again for every bit of Filson Swift's lost treasure. Let alone a pair of shoes."

"I'm still afraid," Quinn said. "For both of us, and Zora, too." His sister was hunkered inside the wagon, feverishly writing on pieces of paper she'd ripped from her logbook. "How do we ward off a spirit that can go around raising elementals from the bedrock?"

Signe gave him a sunny look. "Our predicament may seem dire, but I believe we can bring the Hollows back into balance if we combine Mr. McBrain's knowledge, Zora's ingenuity, and my vision." She twirled her parasol. "The universe has chosen me to do this. I can feel it in my bones."

Bones. Quinn thought of the time he'd accidentally dug up a mass grave of green-tinted skeletons. Victims of spirit-sickness from the Great Wakening, his mom had told him. "I don't know why the universe would choose *me* for this," he said. "I'm no seer, or sage, or inventor."

Signe scooted closer to him on the seat, so that her hip touched his. He rather liked the sensation. "Don't forget how you saved Zora's life," she said. "I saw that. You're part of this for a reason. And"—she hemmed and hawed before pushing on in a rush of words—"maybe destiny has other plans for you, too."

As Quinn floundered for a reply, the horses crested a knoll and began their descent toward the village. "We're here," he shouted back to Zora. "Want to come help explain things to the Stegalls?"

His sister opened the door. "You'll do a better job than I would." She handed him a stack of letters. "While you're at it, could you mail these?"

He thumbed through the envelopes. *To Fiona Coldiron, Lightning Bug Hollow.* Zora's mother would never let her leave the house again if that letter mentioned half of what they'd been through the past few days. *To Emerson Tate, Lost Hollow.* They could use the Ranger's steady presence right about now. *To Viola Mack, Mill Hollow. To Kirk Slocum, Iron Furnace Hollow.* What did Zora want from the merchants? *To Darius Epps, Three Mounds. To Paige Zhu, Cascade Hollow.* The Spotter would appreciate a report on what they'd learned, and Paige would eat up any gossip from her new friend.

"I think we should tag along with Signe to see Nevan McBrain," Quinn said.

"Fine." Zora glared at him, then at the black-clad young woman occupying her usual roost. "Don't bug me till lunchtime." She slammed the door behind her.

Ms. Stegall and Sammie were sitting in the same spot as yesterday, wearing the same clothes. Quinn waved to them and unloaded their belongings from the wagon. Signe helped him lug the trunks to the tavern porch.

Sammie's eyes grew round at his description of the elemental, while Ms. Stegall looked crushed. "Figures, with my luck," she said, dabbing her eyes. "Leastways we weren't asleep in our beds when it laid hold of our place. Thanks for saving our stuff, anyhow. Nothing left for us to do now except go crawling back to my people up the hollow."

"I'm sorry we couldn't save your home," Quinn said, in his best rendition of his mother's graveside manner. "We did all we could." But maybe he and Zora had only stirred up more trouble for everyone.

He left the Stegalls to the task of sorting through their trunks and went to find the post office. By the time he returned, Signe had readied her own one-horse wagon. It was painted white, with black and purple scrollwork around its door and windows.

"You can follow me," she said. "We should arrive at the Big Lake tomorrow afternoon."

Zora was already snuffling in her sleep, so Quinn left the radio off and ruminated about their new traveling companion's theories as the scenery rolled by. Blue chicory and weeds with lacey flowers—the sort the bees seemed to fancy so much— lined the road. Tree-coated ridges fenced them on either side.

Signe called their caravan to a halt at a ramshackle trading post, and Quinn knocked on the wagon's door to rouse his sister. No answer. When he stepped inside, Zora rolled out of bed with a crutch in one hand and the banisher in the other.

"We've stopped to eat," he said, pushing the weapon's snout away from his stomach. "Would you like to join us after you're dressed?"

Zora stared blearily at him, then set the banisher on her bunk and tugged down her nightshirt to cover more of her thin legs. "I *am* ravenous. Also a little jumpy, I'll admit."

Once she was ready, the two of them made their way to the trading post's counter. They both ordered the squirrel stew, seeing as how it was the only item on the chalkboard menu.

In the meantime, Signe had unrolled a large piece of paper. It was a printed map of the Hollows, with indigo handwriting here and there. The sloppy letters surprised Quinn, who'd expected a more flowery script from her.

He inspected the chicken scratches. The ones next to Mill Hollow read, "Orbs, gizes, flambs." Beside that, at a different angle, Signe had added, "Pair of troublemakers." The scrawls under Comet Tail Hollow listed the spirits he and Zora had banished there, along with a question mark. A squiggly line led northward to Clack Mountain. No notes up there about hounts or dahoos. Or conspirators, either.

Signe opened a small metal case and removed a magnifying glass. Holding it to one eye, she peered at the map. "So—"

"What are you doing with that?" asked Zora. "Trying to set your map on fire?"

Quinn shook his head at her. She could at least *try* playing nice for the next two days.

Signe had tightened her lips into a straight line. "No," she said. "I use it to read."

"Oh." Zora's gaze dropped to her lap.

"As I was saying." Signe placed a gloved finger on a tiny X. "We're here." She pointed to a twisty blue shape resembling a two-tailed salamander. "And there's the Big Lake." She brought the magnifying glass closer to the map until she found a dot in the blue. "Witch's Hat Island. That's where my informant said Mr. McBrain would be."

Zora's eyes narrowed. "Remind me who you said this source was."

"I didn't, but I'll tell you if you promise to keep his identity to yourselves. He and Mr. McBrain parted on less-than-amicable terms."

Quinn nodded. "Have it your way," muttered his sister.

"I heard it from a Spotter named Otis Hetfield," said Signe. "A cagey sort of fellow, but his story included some convincing details."

"McBrain's assistant?" Zora sounded taken aback.

"That's right." Signe ran her fingertip from the X to the lake's edge. "If we go thisaway, we should be able to rent a boat at Tater Knob."

"Why's the old man been hiding on an island all these years?" Quinn wanted to know.

"Mr. Hetfield was vague on that point, but he did suggest his former employer had turned strange and secretive."

Zora frowned. "Peachy."

Signe rolled up the map and tied a ribbon around it. "Nevertheless, he's our best hope for clues to solving the problem you've—the problem we're all facing."

The cook brought them each a bowl of thick, brown stew. Quinn tried a spoonful of his and bit down on a hunk of gristle. No wonder they were the only customers.

One disappointing meal later, Quinn and Zora were back in their familiar places on the wagon's seat. A woodpecker's knock rose above the clomping of hooves and the rattling of wheels along Nine Hazel Pike.

"So you trust Signe now?" he asked.

"She was inside the house when the elemental attacked," said Zora. "If not for me, she would've stood there slack-jawed till the thing disintegrated her. Seems like a bad move for a Spiritist plotter."

"And her notion of restoring harmony between humans and spirits?"

Zora shrugged. "I don't know what to think anymore."

That made two of them, for once. "She says it's her fate."

"Ha. A bedtime story she dreamed up to feel better about being different from everyone else." Zora picked up an edge-worn tome and began flipping through pages of schematics.

Quinn held his tongue. When the sunlight waned, he hailed Signe. "Are we coming up on any inns?"

"Not anytime soon," she called back. "We need to look for somewhere to pull over for the night."

They followed the evening star until they sighted a turn-out large enough for both wagons. Quinn freed the horses from their harnesses so they could graze on the patches of grass by the roadside. Then he gathered kindling from the woods while Signe chopped up acorn squash and red bell peppers. Zora sat on a stump, twiddling with one of her illuminators.

"It's a shame we don't have any marshmallows," said Signe, once they'd finished their skewers of campfire-roasted vegetables.

Zora glanced at her wrist. "I'm more concerned about the possibility of that spirit tracking us here from Comet Tail Hollow. I like it better when I'm the one doing the hunting."

Signe stood and faced the darkness. "Nothing out there."

"What do they look like to you?" Quinn asked her.

She played with the ends of her hair. "It's hard to describe. Have you ever seen an ultraviolet photograph?"

"My mom showed me an album of those when she was teaching me how to use her camera." One of the pictures had captured a little waterbound as an opalescent slick on the dark water of a slough pond. "What about the sorts of minerals that glow under black light? We used to find chunks of them—fluorite and gypsum, mostly—on our trips to the local quarry."

Signe nodded. "Kind of like that, too." The fire sparked, casting an orange glow on the lenses of her glasses. "Your mother sounds like a woman of many talents."

"She has to be, in her business," Quinn said. "I guess I learned a lot growing up as her helper. Though I hope we won't need any flower arrangements or embalming fluids on this expedition."

"And how do your gadgets work?" Signe asked, pointing at the small pile of equipment beside the stump.

Zora curled her lip. "I'll try to put it in terms you'll understand. The spirits are so repugnant to nature"—she drew out each syllable—"that their very presence sends vibrations of black magic through the ether. Itsy-bitsy spirits make ripples, and big, nasty spirits make billows."

Signe bridled but didn't interrupt.

"The number of pixie-jewels that twinkle on this enchanted scepter," Zora continued, "tells me how powerful the spirits are." At the push of a button, a light came on. "That's you. One lonely little sparkle." She placed her finger on the switch to the beam, and Signe flinched. "When I push this, it casts a charm that makes them go all shiny-whiny and shaky-achy." Zora put down the illuminator and lifted the banisher. "Next, my wizard-wand blasts out waves of good, pure magic. They collide with the evil ones, and—boom!" Under her breath, she added, "Destructive interference of kirlian energy."

"Very edifying." Signe's expression was tart.

Quinn ended the discussion by suggesting they take turns on lookout. The others agreed, and Zora volunteered to go first.

Signe intercepted him on his way back from grooming the horses. "Good night," she whispered, and took his bare hands in her gloved ones. Her pupils darted toward the woods. Toward Zora. Back to him. Then she turned tail and made for her own wagon before he could say—or do—anything.

He stood there until his pulse slowed back down. No doubt he'd shown her a fine imitation of a bump on a log.

But he still smiled as he climbed up to bed.

The howling started around midnight.

Quinn opened his eyes. An instant later, his sister bawled his name. He dressed in the dark and sprang down from the wagon.

"Two lights," Zora said, as she passed him the banisher. Soft footsteps alerted him to Signe's approach, and he realized he'd put his shirt on backwards.

Another cry came from the forest, an unearthly sound that made him want to cover his ears.

"Do you think"—he began, but then a howl came from the far side of the road. He pulled on his goggles and waved the banisher's beam. All he saw were blue-tinted tree trunks.

"They've encircled us," said Signe.

Zora groaned. "Can you tell what type?"

"Too blurry at this distance. I may have second sight, but I'm *near*-second-sighted." Signe pulled at the corners of her eyes. "They're just flitting back and forth."

"Maybe they're afraid to do anything more," said Zora.

The spirits kept up their caterwauling for the next half hour, sometimes in unison and sometimes as an eerie call-and-response. Signe paced around the campsite, while Zora stayed glued to her stump. Quinn posted himself by the horses, patting them when they grew restless.

Suddenly, the cries broke off. Undine rubbed her head against him, and Ursula fluttered her nostrils. In the heart of the campfire, a log collapsed against the coals with a faint crackle.

"Are they gone?" he asked.

As Signe opened her mouth to speak, the baying started again. "Whatever they are," she said, "they move fast and stick low to the ground."

The banisher beeped again. Quinn swung it left and right at greenish things skulking among the trees. "Still too far," he told Zora.

But the pack of spirits was drawing closer with every passing second, their howls resounding through the forest.

"There!" His sister pointed to a ropey form behind a fallen tree.

"Herns," Signe said, with a trace of dismay.

Quinn's flesh crawled when more shapes came skittering toward them through the brush.

"I've never heard of a pack this large," said Zora.

One by one, the spirits emerged from the forest and formed a ring around the campsite. There were scores of them, each waving a pair of razor-tipped curlicues.

"Too many to shoot them all," he shouted over the din.

Zora used one of the foulest curses in her stockpile. "We should've gone back to my lab. I could've"—she kicked the stump with the back of her foot. "Let's see how many you can get before—"

"Wait," said Signe. She walked toward the edge of the firelight, her palms held high, and Quinn shifted the banisher to cover her. The herns lashed the air with their feelers, then fell silent.

"I hope you can understand me," Signe called out in a clear, if tremulous, voice. "I know you're vexed with us humans, but tonight we can start down a new path."

The spirits howled louder than ever. Quinn's throat constricted as he imagined them swarming her.

Signe stood her ground. "We don't mean to hurt you." She looked over her shoulder at him.

He lowered the banisher. The herns let their barbed limbs droop, and Signe mirrored the gesture. "I believe we can live in peace with one another." She took another step forward.

In the blink of eye, the entire pack of herns vanished. Zora gave a startled meep.

The three of them waited for a long stretch, but the spirits didn't return. At last, Signe wiped her brow. "I thought that went well," she said.

Quinn pulled off his goggles and stared at her in awe. "I think the universe *did* choose you to help fix all this."

She bobbed her head, grinning like a pumpkin carved for the Harvest Festival.

"I'd like to see you try to sweet-talk an elemental that way," said Zora.

Signe tossed her hair. "Maybe it helps not having a potty-mouth, like some folks." She broke into a nervous laugh, and then Zora did, too. Another small step toward harmony in the Hollows, thought Quinn.

He took the next watch. The rest of the night passed quietly.

After a breakfast of buttermilk pancakes, Quinn took the reins again while Zora tinkered inside the wagon. She came outside a few hours later to show him a pistol-sized banisher with a squat glass barrel and a curved bronze grip. "It's not as strong as the big one, but it could come in handy." Her eyes flicked toward the other wagon. "In case she's wrong."

The sun had neared its zenith when the lumpy form of Tater Knob came into view. They found an inn, stabled their horses, and huddled on a deck overlooking an arm of the Big Lake. Quinn caught himself staring at the spiderweb pattern of Signe's dress.

She dimpled at him and pointed toward the calm blue water. "Witch's Hat Island lies thataway. Let's go find ourselves a way to get there."

The three of them walked down to the pier, and Zora tapped out a martial rhythm against its boards as they passed rows of weather-beaten fishing boats. Anglers sitting beside buckets full of worms and coolers full of beer paused in baiting their hooks and winding their reels to rubberneck at the procession along the waterfront: Quinn with his dark hair and clanking gear, his sister with her reddish hair and crutches, Signe with her whitish hair and parasol.

A hulking man at the edge of the dock set down his fishing pole and sauntered toward them. "Looking for something?" he asked, looming over them in his chest-high waders.

"A boat to rent," said Signe. "With a motor that can get us across the lake and back."

The man eyed her, then Quinn and Zora. "I got one that'll work for y'all. Rented it to a young woman about your age the other evening. Apprentice Spotter from Cascade Hollow, as I recall."

"About yea high, with short, black hair?" asked Quinn.

"That's her. She was an uncommon-looking sort of—"

"If you don't mind," said Signe, "we're in a bit of rush." Next to her, Zora smirked.

"Right this way." The man guided them to a small wooden craft with a clockwork motor. The lettering on the side read *HARTBEAT* (Quinn didn't point out the misspelling). "Five bits by the hour or twenty by the day. You won't find a better price."

Zora examined the motor. "Kind of corroded, isn't it?"

The boat's owner snapped his fingers. "Almost slipped my mind." He lumbered over to a nearby shed, then lumbered back and used a pair of long, skinny pliers to adjust the motor's cogwheels. "This baby needs a new regulator. That should hold it for now, though." He wound the mainspring until it clicked. "All ready."

Zora seized command of the tiller, and Signe ensconced herself in the bow. Quinn climbed aboard between them, almost tipping himself—and the equipment—over the side in the process. Skinny gar and shiny bass swam by within arm's reach of the hull.

His sister turned a key that set the motor whirring. The dock slipped behind them, and the boat left the shelter of a cove for the broad body of the lake.

After two-odd moons of tailbone-busting wagon trips, the ride across the water felt like floating on air. Quinn let the rocking motion lull him into a half-sleep. For a moment, he dreamed of captaining a submarine beneath one of the oceans he'd read about in fox-paged books.

A loud whine and a burst of acceleration jolted him awake. Zora snickered from the stern. "Just testing the torque, big brother."

Signe stuck out a hand. "Around that bend." Two symmetrical hills—the Twin Knobs—bookended the parasol in her other hand. The tower of the Ranger Headquarters capped the peak of the left twin. Quinn tried to make out the bottom of the lake, but a greenish-brown murk concealed it.

They cleared the bend and set course for a cone-shaped island with evergreens on its flanks. "Ta-da!" shouted Signe, flourishing her parasol.

Zora steered the boat to a pier with rotted pilings and missing planks. The rocky shore was as still as a snapping turtle waiting on a minnow.

Signe hopped onto the pier before they'd even come to a full stop. "Come on," she said.

"Your sugar-pop needs to stop rushing me," Zora hissed in his ear. He gave her a boost, then hauled himself up and tied the boat to a rusted cleat.

Signe had discovered a weed-choked trail leading away from the pier. She tramped through brambles and creepers, with Quinn and Zora straggling after her, until she came to a wire strung across the path at knee level. Tin cans hung from the barrier. She prodded it with her foot, and the cans jangled in response. The sound quickly faded beneath the relentless buzz of the cicadas.

When nothing else happened, Signe stepped over the wire and led them into the shade of the pines.

Soon the path wound uphill past saplings downed by the last storm. Across gullies cut by rainwater. The afternoon heat traced lines of perspiration on Quinn's brow, and spiny cockle-bur seeds stuck to his trousers. Behind him, Zora was wheezing for breath.

At the top, they found a clearing. Sentinels made from rag-gedy clothes, metal scraps, and animal skulls stood guard along its perimeter. Within their ranks, rows of cabbage heads and carrot tops converged on a gray, windowless building.

"The man likes his privacy," said Zora.

As Signe entered the clearing, chimes rang out from the sur-rounding trees. She started, then squared her shoulders and strode onward. Quinn hurried to catch up with her. The build-ing's walls resolved into sheets of corrugated metal.

A door clanked open, and a figure shambled outside. The first thing Quinn noticed about it was the armor—made of something like tinfoil, but duller—covering it from head to foot. The second thing he noticed was the trident-gun in its right hand, pointed straight at Signe.

"Don't come any closer," said the man inside the armor. "I use this for gigging frogs, but it'll work just fine on intruders."

"Mr. McBrain?" Signe's voice was so high it would've broken glass.

"Shush!" thundered the man. "You're the trespasser here, so how about *you* tell me *your* name."

"Signe—Signe Janasdottir. I'm—"

The man shifted his weapon. "How about you there, with the glass-and-silver firearm?"

"Quinn Prosser." He retreated a few paces. "And this is my sister, Zora Coldiron." She stepped out from behind him to get a better view, and he stepped back in front of her to block the trident-gun.

But its wielder wasn't aiming it at them anymore. "Coldiron? You're Vernon Moss's daughter? The one from Lightning Bug Hollow?" He sounded astonished. "And you—I never knew he had a son, too."

Quinn puffed out his cheeks in indignation.

"I'll tell you who we are," said Zora. "We're the best spirit-hunters in the entire Hollows. Not to mention the only ones."

The man held a gauntlet to his mouth-slit. "If that's so, we have much to discuss." He gave a hollow chuckle. "You two made it here just in time."

"Time?" Quinn said. "For what?"

"Why, the next Wakening. Your father didn't tell you?"

12

"I DISCOVERED THE FIRST PIECE OF EVIDENCE TWENTY YEARS ago," said Nevan McBrain. He closed the door and barred it, then took off his helmet. A goatish beard and unkempt hair framed his face.

Once Zora's eyes adjusted to the dim light inside the bunker, she saw dozens of calendars hanging from the foil-papered walls. A glass star-globe next to a copper astrolabe. A pin-sprinkled diorama of the Hollows that put Signe's map to shame. A brass telescope leaning against a stack of books with tantalizingly unfamiliar titles. *On the Origin of Spirits. A Posthumous Account of a Spire as Seen from a Hot Air Balloon. The Sinking of the Riverboat "Commodore" by an Altie and the Ordeal of Its Crew in the Wastes.*

Quinn and Signe stared at the Master Spotter as he removed his metal suit, piece by piece. "This getup keeps the spirits from sensing my presence when I go outside," he said, and clanged one hand against the wall. "We're safe in here from both them and the two-legged fiends." Quinn and Signe continued staring.

"Twenty years ago?" prompted Zora.

"Ah, yes." Mr. McBrain picked up a sheaf of papers from a frayed ottoman. His fingernails were like claws. "The finding that changed the course of my life's work." He handed her a yellowed, brittle letter. "Careful with that. It's well over a century old."

Zora unfolded the letter. The date at the top—March 19, 1925—followed the pre-Wakening Calendar. She read aloud:

To Professor Maxwell Doran, Department of Atmospheric and Etheric Sciences, Daniel Boone University, Mount Poplar, Kentucky.

A university, thought Zora. How wonderful that must've been.

Dear Professor Doran,

Last month, you visited our fine county to investigate its legendary ghost-lights. You may recall that I dismissed my neighbors' tales of sonorous apparitions as unadulterated balderdash. Indeed, I told you I had lived here my entire life without once witnessing the phenomenon.

If only that were still the case.

For the past three nights, an uncanny noise has disturbed my sleep. To me, it sounds like the thrum of a phantasmal engine. My sister Delia, who came to stay with me yesterday, likens it more to the growl of some strange beast.

Zora traded glances with Quinn.

On the first and second nights, I was too frightened to seek the source of the noise. Last night, Delia—who is bolder than I—armed herself with a lantern and shotgun to pursue it. Unable to dissuade her, I had no choice but to follow. Our search led us into the woods by our property, where we beheld an eldritch, viridescent—

Zora tried to remember what "viridescent" meant. Judging by all the ten-bit words, this letter-writer would've gotten along well with Mr. Epps.

"Green," said Signe, like the show-off she was.

—an eldritch, GREEN glow spinning rapidly upon itself. It possessed a mesmeric power that held us entranced for some time; afterward, neither of us could say for how long . . .

The letter trembled in Zora's grip. "Keep reading," said Mr. McBrain.

I even fancied I heard a voice inside my head deliver a wordless warning—or perhaps a threat. Delia suffered no such experience; thus, I speculate that the light's hypnotic gyrations induced an auditory hallucination on my part.

Once the spell broke, we fled back home—and, I confess, stayed awake until dawn. I fervently hope you can return and provide us with an explanation for this fantastical specter—as well as a method for laying it to rest.

I fear it will come again tonight.

It took Zora a few seconds to decipher the ornate signature: "Kindest regards, Millicent Stackpole."

"Did the professor come back to help them?" asked Quinn.

"Ms. Stackpole wrote that on the last day of winter in the last year of the Old Calendar." Mr. McBrain took the paper from Zora and refolded it. "The Great Wakening began the next night, so she never had the opportunity to mail her letter. I recovered it from a house in the near reaches of the Wastes. A gargantuan elemental had taken possession of the surroundings for as far as the eye could see." He paid no heed to the queasy looks from his guests. "The important point is that she observed an uncatalogued spirit, the manifestation of which *preceded* the Great Wakening."

Signe started to interrupt, but Zora raised a finger to her lips.

"I sent my former assistant"—their host made a face, as though he'd caught a whiff of skunk—"to scour the Hollows for any reports of a spirit matching the one described by the unfortunate Ms. Stackpole. After eight years of fruitless searching, he met a peddler and amateur spirit-chaser named Vernon Moss." The old man nodded at Zora and Quinn. "Your father told us he'd seen our mysterious quarry during his travels."

Quinn clenched his jaw. Zora wished she could punch Dad for the both of them.

"Furthermore," Mr. McBrain said, "he offered to help us study it. We spent the next four years charting its wanderings through the Hollows, and sometimes beyond, until—"

Zora had done the math in her head. "It found me in Lightning Bug Hollow." She disregarded a probing look from Signe.

"Correct." The Spotter stroked his beard. "The incident upset your father a great deal, but we deduced several significant details from the account you gave him. First, the spirit was intelligent. Second, it could communicate telepathically, just as Ms. Stackpole's letter hinted. Third, it could call forth other spirits. Lastly, and most alarmingly, it knew of our efforts to monitor it."

Signe tried to speak, but he talked right over her. "After the spirit's visitation, we experimented with various ways to elude its attention." He gestured to the walls. "Lead shielding seems to do the job."

Heavy metals could block kirlian waves? Useful to know, Zora told herself. As long as she didn't have to spend the rest of her life in a bunker, hiding from spirits and worrying about lead poisoning.

"I secluded myself here," Mr. McBrain went on, "against both the spirits and the spies that had begun to shadow me. Meanwhile, we redoubled our efforts to ferret out records of our otherworldly adversary. Four moons ago, we succeeded." He sifted through the clutter on his desk until he found a leather-bound journal with a gash across its cover. "Something your father purchased from an itinerant bookseller. He brought it to me as soon as he read it."

"This spring," Quinn said, in a low tone.

The Spotter gave Zora the journal. "It's the diary of one Leamon Altizer, who lived in the Pass back when humans still inhabited it. Over the course of a dozen years, he documented nineteen sightings of a spinning, humming spirit—sometimes by itself, sometimes accompanied by other kinds of spirits. The last seven observations date to the year of the Lesser Wakening, ending with one on the eve of the summer solstice. The following night, legions of spirits laid waste to the Pass. And Sylvania as well, if the radio silence since then is any indication. Mr. Altizer fled with his journal, but a roamer of some sort waylaid him during his journey through the Border Hollows."

Zora turned to the entry for the third day of summer, in the year 77 AW. *I feel utterly enervated,* the author had written, *and my flesh has begun to take on the same hue as the monster that stung me. I fear I shall wander no more; nor shall I solve the riddles posed by the Harbinger of Sorrows.*

The rest of the pages were blank.

"Leamon Altizer succumbed to spirit-sickness before he could inform anyone of what he'd seen," said Mr. McBrain.

"Now you think it's happening again." Zora's own voice sounded as though it were coming from far away.

"That would fit the pattern." The old man made his way to the model of the Hollows. "The spirit you encountered as a child manifests intermittently over a twelve-year span, with increasing frequency. Then"—he turned down the lights, and the pins on the diorama glowed in the dark—"a new Wakening occurs."

Signe finally managed to get a word in. "You mean it's some sort of herald?"

"We know it can summon others of its ilk from nearby." Mr. McBrain pressed a wizened talon against the pin that marked Lightning Bug Hollow. "I believe that under certain planetary conditions, it can also open a portal to the realm of the spirits— their own dimension, universe, call it what you like—and allow them into our world." He raised the lights again. "I've identified more than forty spirits in my career. This one, I named the *harbinger*."

"I get why you have all the calendars," said Zora. "You buy into the celestial theory. Year Zero up at the top. Year 77 down there. And now"—she pointed at the final calendar—"Year 143 right here."

That elicited a flummoxed look from Quinn.

"Some spiritologists think the timing of the Wakenings had to do with the earth's alignment," she explained. "The Great one happened on the vernal equinox—the first day of spring— and the Lesser one on the summer solstice. So—" She stopped as her hair stood on end.

Mr. McBrain finished for her. "The next one in the sequence will take place on the autumnal equinox. Given that the Great Wakening also fell on an equinox, I suspect this new one will match its scale." He gave a dry, mirthless laugh. "The current cycle of appearances has already gone on for twelve years, so the harbinger is right on schedule to crash the upcoming All Hollows celebrations."

Quinn counted on his fingers. "That's six days away!"

"As I said, you arrived just in time."

"Why didn't you tell anyone this?" yelled Zora. "The Rangers, or the Judges, or any of the other Spotters?"

"I didn't imagine there was anything I—or they—could do about it. Announcing my findings would've done nothing but set off a season of chaos among the rabble of the Hollows." He steepled his hands. "And given away my location to the harbinger."

Quinn scowled at the diorama. "What'd our father do when y'all figured this out?"

"He deserted me to run back to his old farm. But even that was preferable to how my impertinent assistant reacted. I exiled *him* from this island for making"—his voice was heavy with scorn—"a ludicrous suggestion."

Signe seemed puzzled by that. "What did he—"

"Unfortunately," Mr. McBrain plowed on, "that severed my last contact with the mainland." His eyes glinted from their deep sockets. "So what's this you said about spirit-hunting?"

Zora launched into a rapid-fire description of her inventions. When she ran out of breath, her brother opened his pack and held out an illuminator to Mr. McBrain, who turned it over in his hands and set it on a table. Quinn gave him the banisher next, then a spirit-grenade and the trap prototype.

"We've been using these devices all summer," said Zora. "Do you think we might've triggered a flurry of spirit weather across the Hollows?" She looked at Signe, who frowned back at her.

The Spotter assumed a meditative air. "I doubt it. More likely the harbinger is testing its abilities. Or perhaps it's merely a coincidental fluctuation in spirit activity." He brushed the question away. "In the grand scheme of things, it hardly matters. Provided these weapons work as you say, we may have a chance to stop the cataclysm before it happens, by eliminating the harbinger."

Easier said than done, thought Zora. They'd barely survived their last meeting with it.

"Hold on," said Signe. "I think we should consider a different approach. If we can communicate with this harbinger, then maybe we can persuade it to leave the Hollows in peace." She waved her folded-up parasol like a baton. "On the way here, I—"

Mr. McBrain silenced her with a scoff. "That's almost as outrageous as what my former assistant proposed." He turned to Zora. "Does this young woman work with you?"

"Well . . ." she began.

"Yes," said Quinn. "She has a kind of second sight for spirits."

"A neat trick, I'm sure, though I've never needed anything but ordinary vision to track them myself." The Spotter's voice hardened. "I hope she's also capable of perceiving that her naivety may get herself, and you, killed. During the Wakenings, the spirits wiped out countless humans. Yet *she* believes she can simply ask them to be *nice* to us, the callow little twit."

Color rose in Signe's cheeks, and she blinked rapidly from behind her bottle-thick lenses. Quinn raised a hand in protest, but Zora surprised herself by speaking up first. "Nevertheless, our—um—associate did talk a pack of herns out of attacking us last night."

"Herns are unpredictable brutes," said Mr. McBrain. "I would know, having classified them myself. So long as your friend doesn't hinder our work, I suppose I don't care whether she invites the spirits for punch and cakes. In any event, our biggest problem right now is finding the harbinger."

"We saw it two nights ago in Comet Tail Hollow," Zora said. "Then it set an elemental after us."

The Spotter looked grave. "Its power will wax as the equinox approaches. But at least we know where to begin searching. I believe I can use the data I've gathered to project its likely course." He started filling a crate with photometers, theodolites, and other paraphernalia. "We should leave at once."

Quinn pointed to a grandfather clock standing against a crinkly wall. "It's already evening. Wouldn't it be safer to wait till tomorrow?"

"By then, the new Wakening will be one day closer." Mr. McBrain added books and papers to the crate. "You have a boat down at the pier, I hope?"

Zora smacked her forehead. "The motor! I forgot to wind its mainspring."

"Better go take care of that, then." The Spotter stared at her crutches, as if noticing them for the first time. "Your brother can help bring my equipment when I've finished packing it."

"I guess I'll come with you," Signe told Zora, still sounding flustered.

The two of them left the bunker to troop past Mr. McBrain's scarecrows, which looked even more ghoulish beneath the darkening sky than they had by daylight, and his tin-can trip-wire, which clinked loudly when Signe stumbled over it. By the time Zora reached the pier, all four of her limbs had begun to ache. She dropped her crutches into the boat and lowered herself after them.

Signe joined her in one nimble motion, then picked up the crutches and offered them to her.

Zora tensed. "Don't touch those." Not without her permission.

"Listen, I understand—"

"No, you don't."

Signe put down the crutches. "I was only trying to help." Her hands balled into black fists.

"I know." Zora turned her back and focused on the motor. What a piece of junk. Flawed design, slapdash construction. She whacked it.

Behind her, Signe let out a sob. "This isn't how things were supposed to be," she said, between sniffles.

The boat rocked as Zora shifted next to her and gingerly patted her shoulder blades. "We're going to fix this—me, you, Quinn, and Mr. McBrain. Who, it turns out, is a bit of a pompous"—she considered and rejected several words—"curmudgeon."

"Thanks." Signe gave a weak laugh. "You should wind the motor, remember?"

"Right." The boat's owner had made the task look easy, but Zora found it a challenge even with the arm strength she'd built up over the summer. The mainspring clicked into place just as her brother and Mr. McBrain climbed aboard.

She cranked the drive key. Sprockets clacked inside the clockwork motor, and the boat pulled away from the dock.

Quinn switched on the banisher. When he pointed it toward the opposite shore, one orange bulb lit up on the weapon's stock.

"What's that all about?" asked the Spotter.

Signe waved from the bow. "That's just me."

"She radiates slight levels of spirit energy," Zora said.

Mr. McBrain regarded the pale young woman as though she'd grown a thirteen-point set of antlers. "What manner of chimera *is* she, anyway?"

"You tell us, you conceited windbag," Signe snapped. "I thought you knew everything."

Zora grinned at the Spotter's consternation. Witch's Hat Island was a peaked shadow against the twilight at her back. Ahead and to the right, the gold beacon of the Ranger Headquarters shone above one of the Twin Knobs.

Her wrist-watcher beeped. Two lights: one for Signe, and one for something else. "Quinn?"

"I've got it too, sis."

Zora revved the motor. "I thought Paige and her boss didn't find anything in the lake."

Signe knit her brows. "Who?"

"A Spotter named Darius Epps and his apprentice came here not long ago, searching for a waterbound spirit."

"I must've missed that part of the conversation," said Quinn.

Mr. McBrain drummed his fingers along the side of the boat. "The Big Lake has the least spirit activity of anywhere in the Hollows. That's why I chose the island for my sanctuary." He dug a pair of binoculars from his crate and scanned the lake. "There are a few old rumors to the contrary, which I fanned to scare away busybodies, but I've lived here for years with nary a sighting."

Another beep. Zora looked around the plane of water. All smooth, all black.

"I'm reading spirits in multiple directions," said Quinn. "Signe, do you see anything?"

"No." She leaned over the prow. "Wait." A sharp intake of breath. "They're underwater."

The Spotter lowered his binoculars and arched his eyebrows.

"Dozens of them," Signe added.

Again? This wasn't fair, Zora told herself.

"Perhaps the tales had a kernel of truth, after all," said Mr. McBrain. "But for a shoal of waterbounds to manifest now, after so many decades . . ."

Not just unfair. Suspicious. Zora yanked open the motor's panel to reveal a cluster of whirling cogwheels—and one pulsing red light, identical to the one in Evelyn Fontaine's camera.

"They're coming up toward us," said Signe.

Zora killed the motor and pulled out the flashing device.

"We've stopped!" shouted Quinn.

"Don't you think I know that?" she shouted back. "The overgrown dock rat who rented us this boat planted a spirit-lure on us." Tuning out the racket from the others, she searched for the device's toggle.

This one didn't have an off switch. She smashed the lure against the seat, and its bulb ceased blinking. Had she done it in time?

The water around the boat glowed a deep blue-green. Small bubbles broke the surface, followed by larger bubbles, which gave way to boiling foam.

Nope, not in time. The spirits had already taken to the hunt. She restarted the motor, and the boat shot forward.

"They're staying with us." A note of urgency had entered Signe's voice. "Closing in."

Four orange lights. Zora jammed the remains of the lure down a pocket and pulled out her new banisher-pistol. Five lights. Quinn braced his feet against the sides of the boat. Six.

As spray filled the air, tentacles rose behind them. Their phosphorescence cast a cold, turquoise light across the dark mirror of the lake.

"I gather I'm about to receive a demonstration of your spirit-weapons," said the Spotter. "Preferably sooner rather than later."

Zora pushed down the throttle until the gears made a grinding noise. The tentacles kept pace with them, swaying like rushes in a breeze.

"Let me try first." Signe stood, using her parasol for balance. "Waterbound spirits!" She wobbled, but then righted herself. "We mean you no harm. Go in peace, and let harmony between your kind and ours settle these turbulent waters."

The greenish-blue shapes paused in their motion. Signe smiled, while Mr. McBrain shook his head in disbelief.

Without warning, one of the tentacles whipped through the air toward Signe. The parasol flew from her hand and disappeared into the lake with a plop. She stared after it, her jaw hanging down.

Moving as one, the tentacles slammed into the water. The boat lurched, and Signe toppled forward into the bow. Quinn opened fire with the banisher, vaporizing one of the glistening forms. Zora's first shot with the pistol went wide.

The Spotter pointed toward the signal-lamp on the distant hilltop. "Make for Twin Knobs."

"Take the tiller," Zora said. As she and Mr. McBrain traded places, her brother picked off two more tentacles. She snuffed out another one with her pistol.

"They keep coming," muttered Quinn.

A vertebrae-rattling moan emanated from the depths. What had Paige told her? *The Big Lake—legends—a jumbo-sized waterbound.*

"Not they," said Zora. "It."

Signe peered over the side of the boat, then jerked back her head. "You're right." If possible, she looked whiter than ever. "It's enormous."

"A leviathan!" Mr. McBrain tore at his beard. "Dormant for all these years."

"Hold it off as long as you can," Zora told Quinn. With her free hand, she rooted through the pack until she came up with a grenade. Too small. She activated it and chucked it over her shoulder. An explosion reverberated through the night, answered by a watery blare.

"I've blundered into the snares of my enemies," ranted the Spotter. "I never should've left my island with a pack of juvenile upstarts."

Zora stubbed her fingers against the rim of the trap prototype. But where was the remote? She dropped her pistol to paw inside the pack with growing desperation.

A whistle broke her concentration, and a trail of light appeared above the lakeshore. "Flares!" said Signe. "They've seen us." She sounded overjoyed, but the Ranger station was still only a faraway beacon on the heights.

Zora found the remote. Now they'd see whether that stinking hunk of pond scum liked a taste of what she and Quinn had done to the hount.

Her brother fired again, and again. "Some help—would be—good."

"Watch out!" shrieked Signe. Zora looked up in time to see a tentacle wrap around Mr. McBrain's waist. As the spirit pulled him over the stern of the boat, he flailed his arms and shouted to them.

Then he vanished in their wake.

The boat yawed off course, away from the shore. Quinn blasted the water with bolts of energy. Signe lunged past him toward the tiller, her glasses askew. The leviathan grasped at them with a multitude of arms.

Quashing the instinct to scream, Zora pitched the trap into the lake. It landed with a splash and bobbed for a few seconds before sinking beneath the foam.

A tentacle reached for her throat. She picked up the pistol and shot it, but two more tentacles replaced it.

She pushed the button on the remote.

With a muffled thump, the water around the boat turned a brilliant violet-blue. A tortured bellow sounded from far below as spasms coursed through the leviathan. Signe cried out and doubled over, vomit dribbling down her chin.

Zora squeezed the pistol's trigger. No ray. Dead battery. She grabbed a crutch, swinging it like a club against the nearest tentacle.

The bulk of the leviathan smashed against the bottom of the hull. The world flipped upside-down. Zora's mouth filled with foul-tasting liquid, and she strained to kick her legs.

She surfaced near the overturned boat with a gasp and a cough. The tentacles were gone, and the aquamarine glow had disappeared. Quinn was using one arm to support Signe, whose sodden white hair lay draped over her face.

Through water-clogged ears, Zora heard the purr of an approaching motor. A pair of hands reached under her armpits, lifted her from the lake, and set her down on a dry seat.

"Ms. Coldiron," came a gentle drawl, "we do seem to keep meeting in the oddest circumstances." Ranger Tate placed a blanket over her shoulders. "I got your letter. I'm glad you're still with us among the living."

Signe was lying on the patrol boat's deck, a life jacket under her head for a pillow. A woman with gold braid on her cap said something to Quinn, and he offered her the banisher for inspection.

Zora's mind was blank; her body felt numb. She looked at her hands. One still gripped a crutch, while the other held the pistol.

They'd lost her other crutch. Signe's parasol. Most of their equipment. And the one person who'd known how to find the harbinger before it summoned enough spirits from its world to destroy the Hollows.

13

QUINN PICKED DRIED MUCUS FROM HIS EYELASHES. HALF PAST THE eighth petal on the Daddy Hex clock. Morning already. Five days until the equinox.

"Wake up," he called to Zora. "They'll be waiting for us."

His sister searched through her drawer of overalls until she found what must've been the least grubby pair. She leaned on her remaining crutch as they slowly walked along the base of Tater Knob to the inn they'd stopped at just yesterday. Signe and Emerson Tate were there with Ranger Captain Flores, who tipped her gold-trimmed cap at them. The innkeeper had laid out five plates of bacon and grits on their table.

Quinn and Zora sat down. "We searched for the man who rented you the boat," Captain Flores told them. "He's nowhere to be found."

"Probably on his way back to Evelyn Fontaine." Ranger Tate looked downright baby-faced next to his silver-haired boss. "She's gone underground somewhere. Easy to lay low when you have as much money and as many lackeys as she does."

Across the table, Signe pushed away her untouched plate.

Quinn wasn't hungry either, but he stuffed some grits into his mouth anyhow.

"That's quite a story y'all told us last night." Captain Flores sized them up with bloodshot eyes. "I doubt I'd believe a word of it if I hadn't seen the leviathan for myself." She ate a bite of bacon and wiped her mouth with a napkin. "So, the hermit predicted a bona fide Wakening on All Hollows. And y'all think he was right?"

Zora nodded. "Mr. McBrain might've gone a bit eccentric, but he'd compiled a mountain of data on the harbinger." She rearranged her food with a fork. "All on the bottom of the lake now. With him."

Quinn stared down the slope toward the water. Today it looked as peaceful as any other grave he'd helped dig.

"This harbinger," said Captain Flores. "Can your weapons stop it?"

Zora nodded again, more hesitantly this time. "I have a theory about how to do that, but I need to get back to Lightning Bug Hollow to work on the technology."

"Next question," said the captain. "How do we find the spirit before it's too late?"

Quinn had chewed over the same problem himself. His sister wasn't going to like the solution he'd hit upon.

Zora held up her hands in a helpless gesture. "We were counting on the old man for that."

Captain Flores frowned. "There's a snag, for sure."

"What about his former assistant?" Quinn asked. "What's his name again?"

"Otis Hetfield," said Signe. "I have no idea where he is now. And when I spoke to him earlier, he neglected to tell me about the harbinger."

Which left only one possibility, just as he'd suspected. He sat up straighter. "That means I need to pay a family visit to Sassafras Hollow." The captain cocked her head. "Our father helped Mr. McBrain track the spirit for years," he added, for her benefit.

"But we need to go to my lab," said Zora.

"*You* do. I wouldn't be any help working on your inventions, and you know it."

She grabbed his arm. "You've got to come with me. Besides, we only have the one wagon—"

"I can take him," Signe said, to an empty spot on the wall. "Zora, he's right. Your dad's our best chance of learning how to find the harbinger."

"I can't do this alone." His sister was pleading now. "Not with spirits rising up everywhere and Evelyn Fontaine's cut-throats out to get us."

"With your permission, Captain," said Ranger Tate. "Perhaps I can escort Ms. Coldiron and provide her any assistance she requires."

"Excellent suggestion, officer." Captain Flores stood. "We have a plan, then, and no time to waste. While y'all complete your tasks, I'll place my entire force on night patrol and ask the Judges to declare an emergency throughout the Hollows. If we see this spirit, I'll send word by courier." She rested one hand on her holster. "And if we catch Ms. Fontaine or any of her flun-kies, I'll conduct the interrogation myself."

Zora slouched in her chair, looking defeated.

"I'll join up with you as soon as I talk to our father," Quinn told her. "You can take the banisher I've been using."

"You keep it. The pistol's easier for me to handle, and

I have my wrist-watcher. But I don't like us"—her voice shook—"splitting up."

"I need to do this." He rose to go before his resolve could break.

She tugged at his sleeve. "He's only going to disappoint you again."

Back at the wagon, Quinn unplugged the banisher from the battery and crammed his clothes into his pack. When he returned to the inn, his sister and Signe were standing by the railing and whispering at one another. They both clamped their mouths shut the moment he set foot on the deck.

Zora came over and hugged him with her free arm. "Don't let any spirits catch you with your pants down, big brother."

He kissed her on the forehead. "I love you, too, little sis." Then he shook Ranger Tate's hand. "Thank you, sir."

"Safe travels and good luck, Mr. Prosser." There was the ghost of a tremor in the man's drawl.

Signe donned a black, wide-brimmed hat and set off toward her wagon. As Quinn turned to follow, he saw Zora's face crumple. The image hung in his mind for a long time afterward.

The road to Sassafras Hollow was all hills and potholes. Three hairpin turns into the ride, Quinn found himself struggling to contain his frustration at Signe's horse for being slower than Ursula and Undine. Never mind that the poor beast had to do all the pulling by her lonesome.

Signe was looking wan and listless on the driver's seat. She hadn't said a word since telling Fylgja to go.

"Are you still feeling peaked?" Quinn asked. "That seizure you had on the boat, from the explosion Zora set off—"

"I'm all better from my fainting episode." Her voice was dull. "It's not that. My whole life, I've told myself I was special. The seventh born of a seventh born, gifted like no other. When my parents nagged me to grow up and settle on a respectable apprenticeship, I pitied them for being ordinary. When my brothers and sisters rolled their eyes at me, I said they were only envious." She pulled down the brim of her hat to cover more of her face. "But my childish fantasies got Mr. McBrain killed."

"If you want to lay blame," Quinn said, "I figure Zora and I were the targets of those folks with the lure, so what happened to him is just as much our fault as yours. And who's to say you *weren't* sent here by fate, or what have you, to help save the Hollows? We only know about the new Wakening in the first place because you led us to the old man. All on account of him, this Hetfield person, and my father"—Quinn took a breath to still his resentment—"keeping it a secret from everybody else."

"The leviathan didn't even leave behind a . . . body to bury."

"That might've been a mercy, of sorts." Last summer, Quinn had helped his mother embalm the corpse of a woman who'd drowned in the Great Salt Creek. If he had to die in a few days, he'd rather be cremated by an elemental or picked clean by a hount.

The sun came out from behind a cloud, and Signe squeezed her eyes shut behind her glasses. "The last words I said to him were spiteful ones."

"I reckon he had that coming, at any rate. Leastways

you tried to warn him at the end." He almost gave her a pat on the back, like he would've with Zora, but then thought better of it. "What did you and my sister talk about back there, anyhow?"

"She told me to keep you safe. And that she'd try out the banisher on my face if anything happened to you." The sky turned gray again, and Signe opened her eyes. "You know, she adores you something fierce."

The beginnings of a lump formed in Quinn's throat. "I'm sorry she's been so ornery toward you. My sister's a complicated person, with lots of strong notions."

"That's okay." Signe almost smiled. "So am I."

They drove on between two cliffs of layered shale, and Quinn took a moment to read the words painted on the rocks. *Josie + Harlan Forever* in a rose-colored script, encompassed by a heart shape. Sweet, but the couple who'd left that message had no idea how short their future—and everybody else's— might end up being. *Crooked Branch Hollow is a Rat's Nest,* in blue. Troglodytes, Zora would've sneered. *Hail the Wearer of the Horned Crown* in green, with a design that looked like antlers. Bizarre. Yet familiar, in an unnerving way.

When they passed through to the other side, Signe began to sing. Her voice was reedy and off-key, but Quinn didn't mind. He knew the song by heart. It was the one about how the fiddler girl had saved the people of a cursed hollow by using her music to hold off a spirit-tempest long enough for everyone in its path to escape. Everyone but herself, that is. Signe's voice faltered as she reached the last verse, the one where the girl's final tune ended to the twang of fiddle strings breaking.

"Not the most uplifting choice, I'll grant," she said.

"Maybe so, but it's still one of my favorites." That brought a genuine smile to her face.

Over lunch, they composed letters warning their families of the impending catastrophe. It struck Quinn that he might never see Cascade Hollow again, and for the first time since meeting Zora he longed to go back to his old humdrum life at the funeral home. To admit to his mother he'd jumped in over his head and ask her what he should do.

Come to think of it, what would she make of Signe if the two ever had the chance to meet? The black clothes might go over well, if nothing else did.

At dusk, they came to a trading post that advertised THE BEST FRIED CHICKEN IN THE HOLLOWS, BAR NONE in giant letters, along with *Mail, Stables, & Tolliver's Anti-Spirit Spray* in smaller ones. Zora had told him once that the spray was nothing more than camphor cut with possum urine.

Signe brought the wagon to a stop. "Fylgja needs a break," she said.

He stamped on the footboard, then nodded. "I'll take care of her if you can mail our letters and buy some food for us."

"I'm going to ask whether they have a hot shower, too." She inspected a strand of her hair. "At this point, I'd walk barefoot across the Wastes for one."

Once Signe was gone, Quinn tried to sort through his feelings about her. It seemed wrong to go mooning over a young woman right after he'd abandoned his own sister to unknown dangers.

And yet.

He led Fylgja to the stable, got her situated, and started toward the wagon. Along the way, he unslung the banisher from his shoulder. One orange dot. Signe must be coming back. He promised himself that if they lived to see the first day of fall he'd ask her to do something ordinary with him, like go to the Harvest Festival or the library in Hoary Hollow. Any sort of date would be fine, so long as it didn't have to do with spirits.

Until then, he'd keep his mind on stopping the Wakening.

Two orange dots shone back at him from the banisher's stock. He rubbed his eyes and held the weapon closer to his face. That made no sense. He hadn't heard a thing.

From not so far away, a whistle echoed through the twilight. A third bulb winked on without the usual fuzzy beep.

Quinn swore at himself. With all his pining, he'd gone lackadaisical. The lake water must've damaged the banisher's alarms, and he hadn't even noticed.

A streak of light corkscrewed through the woods. The whistle's pitch swooped and soared. He squeezed off a hasty shot, and the spirit blew up with a bang. It left behind a track of acid-green smoke that soon dwindled to nothingness.

Just as Quinn relaxed, a stench of moldy leaves filled his nostrils. He recognized the odor too late. Saltpeter Hollow, two odd moons ago. His first hunt with Zora.

The other half of the spirit rammed him in the back.

Quinn, shouted Signe from high above. *I can't reach you. You've fallen too far.*

He dreamed of a fox with one leg in a trap, surrounded by flames.

No such thing as premonitions, said Zora from the darkness. *Only the brain replaying things it's already seen and heard, connecting them in random ways. Like this conversation. We had it five days ago, remember? Or was that five days from now?*

He dreamed of a swan writhing as an electric wire pierced its chest.

Time, said a voice that wasn't Signe's or Zora's, or even human. *Space. They twist in ways you can't perceive, ways that will entangle you forever.*

He dreamed of a deer that held a bloody, pulsating heart in its five-fingered hands.

Quinn awoke in a strange bed, still wearing his trousers and flannel shirt. But not his boots, it seemed. Signe lay next to him, hidden by a quilt except for her whitish-gold hair. Her glasses were resting on a bedside table. The air smelled faintly of lavender and sweat.

He listened to her slow, soft breathing for a while before sitting up. Light filtered through gauzy curtains onto lilac-painted walls. Black lacquered furniture. A bone-framed mirror.

Signe had obviously put a fair bit of effort into decorating the interior of her wagon. Unlike, say, him or Zora.

Three shelves lined the near wall. The novels stacked on the top one brought back memories of rainy afternoons in the Prosser Funeral Home. *Song of the Muskellunge Mermaids. The Mystery of the Phantom Zeppelin. Addie the Urchin versus the Pneumatic Necromancer.*

He resisted the temptation to wake Signe and ask which ones she'd read.

The middle shelf sagged beneath copies of the same thick texts Zora doted on so much. *A Taxonomy of Waterbound*

Spirits, by Darius Epps. Alice Feng and Hallie Alston's *Revised Classification of Roamers*. *A Field Guide to the Spirits of the Hollows*, by Nevan McBrain.

A shiver ran through his body at the sight of that last name.

The bottom row was all pink and yellow spines with silver cursive spelling out titles he'd never seen before. *Passions of a Young Wood-Witch*. *Steamy Voyages on the Riverboat of Dreams*. *The Virgin of Hot Springs Hollow*.

Quinn shifted on the bed for a closer view, and then Signe sat up to squint at him with sleepy gray eyes.

"I probably should've put those ones away." She sounded sheepish. "Are you all right?" Her camisole was a faded purple, and so were the stripes running down her bloomers. Goosebumps showed beneath the fine white hairs on her legs. Without her usual neck-to-toe black, she looked naked.

Well, almost naked.

He averted his gaze and reined in his runaway imagination. "Fine. Just a bit shook up."

"What happened to you last night?"

"A spirit snuck up on me. A cousin of one Zora and I hunted earlier this summer. She calls them tangles. Could be just a coincidence it showed up, but I'm starting to think those things like the scent of me." He rubbed his back. "It must've knocked me out. How'd I wind up here?"

Signe leaned closer to him, a concerned expression on her face. She peered into his right eye, then his left. "I heard some sort of pandemonium break out as I was buying dinner," she said. "When I came outside, you were unconscious on the ground. The owner of the trading post helped me carry you into the wagon."

"Which"—he swallowed—"only has one bed."

"I see you've recovered the powers of observation that helped make you a famous spirit-hunter." Signe wrapped the quilt around herself. "I maybe should've brought up the sleeping arrangements earlier. Anyway, you seemed out for the night, so I"—she stopped to yawn.

Quinn stood. "That's all right. We're in a hurry, so I'll get Fylgja ready." He found his boots and the banisher on the floor. "Did you get the chance to take your hot shower?"

"Not even a cold one." She lay back on her pillow and pulled the quilt up to her ears. "My quest continues."

On his way to the door, he lingered to look at a framed photograph of a man and a woman standing behind seven children, all with sandy hair and serious expressions. Except for the youngest, the snowy-locked girl showing off her front teeth.

"I'll be right there," Signe called after him.

Quinn stepped outside into what felt like the first day of fall, come four days early. He buttoned his outer shirt against the chill morning air and combed his hair with his fingers. Overhead, a flock of black-necked geese flew south toward some lost oasis beyond the barrens of the Cumberland Plateau.

As he led Fylgja to the wagon, Signe emerged with a lunch pail. "I saved you a few pieces of chicken from last night," she said. She was wearing her hat and yet another dress, one with a pattern of charcoal-colored vines against black.

He bit into a wing. Not bad, though hardly the best in the Hollows.

This time, Quinn drove and played the quiet one while Signe chatted on about everything except the reason behind their journey. After a lengthy soliloquy on her ideal replacement parasol, she paused and studied him with a thoughtful air. "I take it you and your dad aren't tight," she said.

"Mom pretty much raised me by herself. My father dropped by every so often to give me presents, tell stories about himself, and get his paws all over her." Steady there, Quinn told himself. He loosened his grip on the reins. "Right after my ninth birthday, he vanished from my life completely. I spent the next year holed up in our funeral home with my books and my old crystal radio. Mom got really worried about me."

Signe lifted her eyebrows.

"But I had a friend next door named Paige," he went on. "She kept roping me into little adventures to cheer me up. And eventually it worked."

"That was good of her," said Signe, in an oddly stilted tone. "So you and your father haven't spoken since then?"

"Only once. At the first of this summer, he sent a letter asking me to visit him. I threw it away, but then I changed my mind and went to see him. That's when I found out I had a half-sister."

"You only met Zora a few moons ago?" Signe's eyes were round behind her blue lenses. "The way you two are, I figured you'd known each other your whole lives." Her voice turned wistful. "I suppose it's different when you only have one sibling, and that one's, well . . ."

"On the same page as you?" Quinn smiled through his bitterness. "Though Zora would say the same wavelength, instead. I'm grateful she's in my life now, but we missed fifteen years of knowing one another thanks to my father's fine talent for being so tight-lipped."

"It does seem like something he should've told you."

"He wouldn't explain why he hadn't, either." Quinn was

warming up to his anger. "But that's not the half of it. When I talked to him, he also failed to mention the spirit that's fixing to unleash glowing green doom on us."

Signe blanched, as if she'd forgotten about that part, but then rested a hand on the back of his neck. "Facing him again must be hard for you."

"It beats me and everybody else I know dying, I expect."

Her gloved fingertips were soft against his skin. "We don't have to talk about this if you don't want to." She removed the hand and put it on her lap with her other one. "My own dad, I don't think he's ever understood me. No one back home does. Sometimes I think I'm the family changeling."

Quinn wished she'd kept on touching him.

"But I can't really complain," she added.

"I appreciate what you're doing." He tried to put on a chipper face. "I reckon I ought to wrestle with all this while I have the chance."

A sudden gust yanked at Signe's hat, and she caught it just before it flew away. "Well"—she put the hat back on—"I hope you find what you're searching for when we get to your dad's place."

"So do I, seeing as how our lives depend on it."

"Right," she said, almost too softly to hear. "That, too."

They arrived at Sassafras Hollow in the early evening. Since Quinn's last visit, the rows of corn along the road had grown from knee-high sprouts to stalks that cleared the top of the wagon. The hollow's only store had burned down, and a bare stump squatted in place of a weeping willow.

The air grew colder and the shadows grew longer as they followed the meandering curves past half-decrepit farmhouses and barns emblazoned with sun-bleached hex signs. "Which one is your dad's?" asked Signe.

"You can't see it from here." Quinn's heart was already beating faster, and he couldn't hide the trepidation in his voice. "His place is off a side road toward the head of the hollow."

Signe gave his arm a comforting squeeze.

By the time they reached the next fork, the clouds had turned reddish-pink above the western hills. Lightning Bug Hollow lay on the other side of those peaks, a two-day journey by wagon. Was Zora already there, engineering a way to save them?

Fylgja rounded the final bend, and Quinn guided her toward his father's farm. The house was the same as always—a collection of additions anchored by a stone chimney and topped by a metal roof—but the yard, once neatly cut, had gone to seed. Beyond the tumbledown shed, hemp plants waved their serrated leaves with the wind.

Signe pointed to the lights in the windows. "Looks like he's home."

"Lucky us," Quinn whispered.

He parked the wagon by the paddock where he'd first met Ursula and Undine. Signe set her horse loose to graze, then returned to Quinn's side. Together, the two of them walked toward the house.

A sweet, pungent aroma hung over the pathway. Signe wrinkled her nose and glanced toward the hemp field.

Before they made it to the porch, the front door opened, and a lean, shortish man looked out at them from the threshold. Quinn was shocked at the changes a single season had wrought on him. A beard uncut by razor for three moons or more. Hair untouched by scissors for at least that long. A face with the same nose as his and Zora's but eyes now sunken, skin now gray and blotchy.

Quinn exhaled and stepped forward. "Hi, Dad," he said.

14

"YOU RECKON IT'S TIME TO GO, MS. COLDIRON?" RANGER TATE SAID it casually, but she knew it wasn't a question.

"Yes." She wiped her eyes with a dingy shirtsleeve. "And you can call me Zora, if we're going to be traveling together."

"All right, then, Ms. Zora. I'll collect my gear and meet you at your wagon."

Walking with just the one crutch was tricky for her, so the Ranger ended up beating her there. No more pop-guns for him anymore; he'd armed himself with a revolver and a deer-hunting rifle.

"Need any help?" he asked.

Zora brushed past her self-appointed babysitter. "I can get up by myself, thank you very much. And I know how to use the reins, too." One whole day of practice, but still.

He tugged on the bill of his olive cap. "I was thinking more of the horses."

Oh, right. Quinn usually took care of them. "Be my guest."

Once he'd harnessed Ursula and Undine, Ranger Tate climbed up next to her. She clucked at the horses, and they started down a different road than the one her brother and Signe had taken half an hour ago.

"We ought to arrive tomorrow evening," said the Ranger.

"Which only leaves me a few days to work." Zora's mind began running through all the circuits she needed to wire, all the instruments she needed to calibrate.

"Will that be enough?" His voice sounded almost mellow.

"If they find the harbinger," she said, with a confidence she didn't feel, "I'll take care of my part."

As they rode past hill and valley, Ranger Tate recounted a string of tales about his life patrolling the Hollows. The time he'd busted a ring of moonshiners by hiding inside their still for nine hours straight (Zora felt claustrophobic just listening to him). The time he'd saved a wandering banjoist from the clutches of the notorious Skaggs Gang (she picked up on the undertone of fondness in his telling of how the young man had repaid the favor with an evening of songs by their campfire). Even the time he'd seen a half-sheep, half-human monster hiding beneath an ancient railroad trestle (she didn't believe that one for an instant, but at least it kept her distracted).

In return, Zora told him the full story of how she and Quinn had bushwhacked the tangle (and was the raffish young banjo player she'd crossed paths with in Saltpeter Hollow the man who'd won the Ranger's heart with his music?).

At noontime, he fired up the wagon's stove to cook a lunch of fried tomatoes over cornbread. She was hungry as all get-out from not eating breakfast, so she gobbled down everything he put in front of her.

"Maybe I shouldn't mention it," she said, "but with my know-how I bet I could build a pretty fine still."

He shook his head. "Ms. Zora, you already seem to have a knack for brewing up trouble."

She shuffled her boots and dug her fingernails into her palms, the way she'd done when her teachers had chided her for doodling schematics instead of paying attention in school.

"But a nose for solutions, too," Ranger Tate continued. "I'd sure appreciate hearing more about these inventions of yours. Including that watch you keep looking at."

Zora's mood lifted a little as she described—in simplified terms, of course—the paraphysical principles behind her spirit-tech, and he asked a few sharp questions of his own. She'd always pegged Rangers as thick-skulled snoops, but Emerson Tate was full of surprises.

They stopped for the night at Doe Run. He stayed outside to keep guard, while she went straight to bed.

She left the lamp on and the banisher-pistol beneath her pillow.

A blast of cool air struck Zora's face when she opened the door. "Nothing happened?" she asked. "I slept through the night for the first time in five days?"

"Good morning to you, too," said Emerson, from the wagon's seat.

Maybe this was all a colossal mistake, she told herself. A snipe hunt across the Hollows on the say-so of a hermit who'd locked himself away in a foil bunker. Then she thought of Millicent Stackpole's letter, and Leamon Altizer's diary, and the harbinger's voice-that-wasn't-a-voice ringing inside her head.

She sat down to strap on her braces.

On the second day of driving, Emerson talked about how he'd left his home five summers ago to join the Rangers. "I had this powerful hankering to wander the Hollows and help out folks who needed it," he said. "Along with an equally powerful aversion to hoeing rows on the family farm."

Zora laughed. "Me, I always knew I'd be an inventor. When I was a toddler, I'd sit on Mom's lap while she worked and give her the tools she needed. I must've asked her a thousand questions. Dad was a peddler—among other things, it turns out—so it was usually just the two of us."

The day went by as pleasant as could be. Sometimes she halfway managed to forget that Quinn wasn't there. That the catfish, and the carp, and all the other bottom-feeders in the Big Lake were nibbling the scraps from Nevan McBrain's bones. That the next Wakening was fast on her heels.

Zora shivered—from the unseasonable chill—when they passed the ruin outside Lightning Bug Hollow. The horses plodded on by Hildy's, then the neighbors' fields. Almost home, she thought, and suddenly her heart was in her throat.

As they approached the house, Paige Zhu ran down the front steps and waved, her short hair fluttering in the wind. "Hey, Foxtails! I'm so glad you're here. My boss and your mom keep yammering on about science stuff, and I had to come out here to rest my ears because it was *so* boring. Though the two of them seem to be getting along"—she tilted her head at Emerson. "Wait, who's that? Where's Quinn? Is something wrong?"

"Let's go inside," said Zora. "I'll explain."

Paige nodded, now sober-faced, and lent a hand with her things.

Zora's mom met her at the door with a ferocious hug. "My little fox kit!" She let go and frowned. "Where's your brother? And your other crutch?"

"Misplaced," said Zora. "Both of them."

Mr. Epps scrutinized her with his owlish eyes. "Thank you for your dispatch. We journeyed here as swiftly as circumstances permitted."

"So spill it," Paige said.

Zora led everyone to the living room and plonked herself into her favorite armchair. As she told her story, the faces of her listeners went from mystification to alarm and then horror.

When she was done, Mr. Epps stood and put on his top hat. "We must warn my colleagues. Immediately." He motioned to Paige, who jumped up to follow him.

Zora's mom fetched the Spotter's duster from the coatrack. "Try Hildy's at the mouth of the hollow. She might be able to find a courier."

"It'll be dark soon," said Emerson. "I should go with you, in case the spirits are restless tonight."

"Take this." Zora handed him the banisher-pistol. "But come back as soon as you can."

That left her alone with her mom. Zora tried to speak but started crying instead. Her mom came over and held her tight.

Afterward, Zora blew her nose on the front of her overalls and grabbed her one crutch from the floor. "Come with me to the lab," she said. "I need your help."

The rust-colored barn smelled of ethanol and hay. Everything inside was just as Zora had left it—the mishmash of parts, the notes pinned to the walls, the tools laid out in a pattern that would seem random to anyone else. Several of the goats skipped over to welcome her back with wags of their tails and puffs of their cud-breath.

The generator clunked away in its corner as she set to work on a new banisher. Once she'd configured the sensor panel, she stopped and cracked her knuckles.

Her mom gave her a hard look. "You broke your promise to me," she said, in a too-calm tone. "The orbs were bad enough, but hounts and elementals and leviathans are something else altogether."

"*Those* ones came after *me*," Zora grumbled.

"That just makes it worse!" Her mom slammed down the pair of needle-nose pliers she'd been using to sculpt an arc ladder. "You're not even sixteen, and you've already got spirits and conspirators competing to kill you."

Zora hung her head. "I'm sorry."

"And your brother. I thought he might have more sense, given how he doesn't carry on about harebrained schemes like you, but —"

"Don't lay this on Quinn. He's pulled my butt out of the fire more than once."

"He was supposed to keep your butt and the rest of your parts *away* from fires." Her mom had gone red in the face. "I guess both of you take after Vern too much."

Shut up, shut up, you—Zora wanted to shout back, but she stopped herself. "Please." A pit grew in her stomach, as dense as a chunk of uranium. "Not now."

"We'll discuss this further when everything's settled down." Her mom was back to the fake-calm voice. "Till then, you're not to go past our yard. Not even to the sinkhole."

Maybe the world would end, thought Zora, and she'd get to avoid that conversation.

With one final glower, her mom left to wait for the others at the house. "Just us now," Zora told the goats. She fortified herself with a swig of Earl's Electrified Ginger Ale and hefted a pair of calipers. From there, time blurred as she lost herself in her n-ray detectors and nebulium spectrometers, her magnesium-tungsten filaments and silicon diodes.

"Mind if I watch?" asked Paige, from the doorway.

"Nope," said Zora. "But I may start giving you orders."

"That's most of my life these days, anyhow." The apprentice Spotter strolled into the barn and hugged her bare arms to her side. "Whatcha working on there?"

"An ectoplasma amplification unit, for disrupting kirlian waves with . . ." Zora cut herself off. "For keeping away spirits."

"Swell. Hey, tell me about this uncanny lady-friend of your brother's."

"My theory is that she's a mutant."

Paige giggled. "No, silly, what's she like?"

"I suppose Signe's all right, when she's not pretending to be the Queen of the Storybook Spooks." Zora soldered another platinum wire. "Quinn seems awfully stuck on her. Maybe they can play make-believe together."

Paige peeked over her shoulder. "You mad at her for dragging him away?"

Zora shrugged. "A little. What do *you* think about it?"

"Me? I'll be right tickled if Pine-Box has met his match."

So much for Paige going all green-eyed on his account. "How come you and Quinn didn't work out?" Zora asked.

"Everyone else expected us to wind up together. My

parents. His mom. And he was hoping we would, too." Paige looked up at the rafters. "But I knew we weren't right for each other, not that way. This spring he told me how he felt, and I told him how *I* felt, and he was pretty broken up about it. Things haven't been the same between us since." She gnawed on a finger. "I get that it was tough for him, I do, but I still miss my old friend." Her tone turned gruff. "He'd better hurry his behind over here."

"I just hope he's okay," said Zora. She closed a relay, and a violet arc appeared between the two poles of the etheric coil. "That they're both okay."

"Hey, that's nifty what you did there." The apprentice Spotter bounced from one heel to the other. Her eyes were bright. "You're going to figure this out, Foxtails. I know you can."

Zora woke up alone, face down on her table in a puddle of drool, with a blanket around her. Sunlight shone through the barn's square windows.

Another night with no spirit attacks, but only three more days until the equinox.

She swilled away the rancid taste in her mouth with another drink of caffeinated ginger ale and got back to tinkering. She'd just hooked a cable to the generator when her mom barged in carrying a plate of biscuits drizzled with sorghum syrup. "What can I do?" she asked.

"You build more banishers and grenades," said Zora. "I'll keep working on this project."

Midway through the morning, her mom looked up from a flask of freshly distilled argon gas. "I talked to Paige while you were sleeping. It sounds like you've made quite an impression on her."

Zora grunted. Had the chatterbox apprentice run her mouth about the moonshine-drinking part? Scratch that—she trusted Paige to keep her secret safe.

"It's nice seeing you make new friends," said Zora's mom. "And Mr. Epps says you're—how did he put it—quite the perspicacious young woman."

"That's a good thing, I hope." Zora picked absentmindedly at a new pimple on her forehead as she waited for whatever was coming next.

"I'm still mad at you, but I'm proud of you, too." Her mom's smile brought out her crow's feet. "I didn't mean what I said yesterday, about you and Quinn and your father."

"I know," said Zora. "And I really am sorry about everything."

Her mom plucked up a screwdriver. "But if I ever see Vern again, I'll electrocute him. All those years, sneaking around and meddling with spirits without even telling me. I've tried to forgive him for a lot—the lies, the other women. Not this." She stabbed the air with the tool as she spoke. "I always thought the spirit coming here all those years ago was just happenstance. But no, Vern brought that monster down on *my daughter.*"

Zora had never heard her sound so livid.

Emerson rapped on one of the windows, startling them both. "Some visitors for you, Ms. Zora." He wore a baffled expression. "A whole caravan of them, in fact."

Zora went out to join him. The carriage parked in front of her house had KIRK'S IRON WORKS stenciled on its side in copperplate. "Howdy," said Mr. Slocum, brushing imaginary dust from his dandified clothes. He made to shake her hand, then glanced down at her crutch and stopped in mid-motion.

She pumped his hand with her free one. "Thanks for coming."

"I could hardly do otherwise, my brainy young friend. Business is booming, in no small part to you." The merchant gestured to a row of carts stacked with crates. "I brought everything you asked for in your letter."

"I'll pay you back," said Zora. "You can count on it."

"Consider this delivery a free sample, on speculation of a potential business partnership." Mr. Slocum's cheery tone faded. "You mentioned an unpleasant sort of situation. How's that going?"

She couldn't lie to him. "Even more serious than when I wrote you. Be sure to keep your radio on these next few days."

"I had a notion you might say that." The merchant's breath hissed from him, as though he'd been punctured. "Start moving them there crates," he shouted at his workers. "Take them to"—he looked at Zora, and she pointed to her lab—"that there barn." The yard instantly became a hive of activity.

Once the workers had unloaded the carts, Mr. Slocum gave Zora a farewell dip of his hat. "It's a pleasure to meet you again, my firecracking young spirit-hunter. Or is it spirit-buster? No, spirit-*smasher*."

Zora nodded. That did have a nice ring to it.

"Ms. Mack sends her regards, by the way," the merchant added, more quietly. "She would've come too, but one of us had to stay and ride herd on the railroad project. We're both pulling for you, whatever it is you're up to."

Now that Zora had all the supplies she needed, she set everyone to work. She gave Paige and Emerson spools of wire to string around the yard, and Mr. Epps instructions on how to set up the junction boxes. After that, it was off to the lab again with her mom.

Sometime past sunset, Zora put down her tools and allowed herself a self-congratulatory grin. "We can let the system charge overnight and test it tomorrow," she said. "Then I can start on the portable version."

Her mom pushed strands of orange-gray hair from her face, leaving a grease smudge on one cheek. "I'm going to make supper. Are you done?"

"Not quite yet. Before you go, can you get me that brass pipe over there?"

The replacement crutch would take some getting used to, Zora told herself as she experimented with it on the walk to the house. It was heavier, for one thing. Still, she liked having two of them again.

And she felt safer with this new one in her hand.

Her mom and Mr. Epps were in the living room, poring over star charts and a copy of Clementine Geller's *Atlas of Earthbounds*. Paige was curled up in the armchair like a cat, fast asleep. In the background, the radio sang softly about spirits bright as emerald dew twining among pale wildwood flowers.

"Where's Emerson?" asked Zora. She found her long-cold soup beans on the kitchen table and started eating them.

"He took one of your contrivances on a reconnaissance of the premises," Mr. Epps said.

"Good for him." Her wrist-watcher was showing all clear. "Have you heard from the other Spotters yet?"

He shook his head.

"Have the Rangers made any announcements on the radio?"

"Just music all evening," said her mom.

"I should rest up for the end of the world." Zora swallowed the last bite of her beans. "At least I can sleep in my own bed, for once."

Her shoulders hurt as she walked to the room she'd used ever since she could remember. A haggard, broken-out face looked back at her from the mirror above her desk.

The bed had the same old counterpane, the one with ohm signs and lightning bolts. She sat on it, dropping her old crutch to the floor but setting the new one down gently. One boot off, then the other. One brace off, then the other. The stink of her socks wafted past her nose. She peeled them off, inspected the red marks on her ankles, and bent her toes as far as they would go.

Finally, Zora let herself fall backwards onto the bed and covered her eyes with her palms, blotting out the periodic table on the wall. She imagined an invisible force pulling her body through the mattress, through the floor, through the dirt at the bottom of the cellar she always avoided because of the rickety ladder.

Down the hallway, her mom and Mr. Epps were talking in low voices. Paige had started snoring, from the sound of it.

Zora undid her pigtails and took one more look at her wrist-watcher. This time, there was an orange light.

She pushed herself into a kneeling position. No spirits outside the window. No Ranger, either. Nothing but the barn, and the woods behind it. Could that be Signe? Was Quinn here, too?

Another orange bulb lit up without a noise. Careless girl, Zora scolded herself. She should've tested the sensor alarm after the soaking in the lake.

She held her breath and listened. A mandolin quavered on the radio. Her mom said something, and the Spotter chuckled. Paige snored again.

And underneath the other sounds, so faint as to tease her eardrums, came an all-too-familiar drone.

A few seconds later, she was rushing toward the living room, her boots still untied and the top straps on her braces left undone. "It's here!" she shouted.

Her mom and Mr. Epps popped up from the couch. Even in her frenzy, Zora noticed how closely to one another the two had been sitting.

Paige yelped from the armchair and snapped to attention.

"What is it?" asked the Spotter.

Zora started to hyperventilate, then regained control of herself. "The harbinger." She held up her wrist. "Three lights and counting."

"To the barn," her mom said.

Paige was the first one out the door, followed by her boss. Zora went next, and her mom brought up the rear. The humming had grown loud enough to drown out the generator.

"Most singular," muttered Mr. Epps.

His apprentice pointed in the direction of the sinkhole. "Over there."

A green radiance was spreading through the woods where Zora had seen the spirit as a child. That thing had shadowed her all the way back to her own home. If she botched this tonight, they'd all be dead.

But get things right, and she could save the Hollows with a few days to spare.

"Stop gawking!" barked her mom. "Move!"

The four of them made it to the barn, and Zora's mom snatched a banisher from the workbench. It looked absurdly bulky in her small hands, but her expression was fierce. When she switched on the device, a dozen of its bulbs turned orange with a burst of noise.

Paige scooped up another banisher. "Okay," she said, swinging it wildly. "Okay, okay. I'm ready."

Zora pressed her face against the nearest window. No sight of Emerson. The generator, she reminded herself—check the power level.

"Something is approaching us from the forest," called Mr. Epps from the doorway. "A number of roamers, to be more precise. One matches the description of the harbinger."

"What about the others?" asked Zora's mom.

The system was still charging. *Elementals, stay below,* Zora chanted inside her head, like a superstitious child. *Earthbound spirits, spare us woe.*

"At this distance," said Mr. Epps, "it's difficult to identify them with certainty—"

"Sir," interrupted Paige. "We're not taking notes for the book."

"True. I *conjecture* that those three spiky specimens are shards, and that the blinking one is a pharos. Hazardous, but our armaments should suffice against them. The one behind them"—the Spotter paused. "Dear me. It's summoned a dwayyo. Quite inauspicious. I haven't seen a spirit of such proportions since my trek to the Ruined Town as an apprentice."

The ground shook beneath Zora's feet. That must've been the dwayyo.

"Are they in range?" Paige pushed open a window and aimed her banisher toward the trees. "Or should I go after them?"

"Stay where you are," ordered Mr. Epps. "The efficacy of your weapon against the dwayyo is suspect at best." He turned to Zora. "Is your new apparatus functional?"

She fought the instinct to flip the switch. Too soon, and she'd fry the circuits. "Not yet."

The humming shifted from beyond the far side of the barn to the near one. "Listen to that," Paige said. Green light flickered across her cheeks, and her eyes went glassy. "Kind of puts me in mind of a lullaby . . ."

Zora poked her in the ribs with a crutch. "Don't stare at it."

"Ow, Foxtails. That smarts."

Good. If Emerson would finally show up, and if they could hold off the spirits for just—

Three times now, said a voice that seemed to emanate from everywhere, or nowhere. *This is the last, little one.*

15

"PLEASE, GO ON IN." QUINN'S FATHER HELD THE DOOR OPEN, THEN broke into a hacking cough that cut short anything else he had to say for himself.

Signe took off her hat and stepped inside. Quinn dawdled for a moment before following her. He had to pick his path carefully to avoid the sheets of paper that littered the floor. Dust coated the radio on the sideboard, and the plants by the window had shriveled into brown remnants.

The last time he'd visited, the house had been cleaner. It had smelled better, too.

Signe held out a black-gloved hand and introduced herself. After a glance toward Quinn, she added, "I'm a friend of your son's."

His father shook her hand and flashed a broad grin that made him seem almost like his old self again. "Vernon Moss. It's a privilege to welcome such an enchanting young woman to my home." He picked up a pipe from the coffee table, passed it from one hand to the other, and set it back down. "I apologize for the mess. Haven't had too many visitors lately."

Feeling tongue-tied, Quinn shoved aside a pile of almanacs

to clear a spot for himself on the threadbare sofa. Signe took the cushion next to him and set her hat on an unopened case of Doctor Phineas Pfaff's Famous Cure-All Tonic.

"Can I get you anything?" his father asked. "I've got some beer and leftovers in the cooler."

"If you have a shower or tub I could use," said Signe, "that would be splendid. We've been on the road for quite a while."

"Sure." Quinn's father retrieved a towel for her. "Second door on the right. There's a tub with a solar-powered heater that Fiona—that Zora's mother built for me."

"I'll leave you two to catch up," Signe said, and hurried off toward the bathroom.

"Interesting-looking friend you have there," said his father. "How'd you meet her?"

Quinn locked his jaw until he heard the water running. "I know about everything." He tried to sound matter-of-fact, but it came out as an accusation. "You tracking the harbinger with Nevan McBrain and"—he never could remember that other man's name—"his assistant. The time it came after Zora. What it's going to do on All Hollows."

His father sat in the chair across the coffee table and folded his hands in front of his face. Neither of them said anything. On the mantelpiece, a rosette-faced clock ticked away slowly, as though its gears were winding down.

"Your sister," said his father, at last. "She's okay?"

"Safe in her lab." Quinn hoped that was true.

A faucet squeaked, and the pipes beneath the floorboards stopped rattling. Judging by the splashes from down the hallway, Signe had climbed into her bath and was washing her hair.

He pushed the notion from his mind. The only thing that mattered these next few days was hunting down the harbinger.

"So, you found out." His father's tone was weary. "Mind if I ask how?"

"Zora told me what happened when she was seven. Old Man McBrain told us the rest."

"Is he still hiding out on that island of his?"

Quinn shook his head. "He's dead."

"*Say what?*"

"A waterbound spirit took him." Quinn inhaled some of the burnt-smelling air and blew it back out.

"Well," his father said. "Well. I reckon he should've stayed in his lead-foil bunker." He hunched his shoulders. "Not that it would've made any difference, in the end."

Quinn's vision clouded over, and then he exploded. "Why didn't you tell me about the Wakening?" He kept raising his voice, though Signe could surely hear him all the way from the bathroom. "About me having a sister? *Why did you leave and never come back?*"

His father flinched but didn't look away. "Fair enough. As to the Wakening, I wanted Nevan to warn everyone about it. To give folks a chance to make their peace. But he wouldn't go along with me, no matter how much I argued with him."

"You could've told the Hollows yourself," said Quinn.

"Do you think the Judges or the Rangers would've taken the word of a no-account peddler on that? Without Nevan to back me up, they would've laughed and gone like"—Quinn's father raised a finger to his head and made a circular motion.

"What about his assistant?" asked Quinn. "He was a Spotter, too."

"The two of them had some sort of blowup this spring. I never caught wind of what it was about. Otis hightailed it out of there, and Nevan wouldn't speak the man's name afterward. Or leave his hideout, either. So I came back home to wait for the equinox."

"I might've listened to you." Quinn's voice cracked. "But you didn't even tell me or Zora."

"I know I should've, but I couldn't bring myself to do it. I just wanted my kids to have one last happy summer."

It was almost fully dark outside now. "If you hadn't kept so many secrets," said Quinn, "things might've gone otherwise, and the old man might still be alive. You stay right here, and I'll show you." He jabbed a finger at his father and stormed out to the wagon.

When he marched back into the house with the banisher, Signe was already on the sofa with her towel wrapped around her head. She gave Quinn a questioning look, and he shrugged.

His father stared at him. "What in the Wastes is that?"

"Something your own daughter invented, after you ran off and abandoned her." Quinn brandished the device. "It's a weapon for fighting spirits. Zora's building more of them. If you help us find the harbinger, we may have a chance to defeat it."

"I've tried to puzzle out where it'll be, come All Hollows. Without Nevan's calculations, I can't do it."

"Try harder," snarled Quinn. "You owe us that much."

His father bowed his head. "It's no use. You should go back to Zora, so you can be with her when the Wakening comes. Maybe y'all can save yourselves with those weapons. She always was a smart kid. Tell her I—no, don't bother telling her anything about me."

"So that's it." Quinn slumped onto the sofa. The man had let him down, the same as always, and now they were all finished because of it.

The three of them sat in silence. After a while, Signe rested her head against the cushion behind her. "I'm exhausted," she said, in a small voice. "I'd like to go to sleep now."

"There's a guest bedroom that way." Quinn's father pointed toward a door past the dining room. "Make yourself at home."

She slid her hand to cover Quinn's. "Good night, I guess."

"Good night." He wanted to say more, but it was all he could do to keep from breaking down.

Once Signe had left for the guest room, his father coughed again. "You wanted to know why I didn't tell you and Zora about each other—"

"The way I see it," Quinn broke in, "you were busy two-timing our mothers. Was there more to it than that?"

"That—that was the reason at first," said his father, with a shamefaced expression. "But when the harbinger showed up at your sister's home, I realized I'd put you both in danger. That's why I left and never came back. I wanted to protect you." He pinched the bridge of his nose. "The thing knew about Zora, but I was hoping it didn't know about you. I figured if the two of you never met, at least one of my kids might stay hidden from it. Then I learned about the new Wakening, and it no longer mattered, so I went ahead and told you about her."

Quinn blinked hard and tried to collect his thoughts. "Dad, you left us without saying *anything*."

"I reckoned it was better that way. I was a wretched father. I've never deserved to be a part of your lives."

"It's not about what you deserved." One of the candles on

the mantelpiece guttered and went out. "It's about what Zora and I deserved."

"I'm sorry, son." His father leaned forward, his elbows on his knees. "For everything. But I'm glad for the chance to see you one more time." He made a sort of choking sound.

Quinn took it for another coughing fit until he saw the tears. He turned his face toward the wall. "These past four nights, I've been attacked by an elemental, stalked by herns, dunked by a leviathan, and conked by a tangle. I'm too worn down to talk about this anymore."

"You can take the sofa. Unless you and your friend are . . ."

"The sofa is fine," Quinn said.

"Get yourself some rest, then. I'll take care of that horse in the paddock." His father picked up his pipe again and went out to the front porch.

Quinn lay down on the sofa, but his muscles refused to relax. A whiff of burning hemp drifted through the windows.

Despite everything, he fell asleep before his father came back inside.

Quinn awoke to a quiet, shadow-filled house and an urgent need to pee. Taking his boots in one hand and the banisher in the other, he crept through the dining room. When he reached the guest bedroom, he tapped softly on the door.

Signe poked her head into the hallway. "What is it?" she whispered.

"I want to leave," he whispered back.

"You mean, before your father's up?" She sounded confused, or half-asleep, or both.

"We've wasted enough time here already."

Signe rubbed her eyes. "You're certain that's what you want?"

He nodded.

"Let me get dressed, and I'll be right out."

Signe reemerged wearing her hat along with the plain black shirt and skirt she'd worn the evening they'd first met. The two of them padded out the front door, and she went to harness the horse while Quinn used the hemp field as an outhouse. They were on the road before any of his father's roosters had crowed.

"Now what?" asked Signe. She still smelled of soap from her bath.

He ran his fingers through his hair as he reflected on that. "I reckon we stick with the plan to meet Zora. Maybe the Rangers will get lucky and find the harbinger. You're sure you don't have any clue where Old Man McBrain's former assistant went?"

"Mr. Hetfield was headed north when I met him, but that hardly narrows it down enough to find him in time."

Quinn fumbled over his next words.

"If something's troubling you," said Signe, "you can tell me."

"How much of my conversation with my father did you hear?"

"Pretty much all of it." She hesitated before continuing. "For what it's worth, I think he was wrong to keep you in the dark. And his not telling you about the Wakening has made our task more difficult." Her voice softened. "But perhaps he did have good intentions."

Quinn snorted. A list of excuses, more like it.

"I get the impression your dad does care about you," she said. "He seems remorseful for how he's hurt you."

He threw up his arms. "Stop defending him!"

She scrunched her face at him. Fylgja let out a low nicker, as if offended for Signe's sake.

"I'm sorry," he said. "I just . . . I just need to be angry at him right now."

Quinn brooded for the rest of the morning. After a few attempts at idle conversation, Signe left him alone. When he took a shift at the reins, she used her magnifying glass to skim through spirit-guides until it was her turn to drive again.

In the early afternoon, they came to the rambling marketplace where Big Sister Hollow met Little Sister Hollow. "Whoa, Fylgja," said Signe. "Look, Quinn!"

They'd pulled up between a stand selling watermelon juice and a table overflowing with eggplant. Banners overhead promised HAND-SEWN WEDDING RING QUILTS, CRYSTALS FOR HEXES OF ALL KINDS, and MECHANICAL WONDERS—FROM AUTOMATA TO ZOETROPES. "At what, exactly?" he asked.

"That one." She pointed to a peddler cart displaying an assortment of boots, coats, and umbrellas. Its sign spelled out SALE in still-wet red paint. "I simply *must* stop here." She hopped down and strode toward the cart.

The woman behind the counter tugged at the lapels of her kaleidoscope-patterned jacket. "Step right up," she said. "I've got quality wares in every color of the palette. Along with"—she took a gander at her customer—"black and white, if that's your style."

Her smarmy patter reminded Quinn too much of his father's old sales pitches. "I'll take care of Fylgja while you're shopping," he called after Signe. "And I hope you find what you're searching for."

She looked back with a pleased expression, then commenced

to haggling with the garishly dressed huckster. As it happened, the transaction took long enough for Quinn to get the horse a handful of carrots and still have time to buy a cup of watermelon juice.

Signe returned holding a new parasol. She opened it to show off a white lace design on the black canopy.

"Fancy," was all he could think to say.

"That woman tried to fleece me, but I drove a hard bargain." Signe struck a pose with the parasol over her shoulder and a hand on her hip. "How do you like my purchase?"

His mouth went dry. "You look downright"—he wracked his brain for the right word—"winsome." She laughed, and it occurred to him that he hadn't answered the precise question she'd asked.

"It even has a flashlight built into the handle," she said. "I plan to own this one for a long time."

"I'm happy you found yourself a new parasol," he said, smiling for the first time that day. "It's perfect for you."

They kept traveling well past sunset, but Quinn eventually admitted to himself they couldn't reach Lightning Bug Hollow until tomorrow. When he spotted a pull-off by the edge of a cornfield, he pointed it out. "Should we stop there?"

Signe nodded. The moonlight made her look more ethereal than ever. As she hitched Fylgja to a fence, he checked the banisher. No sign of anything except a young woman with her own invisible halo of spirit energy.

They went inside the wagon, and Signe lit a magenta-shaded lamp.

Quinn glanced from her to the bed he'd woken up in yesterday morning. His throat tightened. "I reckon there's room for me to sleep on the floor," he said.

"I suppose." She bit her lip and stared at the flickering lamp.

Maybe he'd said the wrong thing. He decided to start over. "It means a lot to me, you coming with me on this trip."

"Is that so?" Signe made eye contact with him. "Even with my mysterious talents, it's sometimes a challenge to read your mind."

He breathed in and took her gloved hands in his bare ones. "What I'm thinking right now is that I hope you were right."

"Right about what?" Her voice was just louder than a whisper.

Quinn drew her closer. He was grateful she couldn't feel how clammy his palms were. "Right about fate having other plans for me."

"I am fond of being right," Signe shut her eyes and leaned in toward him.

He kissed her, tentatively at first but more emphatically when she began kissing him back. All his worries about the Wakening fell away.

She drew back and opened her eyes. "That was nice."

Quinn kissed her again. Her mouth tasted faintly of the onions from their supper. He rested his hands on her hips as she wrapped her arms around his back and pressed herself against his chest.

After a minute or so, Signe stopped to touch her chin. "You're a little prickly." Her nostrils flared; her lashes fluttered behind thick blue lenses. "So, do you realize this may be our last night alone together?"

"Yes," he said. His heart was thudding so hard he halfway wondered whether she could hear it.

She removed her glasses and set them down, then pulled her shirt over her head to reveal a gray camisole. Tiny pink blemishes dotted her alabaster shoulders.

Quinn ran his fingers along her collarbone. Her skin felt cool and smooth.

Signe gave him another quick kiss, took off her black gloves, and set to unbuttoning his flannel shirt. Her hands shook as she struggled with the first button. After a few tries, she managed to undo it and moved on to the next one.

They were both breathing faster now. He could scarcely believe this was happening in real life, instead of some book or his own daydreams.

With one button left to go, she stopped and muttered a word as crude as any of Zora's favorite curses.

His stomach dropped. "What is it?"

She put on her glasses and drew back the curtains. "There's a spirit out there."

Quinn picked up the banisher. One light, two lights. Three lights, four.

Signe clutched her new parasol.

Five lights, six lights. Seven lights, more.

From outside, Fylgja squealed in terror.

All the lights.

Quinn pulled open the wagon's door. His knees buckled when he saw the spirit towering over the trees beyond the cornfield. Its aura outshone the moon, and long streamers twisted down from its crown like ribbons from a maypole.

A spire had found them.

His head swam. The folks who scavenged the Wastes for relics feared these things above all other roamers, but he'd never heard of a spire wandering so deep into the Hollows.

Next to him, Signe used a hand to shield her eyes from the yellow-green light. "That doesn't belong here," she murmured.

Over by the fence, Fylgja was rearing and pulling at her lead. Quinn and Signe jumped down from the wagon to unhitch her, and the horse tore away down the road.

Signe gripped his wrist. "We need to go, too."

Together, they bolted into the cornfield. The spirit followed them, narrowing the distance with each passing second. Its utter silence was more terrifying than the hount's roar or the leviathan's bellow.

When the spire reached the cornfield, it began flaying the stalks to shreds with its streamers. Quinn kept running, even as his legs cramped. Everything around him had turned vivid in the glare from the spirit's aura.

There was no crevice to hide in this time, no trap to set. He was going to die tonight.

Still, maybe there was a way for Signe to survive.

"I'll draw it away," he shouted. She opened her mouth, but he swerved to the right before she could argue.

The tall stalks gave way to open meadow. To his left, Signe cleared the cornfield and made for a grove of evergreens.

He looked back, but the spire wasn't behind him.

It was chasing Signe toward the trees. The air around it blurred like a haze on a hot summer day; the earth beneath it lay hidden by clouds of chaff.

Quinn stopped, took aim, and blasted the thing with a ray of violet. The spirit shifted its course straight for him.

He barreled across the meadow, his chest heaving, until something smacked his legs and sent him tumbling into a ditch. The banisher landed in the dirt nearby. He ducked his head as one the spirit's streamers flicked past and curled up into the darkness.

Pain radiated through Quinn's left knee when he put his weight on it. Above him, the spire seemed to fill the sky. He sank back down and braced for the final blow.

"Stop!" Signe shouted in the distance. From the top of a small rise, she waved one white arm and shone her parasol's flashlight in his direction. The spirit bent its crown toward the beam.

Signe swept the light in a figure-eight pattern. "Leave him be," she cried out. "Or, fate willing, I'll . . ."

The spire started after her again, and she resumed her dash for the trees.

Quinn crawled to the banisher. Propping himself on his good knee, he fired at the spirit. Nothing came out, not even a spark.

Just shy of the grove, Signe tripped and fell. The spire closed in on her, soundlessly gliding across the meadow.

"Come get me!" Quinn screamed. He tuned his weapon's coil, like Zora had taught him to do, and fired again. It gave off one arc, then burned out completely.

Signe stood and faced the spirit with one hand held high. Her lips moved, but Quinn couldn't make out her words. As she backed away, the spire raised one of its whip-like streamers and speared her in the chest.

Quinn flung down the banisher with a moan.

Signe took one more step backward and flopped to the ground. The spirit pulled its streamer from her motionless form, picked up something next to her, and held the object in midair for a moment before smashing it into the grass.

The new parasol.

Quinn punched the dirt until the skin on his knuckles tore.

The spire waded into the grove, leaving Signe and the ruined parasol in its wake. Its aura dimmed as it brushed aside branches and crashed through vines.

Gasping from the pain in his knee, Quinn hobbled toward where Signe lay face down in a patch of clover. By the time he reached her, the spirit had already receded into the nearby hills.

He sat beside Signe and rolled her over. Her glasses were gone, her eyes shut. The spire's streamer had left a glowing smear on the front of her camisole, right below her ribcage.

Quinn called her name and shook her by the shoulders, but she didn't move. Please, he thought. Please stop acting like one of the dead bodies in Mom's funeral home.

"Mr. Prosser," said a woman's voice he recognized. "Step away from the young lady and put your hands where we can see them."

"You heard her," said a man. "I've got the drop on you, so get up nice and slow." Quinn knew that voice, too.

His knee throbbed as he rose to his feet and turned to face the hulking man who'd rented Signe the boat at the Big Lake. Who now held a double-barreled shotgun in his bearlike hands.

Three other people were standing behind him. The junk store owner from Saltpeter Hollow. A wild-eyed man Quinn had never met. And a woman in a dark green robe with an antlered design.

Evelyn Fontaine.

She snapped her fingers. "Inspect her, Mr. Hetfield."

The unfamiliar man set down the hurricane lantern he'd been carrying, scuttled over to Signe, and checked her pulse. "Nothing."

The seventh child of a seventh child, she'd said. Quinn pulled at his own hair. *The universe has chosen me to do this. I can feel it in my bones.*

Through stinging eyes, he watched Ms. Fontaine point at Signe. "You're certain that's the seer?" she asked.

"There can't be too many like her in the Hollows." The junk store owner laughed and waggled the broken banisher. His clothes were seedy, but the spiral-shaped amulet he was wearing glittered in the lantern's light.

"Be respectful." Ms. Fontaine's tone had turned wintry. "Our sacrifices to the spirits are a solemn duty, not the occasion for ignorant mockery."

"She's the one I directed to the island," said the man named Otis Hetfield, the one who'd been Nevan McBrain's assistant. "I'd recognize her anywhere, even without those glasses."

The big man nodded. "She was with the other kids at the dock, too."

"So our peddler recruit completed her assignment." Ms. Fontaine sounded deep in thought. "Two down, with just the inventor girl to go. And the Voice said it would deal with her tonight."

"You"—Quinn started to cry. "You're worse than the spirits."

"Don't blaspheme." The woman smiled as she said it. "The Voice doesn't care whether *you* live or die, so you're coming with us until it's time for the ceremony."

"What should we do with the body and the wagon?" asked the big man, keeping his shotgun trained on Quinn.

"Forget the wagon," said Ms. Fontaine. "We've no use for it. As for the corpse, in a few days it will be but one among multitudes. Leave it." She gestured to the remains of the parasol. "But take that. We don't want any of our beckoners falling into the wrong hands."

Mr. Hetfield frowned. "Pity we can't preserve her for study."

Bile rose in Quinn's gorge.

The woman's expression showed a trace of annoyance. "I seem to have left my refrigerator back at the house."

"Her eyes, at least," said Mr. Hetfield, longingly.

"I didn't bring my ice-box and melon-baller, either." Ms. Fontaine waved away any further comments on the subject. "This way, young man," she said, as the junk store owner locked a set of handcuffs around Quinn's wrists. "I'd like to show you the part of my home those irksome Rangers never found."

Quinn looked down at Signe one last time before they dragged him away. Her elfin face stayed frozen in a slight frown.

PART FOUR

THE HIEROPHANT & THE HARBINGER

16

THE ROOF OF THE BARN RIPPED OPEN, AND A WOODEN SLAT WENT flying past Zora's head. Above her, green spikes gleamed against a backdrop of stars.

"One of the shards," bellowed Mr. Epps.

Paige hoisted her weapon and fired. A shaft of violet swept across the rafters, but the shard flitted out of its path. Then the spirit gave a steam-kettle whistle as its spikes evaporated. Zora blinked at the sight of her mom blasting away with a banisher, her hair spilling over her copper-framed glasses.

"Where's that dwayyo?" shouted Paige.

"Still a safe interval away," said Mr. Epps, from the doorway. "But"—the walls of the barn quivered—"increasingly proximate."

The goats herded toward their pen, bleating with fright. One seized up and tipped onto its side.

Zora glanced at the meter on the generator. "If y'all can keep the spirits from causing any damage for a few more minutes, we should—"

Glass shattered as the night turned a dazzling green. "That's the pharos," she called out.

"I've got it." Paige stuck her banisher through a broken window. An instant later, she flew across the barn and landed in a pile of hay.

Zora's mom hurled a grenade toward the pharos. The spirit flickered like a stroboscope and gave the most haunting cry Zora had ever heard. *My grandmother used to say our family has its own banshee,* Quinn had told her once. *When it wails, that means someone's going to die.*

Mr. Epps ran over to Paige, who'd already climbed to her feet and was picking bits of straw from her hair. "I'm fine," she growled at her boss.

Zora checked the meter again, then the window. She couldn't see the pharos. Or the Ranger. "Where are you, Emerson?" she said under her breath.

Lost, replied a voice in her head.

Zora closed her eyes before the pharos flared again.

You are lost.

The dirt floor quaked from the dwayyo's tread.

All lost, little—

Zora threw a switch, and the bulbs overhead dimmed as the power from the generator flowed through Mr. Slocum's cables to Ms. Mack's coils. A violet ring formed around the barn, slicing through the second shard. The spirit splintered into green fireworks.

Paige let out a hoot. "Foxtails, you're a genius."

"Your revelry may be premature," said Mr. Epps. "The dwayyo is upon us."

A translucent shape as broad as a house lumbered toward the energy-fence. Here comes the real test, thought Zora. One of the dwayyo's massive spurs came down on the violet band—

—and sizzled to cinders. With a shriek, the spirit rammed itself against the earth hard enough to send nails popping from the barn's timbers.

The energy-fence held, and so did the walls. As the dwayyo retreated down the slope, a wordless cry of rage echoed inside Zora's skull.

"Ha!" she yelled at the whorl of light hovering between the barn and the barrier. "You're caught in my net now, you whirligig." She motioned to the others. "The harbinger's out there. Shoot it."

Her mom and Paige took off in pursuit. Zora made it out the door just as they leveled their banishers at the spirit. "Got you," she said.

A dissonant hum filled the air, and her brain went fuzzy.

Look upon these specters, whispered the harbinger.

Zora was underwater, pinned beneath a sunken wreck. A skeleton with a beard of algae raised itself from the silt to wink a ruby eye at her.

None of your kind can bar my way.

She was in a coffin, but not alone. The shadow beside her traced a hex sign over its heart, then brushed back its mane of lichen and pulled off its pallid mask.

You will fall, too.

She was flat on the ground. Her mom and Paige were sitting up and rubbing their heads, as Mr. Epps watched like a nervous owl.

Zora's skin prickled. The brass of her crutches caught a glint of reflected green: the third shard, looming behind her. It surged forward, and she rolled sideways in a hopeless effort to avoid its saw-toothed skewers.

With a crackling noise, the shard burst apart. Slivers of it jabbed her skin like icicles before melting away.

"Ms. Zora." Emerson Tate lowered his banisher and smiled down at her. "My apologies for showing up late. I ran into a few spirits along the way."

"I appreciate you bailing me out again." She pushed herself to her feet. "But the harbinger got away, didn't it?"

Mr. Epps nodded. "It dematerialized after emitting that blast of cacophony."

"I thought it was trapped inside the spirit-fence," said Zora's mom. "How'd it escape?"

Zora felt like cursing a blue streak. In deference to her mom's presence, she spat at the ground instead. "It must be able to phase back and forth between our universe and whatever netherworld it calls home."

"In any event," said Mr. Epps, "I am jubilant that all of us remain extant."

Zora spent the night on a bed of hay beside the generator. At the break of dawn, she staggered to her worktable like a sleepwalker.

She was still there when Paige came by to pace around the barn and gripe about how long Quinn was taking to arrive. After a few hundred laps, the apprentice switched to lambasting her fellow Spotters for failing to dig up any new leads.

Zora mumbled in acknowledgment. She had one more set of vacuum tubes to plug into their sockets.

The music on the radio stopped, and a voice came on the air. "*People of the Hollows, this is an important announcement. The*

Judges have postponed the All Hollows celebrations due to the threat of severe spirit weather. Ranger Captain Sylvia Flores urges everyone to remain calm, stay home until further notice, and listen to this station for further instructions. I repeat—"

Paige kicked the hay. "I wish I could do something right now." One of the goats wandered toward her, and she engaged it in a staring contest.

"Once we know how to track the harbinger," Zora said, "we'll catch it unawares, and it won't be able to pull any of its tricks on us." But they only had two days left, with no word from the Rangers on its whereabouts. Dad had better come through, just this once. She'd tried, and failed, to find a pattern in the spirit-trails and ley-lines she'd drawn on Quinn's map. "It stinks that we blew our chance last night."

"*You* did your part just fine. *I* missed every shot I took, unlike your mom and Deputy Drawly."

"I'm betting you'll get another crack at it, soon enough." Zora connected the final cathode and double-checked her work. All good, though whether she'd trust her life to it was a whole nother thing. "Let's take a look at this," she said, emptying the contents of a small case onto her worktable.

"Seems like you've got a mighty nice collection of junk there," said Paige.

"Maybe, maybe not. I saved parts from two different spirit-lures—the one in Evelyn Fontaine's camera, and the one in the dock rat's outboard motor. I'm hoping I can use them to reconstruct a working model." As Zora sorted through the pieces, the radio started playing a song about that magic fiddler girl—something about how she'd invented a new musical technique on the night of the Great Wakening, after a spire had killed her parents and her siblings and everyone else in her hollow. How she'd crawled from the wreckage of her house and dispelled the spirit with seven scrapes of her bow.

"Pine-Box would like that tune," said Paige, when it ended.

"It's funny." Zora held a pin-sized capacitor to the light. "I never cared for those songs before I met him, but one of them gave me the inspiration for the spirit-fence. So maybe music does have charms to—wait." Were those hooves in the distance?

Zora and Paige rushed from the barn to the roadside. Zora's mom, Emerson, and Mr. Epps stepped out of the house to join them. Moments later, Signe's white and purple wagon rolled into view. At first, Zora didn't recognize the gray-bearded, shaggy-haired driver.

Then she laughed in relief. "Hey, Dad!" she shouted. "You picked a good time to drop by." Only eight years late, but still. Quinn had pulled it off, and she owed him an apology.

Her mom crossed her arms and made a face like a boiler about to blow. The others watched with curious expressions as Fylgja came to a halt.

Zora's stomach turned when she realized her brother and Signe were nowhere in sight. They must be resting inside the wagon, she told herself, but her heart began racing. "Where's Quinn?"

"Zora." Her dad ran his fingers through his hair, the way Quinn always did. "He's not with me. I don't know where he is. He took off while I was sleeping, after I said I couldn't help him."

She shook her head. "But you're driving—"

"Hold up a second." Her dad ducked into the wagon and

came back out carrying a limp figure with long, white hair. It was Signe, looking unconscious. Or dead.

Zora swallowed. Had the harbinger laid an ambush along the road from Sassafras Hollow? Quinn's banisher would've been a pea-shooter to the dwayyo, and Signe's stunt with the herns had failed the time she'd tried it on the giant lake spirit.

"You can hand her down to me," said the Ranger. Zora and Paige followed close behind him as he brought Signe to the porch. Her face was a bright reddish-pink. So were her bare arms and shoulders.

"I reckoned Quinn might come here." Zora's dad tied Fylgja to the post. "So I set out on foot as fast as I could. I didn't find any trace of him, but I found his friend, and her horse, and her wagon. She was with Quinn at my house. I think her name's Siggie."

"Signe," said Emerson. "Is she—"

"Still breathing, but barely. I took her for dead at first. When I saw her sunburn, though, I did a few tests that Anne—that Quinn's mom—taught me." Zora's dad reached into his pocket and pulled out a pair of blue glasses with one cracked lens. "I found these, too."

"Bring her into the house," Zora's mom told Emerson. She led them to the spare room and opened the door for the Ranger, who laid Signe on the bed.

Zora squeezed through the others to get a better view. The moons of Signe's fingernails were dark, and her clothes smelled of crushed lightning bugs. Her chest didn't stir, not even a little.

"Allow me." Mr. Epps lifted the bottom of Signe's camisole. The flesh on her belly had a greenish tint.

"What in the Hollows happened to her?" asked Zora's mom, with a hand over her mouth.

"Spirit-sickness," said the Spotter. "Certain rare varieties of roamers can implant fragments of themselves inside a terrestrial host. The infection saps the victim's vitality, inducing a coma and, ultimately, death."

"Is there a cure?" asked Emerson.

Mr. Epps shook his head. "The condition is invariably fatal."

"But, sir," said Paige. "Surely . . ."

The Spotter took off his hat and gave his apprentice a sorrowful look. "It grieves me to say that she may not survive the night."

Zora rapped a crutch—the old one—on the floor, like a gavel. "In that case, I'm going to try an experiment." Everyone stared at her. "Mom," she said, "can you go to the barn and get me some goggles, an illuminator, and a banisher? Oh, and some eye shields."

"I see what you're thinking." Her mom hurried out of the room, talking to herself as she went.

"You three," Zora told her father, Emerson, and Mr. Epps. "Wait outside."

The Spotter looked skeptical; the Ranger looked uneasy; her dad looked confused. But all of them obeyed.

She turned to Paige. "I need you to take off her clothes."

The apprentice went bug-eyed.

"Do it," Zora said.

Paige pulled off Signe's skirt, stockings, and camisole. The angry sunburn clashed with the sickly green hue everywhere else.

Zora's mom returned with a sack full of equipment, set it down, and glanced at the bed with shining eyes. "Poor kid."

"We're going to fix her," said Zora, trying not to think of the unkind things she'd said about Signe. And to her. "Then she's going to tell us what's happened to Quinn."

At Zora's command, Paige closed the shutters and switched off the lamp. Signe's body glowed faintly in the dark, as though someone had coated her with radium paint.

"This is mighty peculiar," muttered Paige.

The three of them put on their goggles, and Zora picked up the illuminator. Steadying her nerves, she activated the device. A blue glow suffused the room, and seven orange lights appeared to the sound of a grainy purr.

"Look at that," said Zora's mom.

A fluorescent lump the size of a fist pulsated beneath Signe's skin, just below her sternum. Blue tendrils stretched up her ribcage to the collarbone and down her stomach as far as the navel.

The mass twitched when Zora shone the beam on it, sending a shudder through Signe's body. Paige turned away and retched.

Zora ran the beam over Signe's legs, all the way to her toes, but nothing happened. She shifted it upward and sucked in her breath.

Light was shining through Signe's closed eyelids—a vibrant indigo, with blood vessels standing out as dark streaks against it.

"That's . . . unusual," said Zora's mom. "Is it spirit energy, or something else?"

Signe whimpered softly, like a sleeper trapped in a nightmare.

"I'm not sure." Zora turned off the illuminator. "That must be how she can see spirits, and how she spooked those herns. But I still have no idea what makes her eyeballs do that."

"Hey, Foxtails," said Paige. "If the rules of nature changed back when the spirits first showed up, do you reckon humans"—she pointed at Signe—"might start changing, too?"

Zora nodded. "You're thinking like a paraphysicist now."

"A mystery for another day," said her mom. "Time to find out whether this works." She placed the shields over Signe's eyes. "That should protect them from the banisher." Then she took a lead smock from the bag and tucked it around Signe's waist.

"Why the apron, Ms. Coldiron?" asked Paige.

"In case her gift is something she can pass along someday."

"Ah," said Zora. She hadn't thought of that. "Based on what we've seen so far, y'all should hold her down for the next part."

Her mom took Signe's ankles, while Paige stationed herself at the head of the bed. Zora picked up the banisher, aimed its tracer beam, and pulled the trigger.

As violet bathed Signe's chest, her limbs began to jerk. Zora's mom and Paige struggled to keep a grip on her. "Is it working?" asked the apprentice, between gasps.

"Yes." Zora's hands had gone damp. "That—that parasite is just so strong." Whatever implanted it must've been a monster.

Signe's lips pulled back from her teeth, and her windpipe rattled. The thing inside her twisted its veins around her heart.

"It's killing her!" shouted Paige.

Zora focused the banisher's ray until it was a needle of light. The spirit-mass turned purple, wriggling like a knot of worms. Signe broke free from Paige's grasp, contorted herself into an upright position, and thrashed her legs.

Zora's mom dodged a kick to the gut. "The lump's shrinking," she said. "It's breaking up. . ."

Signe fell back onto her pillow, foaming at the mouth. Chlorine-colored mist rose from her chest, then dissipated.

Zora let up on the trigger, and her mom lowered Signe's feet onto the bed. "Snakes alive," said Paige, wiping her forehead. The three of them gazed at Signe's now-motionless body. The glow from her skin was already disappearing.

"I'm reading low-level spirit-energy," said Zora. "That's normal for her."

Paige flipped on the lamp. Signe's face had relaxed, and the parts of her that weren't sunburnt had reverted to a healthy pallor, but she was as still and silent as a corpse.

Zora's mom searched for a pulse. "I can't feel any—oh! She's awake."

Signe pushed the shields from her eyes. "Zora?" she rasped. "Thank the universe, you're okay."

"Good to see you, too." Zora's own eyes were blurry all of a sudden.

Signe squinted down at herself with a bewildered expression. "Where am I, and why am I—Quinn!" She tried to sit up, and her pupils rolled back into her head.

"I'll get some water," said Paige. She ran to the kitchen and back, shouting, "It worked! It worked!"

Zora's mom pulled a quilt up to Signe's armpits before calling the others into the room. They all crowded around the bed while Mr. Epps slid a pair of fingers under Signe's jaw, took out a pocket-watch, and counted to twenty. "Astounding," said the Spotter. "You've discovered a cure for spirit-sickness. We positively must collaborate on a monograph about this." Paige nudged him. "At a more opportune time," he added.

Zora's dad cleared his throat and looked at her mom. "Good to see you again, Fiona." She gave him the slightest of nods.

Every second of the vigil that followed was a torment to

Zora. For her dad, too, judging by the way he kept wringing his hands.

Then Signe opened her eyes again.

"Stay down this time," ordered Zora's mom. She took the glass of water Paige had brought and held it to Signe's lips. "Drink. Just a little."

"And tell us what happened," said Zora, as calmly as she could.

Signe sipped from the glass. "Those people with the spirit-lures captured Quinn. They duped me into taking one of their devices, just like they'd duped me into helping draw Mr. McBrain out of his bunker. He was right about how naive I've been." She took another drink. "A spire came after us."

"Son of a biscuit," said Paige.

"I did my best. I really did." Signe started to cry, but no tears came out.

"I believe you." Zora placed a hand on her shoulder. "Did you recognize any of the people who have my brother?"

"After the spire stabbed me," said Signe, "I couldn't move, but I could hear them talking. The man with the boat was there, along with Mr. Hetfield. And a third man, too. Their leader was a woman I didn't know. She sounded so . . . sophisticated."

"Evelyn Fontaine," said Emerson. "I presume."

Signe touched her cheeks and winced. "The way they talked, I think they're honest-to-goodness *Spiritists*."

"I knew it!" shouted Zora. The Ranger raised his eyebrows at her.

"I heard something else, too," said Signe. "Right before I went all the way under. They're taking Quinn to their leader's home, wherever that is."

Clack Mountain, thought Zora. She knew what she had to do, regardless of what her mom, the Rangers, or anyone else said.

Now she just needed to figure out how.

17

QUINN PULLED AGAINST THE HANDCUFFS UNTIL THEY BIT INTO HIS wrists. His feet had gone numb from the ropes around his ankles, and his knee ached every time the wagon jounced.

He never should've left Zora.

Across from him, Evelyn Fontaine was toying with the broken banisher. Behind her velvet-padded seat hung a tapestry of an antlered woman surrounded by spirits. Emerald light glinted from its metallic threads.

"We should stop by the Prosser Funeral Home," Quinn said, with false bravado. "I can measure you for the casket you'll be needing on All Hollows."

"I'm afraid we can't make any detours on our way to Clack Mountain." His captor's powdered face showed no hint of emotion. "I'd just as soon avoid meeting your Ranger friends."

"I don't give a dead rat what a murderer like you wants," he said.

"You misjudge me." She ran a green-painted fingernail along the weapon's barrel. "I've never harmed a hair on a single person's head."

"The spirits do your dirty work for you, don't they?" He

thought of Signe, all by herself in the meadow, and fresh tears formed in his eyes.

"I merely summon them, and they act as they will." Ms. Fontaine's tone softened. "I regret what happened to your friend. I wanted to spare her, and your sister, but the Voice insisted they be eliminated." She looked off into the darkness beyond the barred windows. "You may not believe me, but I understand your suffering. Years ago, I lost the people I loved most to the spirits."

"So how is it you became—what are you, anyhow? The high priest of the Spiritists?" Keep casting her lines, Quinn told himself. Maybe she'll bite down on a hook.

"That *is* what I am." She turned to face him again. "And that *is* why I chose my path. When the spirits killed my brother and my fiancé on one of our expeditions to the Wastes, I realized the only way to prevail against those abominations is through guile. For now."

"That sounds mighty irreverent of you," he said.

"You think I actually worship the spirits?" Ms. Fontaine shook her head. "I've spent years trying to discover how to bend them to *my* will. As for my followers, they were nothing but a band of pathetic crackpots before I came along. With my knowledge and resources, I had no trouble establishing myself as the leader of their cult. I even dressed up their crude rites with more refined trappings." She pointed at the tapestry. "Inspired by a grander calling, my new devotees went forth to spy on the Rangers and Spotters. Including the illustrious Nevan McBrain, until he gave us the slip."

The hermit's ramblings about two-legged stalkers suddenly made more sense to Quinn.

"My followers also gathered data on the spirits," she went on. "Observations and photographs. All the while, I worked at perfecting my beckoners." She resumed tinkering with the banisher. "Then a disgruntled Spotter named Otis Hetfield visited me this spring."

"He told you about the new Wakening. And where to find his boss." Old Man McBrain's assistant had gone and betrayed him to the Spiritists.

"Indeed. He hoped to save his own neck by coming to a, shall we say, understanding with the Voice of the Spirits. His reclusive employer refused to entertain the idea, so Mr. Hetfield traced my network of moles all the way back to me. I found his proposal intriguing."

"He wanted to strike a *deal* with the harbinger?"

"A strategic alliance," countered Ms. Fontaine. "Mr. Hetfield helped me track the Voice, and then I used one of my beckoners to attract its attention. A terrible risk, to be sure, but I spoke— or, rather, *communed*—with it, and we came to mutually agreeable terms." She held up the banisher's barrel in one hand and its fan-shaped muzzle in the other. "Does this piece go here?"

Quinn was so startled that he nodded without thinking.

"Much obliged." The muzzle clicked into place. "The Voice intended to release enough spirits from its realm to massacre everyone in the Hollows, but I persuaded it to show a modicum of restraint. Of course, I gave it advice on the best places to target this time around. The Spotters' lodge. The Rangers' headquarters. The Grand Hall where the Judges speechify for votes and squabble over petty laws. With each of those orders in disarray, I'll have a clear path to controlling what remains of the Hollows."

Quinn thumped his feet against the floor. Be patient, he reminded himself. Zora would find a way to stop the harbinger.

If it didn't catch her first.

"In return, the Voice asked for help in disposing of the three people it perceived as the greatest threats to itself." Ms. Fontaine raised two fingers and a thumb. "The Spotter who'd analyzed its ways." She folded back the thumb. "A young clairvoyant with abilities the Voice itself didn't understand." She lowered one finger. "An even younger inventor who'd developed weaponry for fighting spirits." She lowered the other finger. "Mr. McBrain's bunker presented a challenge, but all we needed was a way to flush him out. As for your sister and your sweetheart, they were simple to find. One adolescent with crutches, another with albinism, both fond of boasting about what special darlings they were."

"You sold out two teenagers to that thing." Quinn put every bit of venom into the words he could.

"To save thousands of lives. Condemn me if you wish, but I made the best choice available under desperate circumstances. Instead of hiding myself in a lead box like Nevan McBrain or waiting around to die like your dear wayward father, I've guaranteed that a portion of humanity will endure to conquer the spirits. Under my leadership."

He laughed raggedly. "What if the harbinger—pardon me, the Voice of the Spirits—double-crosses you? What if it decides to kill you, too?"

"I trust neither human nor spirit," said Ms. Fontaine. "My followers and I will be safe, no matter what. You'll see what I mean. If we're the only survivors, perhaps we can find other people beyond the Wastes." She patted the banisher. "Either way, this technology of your sister's will prove useful, now that I have my hands on it. After the equinox, the Voice will retreat to its own world again for years to come. Long before it returns on the next celestial alignment, I'll finish devising a means to subjugate the spirits."

She opened a trunk and took out an object wrapped in black cloth. Then she turned off the wagon's mercury-vapor lamps and removed the cloth to unveil a foil-lined jar. Within it twinkled a tiny, greenish spirit.

A boge, like the one he'd help chase on the night of the Harvest Festival, with Paige. He'd probably never see her again, never get the chance to patch up their friendship.

Ms. Fontaine removed the jar's stopper. The little spirit drifted past the rim to flitter around her, trilling softly.

She fired the banisher, and the boge winked out of existence.

Quinn glanced toward the wagon's door. Would the other Spiritists turn against her if they learned how she'd played on their faith?

"Go ahead and tell them," said Ms. Fontaine, as if she'd read his mind. "Do you suppose they'll believe you, or their own high priest? But thank you for listening to me." She sighed. "It's a relief to speak freely for once. The fate of the Hollows is a heavy burden to bear."

"I hope an elemental comes knocking at your mansion someday," he said. "I hope it turns you to dust amid all your fancy things."

The crickets outside fell silent, and daylight streamed into the wagon. Quinn bided his time until he heard a rider approaching from the other direction. Just a little closer, and he could shout a message for the Rangers—

"Don't do anything rash," said Ms. Fontaine, "Otherwise, my followers will take it upon themselves to shoot that innocent young traveler. They're quite bloodthirsty, despite my benevolent influence."

The rider passed by, and Quinn went back to dwelling on what might've happened if he'd gone with Zora to Lightning Bug Hollow. Or stuck by Signe's side last night instead of trying to lead away the spire.

At some point, he fell into a deep sleep. When he awoke, his knee felt swollen and stiff; his wrist was raw from the cuff. Dark blue sky lay past the grillwork on the windows.

Ms. Fontaine lifted a speaking-tube to her mouth. "Open in the name of the Horned Crown."

Gears rumbled up ahead, and the world outside turned pitch black. The horses' hoofbeats echoed strangely, then stopped.

"Now you'll understand why I don't fear the Wakening," said Ms. Fontaine. "Nothing can harm us in here."

The junk store owner entered the wagon to untie Quinn and unlock the cuffs while the big man brandished his shotgun from the seat. Quinn's feet tingled when he tried to stand. The junk store owner shoved him through the doorway, and he stumbled to the ground.

They'd driven into a rock-strewn tunnel lined with rail tracks. Mr. Hetfield shone a flashlight at the wooden beams along the walls and roof.

"The Clack Mountain coal mine." Ms. Fontaine held out her arms. "It's belonged to my family since before the Great Wakening. My ancestors sealed it after the main seam ran out, and everyone else forgot it existed." Her laugh rang through the gloom. "The Rangers overlooked the hidden entrances when they came searching for me."

She led them along the tracks past cross-tunnels filled with rubble and shafts that gaped like the bottomless pit in Pipe Organ Cavern. Quinn did his best to memorize their path through the maze, but soon lost count of the turns they'd taken.

As they spiraled higher and higher into the mountain, he caught the sound of a generator thrumming from above. "I found another vein of coal," explained Ms. Fontaine. "Enough to provide all the power required for my sanctum."

"More of a lair, really," Quinn said. "Seeing as how you're the villain here."

She chuckled. "You've read too many fanciful tales, young man."

Mr. Hetfield pulled a lever, and incandescent bulbs strung from the ceiling cast harsh light through the tunnel.

"We're below my house now." Ms. Fontaine pointed at a metal door with a slot for a window. "Here's where you'll be staying until the ceremony."

The junk store owner opened the door to reveal a narrow cell. Its walls were blank except for a stick-figure painting of a girl holding a fiddle. Her eyes had been scratched out, and antler-like gouges rose above her head.

"Go ahead," said the man with the shotgun. Quinn obeyed, and they locked him inside.

Four sets of footsteps receded into the tunnel. Once they were gone, the thin ray of light from the slot disappeared. A ghostly afterimage of the fiddler girl lingered on the wall for a few moments more.

Alone in the dark, Quinn had nothing to do except worry about Zora. His mother. Paige and his other classmates from Cascade Hollow. Everyone else he knew in the Hollows. Even his father.

Not to mention himself.

An uncertain amount of time later, the light reappeared outside the cell. Somebody with a light tread walked to the door and slid one end of a tray through the opening.

"Your breakfast, unbeliever," said a woman's voice.

Quinn took the tray. Grits, blackberries and a cup of water. He wolfed down the food, and only afterward did it cross his mind that the Spiritists might've stirred cyanide into the grits or sprinkled arsenic on the berries.

"No moonshine for you today," his visitor said, and then started to leave.

"Wait," he called out. "Don't I know you?" He'd heard that flat twang before, from the dour young bartender in Comet Tail Hollow.

She halted a few paces down the tunnel. "That's right. Y'all ruined the hullaballoo I raised."

"You used a lure that night. A beckoner, I mean. To set off the spirit storm and bait us." Straight from the hount into the harbinger's web.

"Right again."

"You told Signe where to find us, so we'd go with her to Nevan McBrain." To lead the hermit into the arms of the leviathan.

The young woman sniffed. "And y'all thought you were so crafty."

"Here's what I don't get," he said. "Why in the Wastes would you serve something that wants to kill us all?"

"I'd rather serve the Voice than the likes of *you*, or your mouthy Spotter friend, or her high-hatted boss. And once the new age dawns, I'll be one of the masters of the Hollows."

Darkness filled the cell once more.

When the young Spiritist came back with a bowl of stew, Quinn asked her how long it was until the equinox.

"Tomorrow. Lost your sense of time down here, have you?"

"Do you have any news about Zora?" He started to choke up. "Please, she's my kid sister." Silence followed, and he figured his jailor was fixing to leave.

"Sorry," she said, at last. "The folks in charge don't tell me that stuff."

"Did they tell you what happened to Mr. McBrain and Signe?" Silence again. "Spirits killed them both, you know."

"That's the will of the Voice."

Quinn tightened his fists. "How old are you, anyhow?"

"Seventeen, this past moon." She sounded puzzled. "Why?"

"Signe was your age." He fought to keep from shouting at her. "How does it feel, knowing you helped send her to her death?"

She left without answering.

The young woman went on ignoring him as she delivered his supper. Quinn ate and stretched out on the dirt to rest up for what looked to be his last day alive.

"Happy All Hollows," he told her at breakfast. All she did was grunt.

The next time she visited, he put his face against the slot before she could push his lunch through. "If you unlocked this door," he said, "nobody would miss me. The Voice doesn't care about me. Your high priest said so herself."

"She did?" Doubt flickered across the young woman's pointy features.

"I haven't spent my life studying the spirits. I don't have a gift for seeing them, or for building weapons to stop them." He peered out at her. "I'm no threat to y'all. Please let me go."

"I can't." Her eyes shifted away from his, toward the painting behind him. "They've got plans for you at the ritual."

"What plans?" he asked, but she'd already skittered away.

As time dragged along, Quinn began to suspect that the Wakening had come and gone. That the Spiritists' plans had gone awry, leaving them slaughtered and him buried alive. That he would die of thirst in this hole, with a mountain for a tomb.

Finally, the light returned, and footsteps approached. Another tray slid through the door. Fried steak, mashed potatoes, and green beans, with a shot of bourbon.

His stomach curdled. "My last meal, I take it."

"Be quiet," muttered the bartender-turned-jailor. "I'm giving you a chance to get away. If the spirits hunt you down tonight, that'll be on them and you. Not me." A key turned in the lock. "Wait fifteen minutes, but don't take too long. The others will be coming for you."

Quinn held his breath as he listened to her walk away. After the light disappeared, he began counting. At a thousand, he tested the door.

It opened with a clang that resounded through the tunnel.

He cringed, but then set off into the blackness with one hand touching the wall. His fingertips sank into something squishy. Stale air filled his lungs, and gravel crunched beneath his feet.

By the third fork in the tunnel, he was lost.

His heart hammered as he staggered through the lightless mine. He tried not to imagine himself wandering into one of the open shafts and plunging toward the depths of the earth.

Don't be such a scaredy-cat, Paige would've told him, like she had on their school trip to the caverns. *There's no Gateway of the Spirits down here, Pine-Box. Watch this . . .*

Quinn rounded a turn and froze. Greenish splotches clung to the sides and roof of the tunnel in front of him. He reached over his shoulder for the banisher, but it wasn't there.

The splotches didn't budge. What kind of earthbounds were they? Not lares, or landwights, or anything else in the *Handbook of Subterranean Spirits*.

He walked toward them, primed to sprint as fast as he could on his bad knee. Then he kicked himself. They weren't spirits — just bioluminescent mushrooms growing on the beams.

A wooden stake lay nearby. He used it to tap out a path through the ring of fungi. Around a rockfall that blocked half the tunnel. Past a graveyard for abandoned mine carts.

Water dripped into an unseen pool, and a musty breeze ruffled his hair. The mine had become a cave. He followed it until he saw amber rays shining down from the stalactites and a ladder extending upward from the stalagmites.

He crept forward, holding the stake in front of him pointy-end first. Ahead of him, light was leaking between the planks of a trapdoor. He put one foot on the bottom rung of the ladder and started climbing.

At the top, Quinn pressed his ear against the door, but the world above was as quiet as the family crypt back home. He pushed open the trapdoor, heaved himself onto a wide slab of limestone, and blinked at the red sunset.

His escape had failed.

To his left sat dozens of people in yellow gowns, their hands folded on their laps. To his right stood Evelyn Fontaine, wearing her green robe and an antlered crown. Surprise showed in her eyes, but only for an instant.

"Behold," she proclaimed. "Our sacrifice comes of his own free will, without waiting to be fetched." She lifted her palms, and her congregation rose as one. Quinn spotted the big man from the lake. The junk store owner. The peddler who'd sold Signe the parasol. Otis Hetfield. A few other faces he'd seen around the Hollows these past few moons.

When he looked at the bartender, she lowered her eyes and made a spiral gesture over her chest.

The big man raised his double-barreled shotgun. Quinn dropped the stake, and it clattered by his feet.

"Prepare the torches," Ms. Fontaine told her followers. They scurried to arrange wicker-topped staves along the edge of the limestone shelf while she bound Quinn's wrists behind his back. "I instructed that young acolyte to set you free," she whispered in his ear. "But you had to blunder through the wrong exit. Now I have no choice but to make an example of you for my flock, after I'd already picked a deserving scapegoat. An outsider among us, a man who turned on his previous master." She flicked her hand in Mr. Hetfield's direction.

The renegade Spotter bustled forward. "I'll tie the kid to the altar for you, my Lady of the Spirits."

"Why are you spouting that hooey?" Quinn asked him. "You don't believe anything she says, do you?"

"I believe I'll be alive come tomorrow," sneered the man, as he trussed Quinn to a standing stone near the edge of the slab. The wooded slope of Clack Mountain stretched out below them. "I can't say the same for you, or my pigheaded former boss, or your philandering, hemp-smoking daddy."

Ms. Fontaine ascended to the top of a rock platform. "Defenders of the Glowing Path," she intoned.

"Hierophant of the Horned Crown," her followers chanted in reply.

She smiled down at them. "The night of the equinox is upon us. The old season ends, and the fall begins. The Voice will send its kindred to cleanse the wicked from the Hollows, but your faith has inspired its mercy."

"All hail the Voice of the Spirits!" shouted her flock.

Quinn tugged at the ropes, but the knots held fast. The soles of his boots scraped against chalk-white pebbles that looked disturbingly like chips of bone.

"Tomorrow," said Ms. Fontaine, "you shall take your rightful place as the elect of the Hollows. Never forget, the Voice chose you for your devotion."

"We welcome the Rewakening!" The gowned figures were shadows against the sinking sun.

Her face turned somber. "Sadly, not everyone is worthy of its grace. Tonight, we must punish one of those who has traveled the Hollows slaying the Radiant Ones."

Sweat ran down Quinn's forehead and burned his eyes. His

grandmother had told him tales about the Spiritists perform-
ing sacrifices with daggers made from broken bottles, or with
copper blades soaked in salt and vinegar, but other legends—
ones he'd heard from Paige's morbid little sister—hinted at even
worse rituals.

The high priest brought her arms above her antlered head.
"Keepers of the Shrouded Way, prepare to invoke the spirits
when I give the word." She clasped her hands. "Now!"

A red bulb pulsed at the top of each staff.

Ms. Fontaine pointed to the junk store owner. "Stand guard
here until the Legions of the Wastes come forth." He kneeled before her, then stood and gave Quinn a feral smile.

"You two." She motioned to Mr. Hetfield and the weasel-faced
bartender. "Check for interlopers around the base of the outcrop. But don't take too long. Tonight, the spirits will smite anyone who scorns the Voice's command to take refuge."

The young woman bowed and strode off toward the north.
Mr. Hetfield frowned, drew a wide-mouthed pistol from beneath his gown, and headed in the opposite direction.

The rest of the Spiritists disappeared down the trap door,
one by one. On her way after them, Ms. Fontaine placed a hand
on Quinn's shoulder. "Goodbye, young man. I wish things
could be otherwise. At least you'll be joining your sister and
your sweetheart soon."

He tried to curse at her, but the words came out hoarse and
unintelligible. She shook her antlered head as she followed her
flock into the mountain. The trapdoor slammed shut behind her.

The sun dipped below the hills, and the shimmering curtain
of the spirit aurora swept across the northern horizon.

18

"DID YOU FIND EVERYTHING?" ASKED ZORA FROM HER POST BY THE living room window. The goats were munching on the thistles in the yard, and a hen was pecking near the little plot where she'd held her funeral for Static last winter.

"Two fully-juiced spirit shooters." Paige held up a pair of banishers. "The other contraption's in my backpack. We should get going—daylight's burning, and they'll be back soon."

Zora stroked the edge of a quilt and imagined it was Static's fur. He'd never chased another spirit after his run-in with the harbinger—not even a boge straying through the woods behind the barn—but he'd sat by her feet through all the long nights she'd spent building her first illuminator.

"Not yet," she said. "I want to invite Signe, too."

"Last I checked she was still in rough shape. I almost had to carry her to the bathroom. She won't be much help if she can't walk on her own two—"

Zora tapped a crutch against the floor and gave her a withering look.

Paige reddened beneath her tan. "Sorry. Forgot."

"Never mind that." Zora marched to the spare room and knocked.

"Come in," said a scratchy-sounding voice.

They went in. Signe had put on a long-sleeved nightgown and propped herself up against a pillow. Blisters mottled her face and hands.

"We're leaving," Zora said. "To rescue Quinn and stop the Wakening. I figure the harbinger plans to stage its big show at Clack Mountain." More of a hunch than a hypothesis, but better than nothing. "Want to come with us?"

Signe put on her cracked glasses. "Where's your mother?" She turned to Paige. "And your mentor?"

"Away helping rustle up a pair of saddle horses," said the apprentice. "So Zora's dad and the Ranger can ride off to try and catch the Spiritists."

"They're meeting Captain Flores along the way," added Zora.

"You didn't go with them?" asked Signe.

"My mom and Paige's boss ordered us to stay here," said Zora. Safe inside the spirit-fence, while the fight to save the Hollows—and her brother—went on elsewhere. "That's why we're leaving now, before they get back."

"I see." Signe smiled. "I'd be delighted to accompany you." As she stood and shuffled toward the door, Paige rushed to aid her.

Zora led them to the wagon, wishing she'd had time to disguise the blue lettering on its sides. If Evelyn Fontaine's spies were watching the road, they'd have no problem reading the names COLDIRON and PROSSER.

"Should I fetch another banisher?" asked Paige.

"Not on my account," said Signe. "I won't use it. Though I'd appreciate it if you could bring some of my clothes."

Paige trotted over to the white and purple wagon. A minute later, she reappeared with an armful of black dresses. A few minutes more, and she'd harnessed the horses.

"This'll be a rough ride." Zora steered Ursula and Undine toward the back way out of Lightning Bug Hollow. "On the plus side, we should miss running into anyone who might try to stop us."

Paige looked over her shoulder. "What'll your mom do when she finds out you've split?"

"If we make it back alive, I expect she'll lock me in my room till I turn seventeen. How about your boss?"

"Ditch me as an apprentice, maybe. He's generally a softy, but I've never crossed him like this before."

Zora squirmed. "It's not too late to change your mind."

"Stow that talk. I care more about your big brother's life than my job." Paige ran a hand along her banisher's stock. "And I'll aim better this time if we butt heads with any spirits. Say, how was it talking to your dad?"

"Hard," Zora admitted. "But at least I heard the full story of why he left us eight years ago." She shook her head. "I'd convinced myself I never wanted to see him again. Now I'm angry at him for running off again so soon."

"He does seem prone to sudden departures," said Signe. "I hope it's not contagious."

When night fell, Zora switched on the headlamps. Paige used the banisher to scan the road ahead, and Signe kept watch over the dark woods. Above them, the pole star lit the way toward Clack Mountain.

◎

"So there I am," said Paige, "at the bottom of the cistern in my skivvies, while your brother tries to pull the wool over the Ranger's eyes. Right as I'm fixing to run out of breath, the firecrackers explode on yonder rooftop. Deputy Killjoy goes that-away, and I climb out of the tank, all stealthy-like." She stifled a snicker. "Only Pine-Box doesn't cotton on that I'm gone, so he dives into the water, costume and all, to try and save me."

Zora grinned. Then she saw Signe's folded arms and pursed lips.

"We're all worried about him," Paige said. "Just trying to lighten the mood, Fairy Eyes."

"Pardon me for being such a wet blanket, then," croaked Signe, "but I've had enough story time. And I certainly don't need one of your clever nicknames." She got up and tottered into the wagon.

Paige looked stricken. "I didn't—I hope she isn't—"

"Let me talk to her." Zora handed over the reins. She found Signe on Quinn's bunk, hugging his pillow to her chest. One of his old paperbacks was still lying beside his bed where Evelyn Fontaine's underlings had left it: *Addie the Urchin versus the Ionized Illusionist.*

Zora tried to think of what her brother might say. "Paige wasn't trying to be hurtful," she began. "She's not that sort of person. Not like I can be."

Signe sat up and squinched her eyes.

"I apologize for the way I've treated you," Zora went on. "For the thoughtless words I've said. I'd like to be friends."

"I'd like that, too," Signe said. "And I've been called worse names." She pulled her hair over her face and dropped her voice. "The way I reacted out there, it's just—I can get a bit of a jealous streak."

"You mean about Paige? Trust me, you don't need to lose sleep over the prospect of her cutting in on you. Speaking of which, are you and my big brother, you know"—she caught herself. "None of my business."

Signe got a moony look. "Everything was going so wonderfully with him, as if we were alone together in our own enchanted hollow. It was just like I'd envisioned it would be." Her expression clouded. "Then the spire ruined everything. Thanks again for saving my life, by the way. I wish I could've stopped those horrid people from taking Quinn."

"Well," said Zora, "I did promise I'd shoot you with a banisher if anything happened to him."

While Paige drove and Signe dozed, Zora experimented with the broken spirit lures. No matter what she tried, they refused to work.

She felt like screaming. Instead, she put away the parts and closed her eyes.

The answer came to her as she was falling asleep. Ectoradiation had its own equivalent to infrared light: at a low enough wavelength, it resonated with the spirits. That's why they found the lures so irresistible.

Zora turned on the lamp and went to work. By the time the little hand on the clock had reached the next petal of the rosette, she'd finished a hodgepodge device. At the flip of a switch, it flashed red.

She jabbed the switch again, and the lure went dead. The last thing they wanted was another dustup with a hount. Or worse.

The wrist-watcher showed a solitary orange light for Signe, still hibernating on Quinn's bed. Zora tucked the lure in her backpack.

Another idea came to her. What if the ectospectrum had its own counterpart to ultraviolet, too? Wait, it *did*—and she'd seen it before. That indigo light from Signe's eyes had been high-frequency ectoradiation.

Zora grabbed a pair of goggles. An hour later, she scrutinized her handiwork and then lay down on her bunk.

She dreamed of a sky filled with crimson stars.

The celestial alignment draws near, said a distant voice.

She dreamed of a swirling green abyss.

We will meet again two nights from now.

She dreamed of a world buried in ashes.

Wheels thumped along a wooden bridge, and voices murmured beyond the door. The goggles on Zora's bedside table reflected morning light into her eyes.

One day until the equinox.

She listened to her companions talk while she strapped on her braces.

"Well, lightning strike my nose," Paige was saying. "I never would've thunk it."

"I swear by the universe." Signe sounded more animated today, and less like she'd swallowed a porcupine.

When Zora opened the door, they both turned toward

her. The apprentice gave her a wolfish look. "Your turn to spill."

"What do you mean?"

Signe pounced on her from the left. "Do *you* have your heart set on anyone?"

"Or at least your eyes?" added Paige.

Zora stammered. "I've been so busy with my inventions, and the spirit hunting." She stuck her hands in her pockets. "Besides, I'm not sure there's anyone in the Hollows who'd be right for me."

"Fate may have other ideas." Signe smiled beneath the tattered umbrella she'd rummaged from Quinn's drawer.

"In the meantime, you have us." Paige leaned into Zora and wedged her against Signe, who pushed back to squash her in the middle. All three of them laughed.

A logging road took them up one set of switchbacks and down another. Zora brought the horses to a halt at the bottom. A lone walker dressed in white was approaching across a valley of bare stumps.

"First person we've seen all day," said Paige. "Let's watch out, in case the Spiritists are still searching for Foxtails." She raised a banged-up spyglass to one eye. "Funny-looking fellow, with marks all over him."

"Let me see," said Zora. The apprentice handed over the spyglass. Sure enough, it was that spell-chanter they'd met in Mill Hollow, the one who'd fled from the orbs like a bat out of the Wastes.

"Mr. Crouch," Signe called out to him.

"Howdy." The man waved one of his tattooed arms. "Jinx begone, it's the seer and the scientist. The whispers through the hills say your talismans work better than mine."

"You've heard the warnings about tomorrow, mister?" Paige asked.

He nodded. "Would that I could serve the Hollows in their time of need, but a vindictive star guides my destiny. The path to redemption eludes me."

For once, the apprentice was at a loss for words.

Zora held up her banisher. "This is one of the inventions I used against the spirits in Deadfall Wood." She gave a quick demonstration of how it worked and offered it to Mr. Crouch. "If you want to help, take it and go to Comet Tail Hollow. Find Cora Stegall and her daughter. Keep them safe tomorrow night."

The tattooed man accepted the device with an air of veneration. "I shan't fail in this charge you've bestowed upon me." Then he set off again, mumbling charms about swords and scythes.

Paige gave Zora a sidelong look. "That was big-hearted of you, but now we only have one spirit-shooter."

"It's okay. You still have the one with the polarized scope, and I have my new invention. Which reminds me." Zora pulled out the goggles she'd modified last night and handed them to Signe. "I made these for you."

Signe examined them with a bemused expression. "What are they, exactly?"

"Remember the time you scared away those herns? And how the leviathan hesitated when you stood up to it? I think you can stare down spirits. Literally." She pointed at the goggles. "The lenses should amplify the effect."

"What in the Hollows is that about?" asked Paige.

"I have a theory," said Zora. "I've been thinking about lightning bugs, and how they glow by synthesizing a compound called luciferin. If I'm right, our friend here can do something like that. You might say she has ectoluminescent retinas."

Signe lifted her chin. "On further consideration, I prefer Fairy Eyes."

They stuck to back roads. Along the way, they passed silent, boarded-up houses.

Paige gestured to a hex sign painted on one door. "That won't do any good, will it?"

Zora shook her head. "These people are helpless against what's coming."

After lunch, Paige slept and Zora switched on the radio. *"Please stay in your homes tomorrow night,"* said the announcer. *"If you have a cellar, take shelter there."*

"I gather they didn't find the harbinger yesterday," said Signe.

"They won't find it tonight, either." Zora felt certain of that.

The sun went down, and Paige took the reins. They rode on through darkness, meeting neither human nor spirit, while the radio alternated between staccato warnings and doleful ballads. Zora found herself hoping for one of those songs about the fiddler girl, but the station didn't play one.

As her head began to droop, the first hints of blue appeared in the eastern sky. All Hollows Day had arrived.

She went inside and collapsed on her bunk. This time, she didn't dream at all.

◎

A hand shook Zora's shoulder. She opened her eyes to a pair of refracted pupils looking down at her.

"We're at the foot of Clack Mountain," said Signe. Her nose and cheeks had begun to peel where they'd burned, sprinkling white specks across the front of her cobwebby dress. "Paige found an abandoned barn for the horses."

Zora pulled up the straps of her overalls and checked her illuminators. Her new crutch. The lure in her backpack. All good. She restored her pigtails and scowled into the bronze compact her grandma had given her for her fifteenth birthday. Once this was over, maybe she'd try out a different hairstyle.

When she stepped outside, she cast a long, skinny shadow that held two long, skinny shadow-crutches. So late in the day, already.

She leaned over the side of the wagon just in time to miss throwing up on the seat.

"You and me both," said Paige, zipping up an ancient-looking aviator's jacket.

Zora wiped her mouth, and the three of them started hiking up the mountainside. Every so often, Paige scaled one of the limestone formations to look for any sign of Quinn or the Spiritists.

As late afternoon gave way to evening, they reached the rock where Zora and her brother had taken cover from the hount. That seemed like ten moons ago, instead of ten days.

Signe rested against the mossy stone and panted. "We should keep going," she said, once she'd caught her breath.

"How long till the Wakening starts?" asked Paige.

"If Old Man McBrain calculated that," Zora said, "he didn't get the chance to tell us. All I know is it'll happen sometime between dusk and dawn."

They continued up the slope. Near the summit, they came across a giant limestone outcrop.

Paige clambered to the top of a nearby boulder and peered through her spyglass. "Found them," she whispered.

Zora crawled next to her and took the spyglass. Dozens of figures were standing along the crest of the outcrop, their gold robes glinting from the sun at Zora's back. Behind them, bound to a rock pillar, was a dark-haired captive dressed in sooty clothes.

Her brother.

She shifted the spyglass upward until she saw a green form with the head of a deer and the hands of a human: Evelyn Fontaine, wearing a headdress.

Zora bit her lip so hard she tasted the iron in her blood.

The antlered woman brought her arms together, and a row of red lights blinked along the edge of the cliff.

"Lures," Zora said. "Stronger than the ones in the camera and the motor. Once it's dark, spirits will swarm here from the Wastes."

Paige took another turn with the spyglass. "Those folks in the funny outfits are leaving. I can't tell where to." Her voice went high-pitched with excitement. "They're all gone except one. And Quinn." She jumped from the boulder. "I'm going to get him."

Signe slid after her. "I'm coming with you."

Paige opened her mouth as if to argue, but then she nodded.

Zora lowered herself to the ground and looked at the craggy

face of the outcrop. "I don't think I can make it up that." She kicked a small rock, and it tumbled down the mountainside. "You'll need to go without me."

Paige squeezed her arm. "Don't worry. We'll be right back with your big brother. In the meantime, you can keep a lookout for the harbinger." She holstered the banisher over her shoulder and started climbing.

Signe pulled her new goggles over her head so that they dangled around her neck. "I like your present," she said, before following Paige up the rocks.

Zora lost sight of them when they reached the top of the first ledge. The orange dot on her wrist went dark a few seconds later.

She was alone.

The hills eclipsed the last sliver of sun. Night fell on Clack Mountain, and green fire blazed in the sky above the Wastes. Zora paced along the base of the outcrop, scouting for any roamers drawn by the lures.

Footsteps, coming her way. Had the Spiritists found her? She flattened herself against the rock wall and raised a crutch (the old one, not the new one). A gold shape rounded the corner—

She swung the crutch as hard as she could. The blow landed with a dull crack, and a robed figure fell to the dirt: a sharp-nosed, beady-eyed young woman.

Zora stared down at the snotty bartender from Comet Tail Hollow.

"Heretic!" squealed Ferret-Face. She staggered away, holding her ribs and mewling.

Zora watched her go, too dazed to follow or even say

anything. Evelyn Fontaine must've planted moles all along the route from her mansion to the Big Lake.

Once Ferret-Face's whimpering blended into the sounds of the forest, Zora went back to searching for spirits. To the north, a falling star slashed through the bowl of the Little Dipper. *I wish I may*, she thought. *I wish I might—*

A scream rang out from the top of the outcrop—a lingering, agonized howl. Not Quinn, or Paige, or Signe, but human for sure.

Zora craned her neck. Green and violet lightning flashed as unnatural shrieks filled the air. Her lungs ached from holding in her breath.

All at once, the noises stopped, and darkness settled over the mountainside.

The constellations rotated slowly around the North Star. She waited, but her friends did not return.

Everything depended on her, whether she was ready or not.

Zora exhaled and set out through the fallen chunks of limestone to find the harbinger. The spirit-aurora shone brighter— or maybe it was drawing closer, like the edge of a storm.

An orange light appeared on her wrist. And another, and another. She hid them with the cuff of her shirt.

Then a telltale drone set her spine tingling, from her neck down to her tailbone.

19

"A BEWITCHING SIGHT, ISN'T IT?" SAID THE JUNK STORE OWNER. "Some evenings I come here just to take it in. No photograph can capture its full glory. No painting, either." His voice fell to a hush. "Tomorrow night, you'll be able to see it in every direction from this spot."

Quinn didn't reply. He'd stopped looking at the aurora. Instead, he was watching the dark hills that marked the border of the Wastes.

"Well, I reckon *you* won't be seeing it, not after our visitors are done." The man chortled as he swaggered up to the standing stone. "Fitting how they're drawn to the color of blood, like other predators." His breath reeked in Quinn's nostrils. "They'll come for the beckoners, but they'll stay to feast on you. Our offering. And when the Voice opens the gates to the sky, its brethren will hunt down all the other prey in the Hollows."

"Maybe you, too," said Quinn, with a shakiness that robbed the bite from his words.

"Not me. I belong to the Kinfolk of the Doe and the Stag. You and your sort are just the goats."

"My sister's smarter than your priest, or that monster you bow down to."

Points of green glimmered along the range to the north, like lightning bugs. Or the wisps in the pit behind Zora's home. Except big enough to be visible from far, far away.

"I'll leave you to tell our callers that," said the junk store owner. "It's time for me to go underground." He laughed again and walked away.

As the lures beat steadily, a faint roar echoed from the direction of the Wastes.

Quinn strained against his bindings until the rope burned the skin on his arms and the rock scraped the backs of his hands. He gave up and sagged against the standing stone.

The lights on the hills were already closer.

Something scuffed along the rim of the outcrop. He twisted his neck as far as he could, trying to see around the stone. Two smallish figures were skulking toward him: one with short, black hair, and one with long, white hair.

When the first figure entered the circle of red light and raised a finger to its lips, Quinn held back a shout. How in the Hollows had Paige found him here?

The other figure stepped out of the darkness. At first, he took it for a ghost—or a walking corpse, wearing broken glasses and a mask of shedding skin. His heart pounded. It was Signe, back from the dead.

She and Paige snuck over and began untying him, but an angry bray stopped them short. The junk store owner charged, his stringy hair flapping. Paige spun on her heels to face him. As the man reached out to grab her, she ducked under his arms and punched him in the jaw.

A stone's throw away, metal clanked beneath the surface of the outcrop.

Paige's opponent snarled and threw a haymaker that caught her in the eye, slamming her against the ground. He tried to kick her in the face while she was down, but she flung a handful of grit into his eyes before he could land a boot on her.

"We only need one sacrifice," he said, drawing a shock prod from beneath the folds of his robe.

Through it all, Signe kept on untangling the knots.

The junk store owner swung the prod at Paige's chest. She rolled out of its path, then snatched the wooden stake lying next to her and drove its dull end into the man's stomach. He fell backwards with a groan.

The cords around Quinn's body went slack. His knee gave out beneath him, and he keeled into Signe's arms.

"Barnyard trash-eaters." Spittle flew from the junk store owner's mouth. "When the spirits come, they'll butcher y'all like the beasts you are."

Paige bared her teeth and raised the stake for another blow. The man scuttled away toward the trap door, muttering threats and obscenities.

"Let him go," said Signe. "We need to get back to Zora."

"She's here?" Quinn felt lightheaded. "She's all right?" He stared at Signe's peeling face. "You're all right?"

She pulled him closer. "Your dad and Zora saved me."

"I thought I'd never see you again." His eyes misted, and his nose went runny. "You came for me. Both of you."

"Of course, you goof." Paige touched her eye socket, grimaced, and unholstered a banisher from her shoulder. "Now hustle. We've got a Wakening to stop."

A heavy thud made all three of them jump. The junk store owner had started battering the trap door. "Open up," he barked. The man didn't sound so smug now. More like terror-stricken.

Paige's banisher gave a warning signal: a clear ping, instead of a fuzzy beep. She looked through a blue-lensed scope on the weapon's stock. "Can't see a thing down the mountain," she said.

The Spiritist waved his arms and stomped on the ground. "In the name of the Antlered Lady, it's me!"

A whirring came from above. Crouching beside the rock altar, Quinn glanced up at the stars that formed the coils of the Dragon and the staff of the Shepherd. A greenish-white fireball was streaking past them, straight toward the robed man.

"Let me in!"

The flaming spirit swooped down and seized the junk store owner. He screamed as it carried him into the sky. He went on screaming as it drained the life from him.

Signe clamped her fingers around Quinn's arm. "That's a bolide," she murmured.

The junk store owner's howls gave way to wheezes and, finally, nothing. The spirit dropped his mummified husk onto the outcrop, where it burst into a cloud of dust.

The bolide looped around and dove again, this time at Quinn and Signe. He yanked her toward the standing stone. The two of them landed in a heap behind it, with her on top of him. The whirring grew louder and louder.

Then it ended in a screech, as violet flashed through the air. Paige ran over to them, carrying her banisher in one hand. Her complexion was a few shades paler than usual. "You okay?"

Quinn collected his bearings and nodded. "Great shot."

"Thanks, but this is all yours now." She thrust the device at him. "I don't want to push my luck at shooting lefty. Turns out I busted my right hand socking that creep." She looked at the junk store owner's empty gold robe. "I hope that spirit dragged his soul away with it."

As soon as Quinn took the banisher, half its sensors turned orange. Signe pointed to an entire swarm of bolides, plummeting from the aurora like a meteor shower.

"Stay still," he whispered. "And stay quiet." His companions huddled behind the standing stone while he poked his head around the side.

The airbounds flew through a low-hanging cloud, lighting it up from within, and hurtled toward the outcrop in a v-shaped formation. Long tails of spirit-shine fanned out behind them.

Quinn balanced the banisher in his hands. It felt lighter than his old weapon, the one Evelyn Fontaine had stolen.

The bolides smashed into the row of lures. The red beacons went dark, and the staves toppled. A blast of hot wind blew the smell of brimstone across the outcrop.

Paige made a startled noise, then covered her mouth with her hand. Beside her, Signe fumbled with something hanging around her neck.

The spirits rose again to hover in midair.

Quinn swept the banisher in a series of arcs, and the bolides shrieked as the ray cut them apart. He didn't stop until all of them were gone.

Paige raised a spyglass to her eye. "Clear skies. You're a spirit sharpshooter. And there I was, getting all puffed up about my aim." She put away the spyglass and slapped him on the back with her left hand. "Never seen an airbound before. I think I'll stick to waterbounds."

"Speak for yourself," said Signe.

Quinn peered over the cliff. Dozens of glowing shapes had begun crossing the valley between the Wastes and Clack Mountain. Some were gossamery and translucent; others were thick and opaque. They leaped from treetop to treetop, or threaded through the canopy below, or flowed like quicksilver along the forest floor.

The largest of the spirits was skinny as a snake—if snakes grew wide as rivers. It raised its front end and called out in the voice of a distant cataract.

A hount. Maybe even the one that had nearly killed him and his sister.

"Let's find Zora," he said, "and get as far from this place as possible."

Paige retrieved the wooden stake and led the way down. Quinn followed, holding the banisher with one hand and Signe's hand with the other. His knee twinged with every step.

"My dad rescued you?" he asked Signe, still not quite believing it.

"He found me in the meadow," she said. "Then Zora cured me with a shot to the chest."

"She what?" Quinn tried to unscramble his thoughts. "Never mind, you can explain later." If there was a later.

"Your father and the Rangers may show up here tonight, too," Signe added.

Halfway to the bottom, he heard someone crying. A gold-gowned young woman shambled toward them through a small rock arch. His jailor from under the mountain.

"You," said Signe and Paige, at the same time.

The young Spiritist jerked her head back and forth. "I—we—need to get to the cave before the Wakening begins."

"Too late," he told her. "Your friends locked you out."

"But the man guarding the door . . ."

"You could fit what's left of him in an urn," Quinn said.

She sank into a fetal position. "I've messed up bad," she moaned. "I'm going to die."

"Did you see anybody down there?" Paige asked. "Speak up, or we'll throw you to those things when they get here."

"I did." The Spiritist had the look of a cornered weasel. "The girl with the crutches." She turned to Quinn. "Your sister."

"Where?" he demanded.

"The far side of the outcrop. She went berserk and broke a bunch of my ribs."

Good for Zora, he thought. "And then?"

"And then I ran away from the little barbarian."

Paige waved the stake like a sword. "Keep your trap shut the next time you feel like bad-mouthing my friend."

"And stick with us if you want to live." Quinn eased himself onto the ledge below, keeping his weight on his good knee. Paige and Signe climbed down next to him, and the young Spiritist joined them, sniffling to herself.

Signe placed a hand on her back. "What's your name?"

"L—Lurana."

"Lurana, tonight you can atone for your mistakes and help preserve the Hollows."

Paige dragged the tip of the stake along the rock. "Or else."

"Which way?" Quinn asked the Spiritist, when they reached the foot of the outcrop.

"Toward the Wastes."

He took off in that direction, with Signe right behind him. Lurana hurried after them, and Paige came last. The Milky Way cast dim starlight across their path.

The banisher pinged once. Twice. Three times.

He started to call out a warning, but a frantic yell cut him off. A gleaming lasso had snared Paige by her ankle and pulled her into the air. She flailed the stake as she dangled upside down.

First bolides, now a roperite. Those lures must've summoned half the spirits listed in poor Nevan McBrain's books.

Quinn held his fire when he saw the jagged rocks below Paige's head. While he hesitated, another lasso whipped from behind a nearby boulder and plucked the stake from her grip. "If I can get a line of sight—" said Signe, but her next words were lost beneath Paige's hollering, Lurana's bawling, and a new volley of pings from the banisher. The roperite began hauling its catch toward the boulder.

Once the spirit swaddled Paige in its arms, it would shrivel her to ashes.

The clamor around Quinn faded away, and his vision turned crystalline. He squeezed off two shots. The lassos thrashed as they boiled into luminous steam. The stake sailed down the mountainside, but Paige landed in front of him, square on her bottom.

Signe helped her up. "Are you injured?"

"No," said Paige, rubbing her behind with one hand. "Besides some new bruises to match my shiner. Though I feel weird all over."

Quinn checked the sensors on the banisher. More spirits were closing in. "Go," he said, plugging another lasso. "Fast."

The roperite yowled from behind the boulder and lobbed a stone over his head.

That sent him retreating after the others. He caught up with them as they were scrambling along a wide, flat rock.

Signe went rigid. "In front of us," she said.

A yellowish-green aura formed in the woods ahead. An instant later, a spirit materialized at its center and knocked over a tree with its writhing limbs.

Paige swore loudly.

"And below us." Signe gestured to a host of roamers streaming up the slope. They buzzed, and gibbered, and screaked as they came. One was the size of a barn.

Paige and Lurana backed against the face of the outcrop. The spirits drew nearer on all sides, reaching out with wraithlike tentacles. Dripping pseudopods. Glistening tines.

"We're boxed in," Quinn said, hefting the banisher.

"No." Signe's tone was calm, her expression serene. She took his chin in her palms and kissed him. Her lips felt dry and cracked against his.

For a moment, he let himself imagine that nothing was real except her. That when he opened his eyes, the two of them would be in a different world—a charmed place where the sun never rose high enough to burn her skin nor sank low enough for night, and the spirits, to come.

Signe released him. "No matter what happens," she said, "keep behind me." She removed her glasses and held them out.

He took the glasses but shook his head. "I—"

"Trust me. I was born to do this. I can feel it in my heart." She pulled on a pair of indigo-lensed goggles. "A gift from Zora," she said, and strode forward to face the spirit horde.

"What's she doing?" asked Lurana.

"Shut up," said Paige.

Signe walked to the edge of the rock, close enough to the spirits that her hair took on their greenish hue. "Denizens of the Wastes," she called out. "You're trespassing here. The Hollows are our home, not yours."

The spirits halted and fell quiet. Some billowed along the ground, while others levitated among the trees.

Quinn thought of the leviathan. Of the spire. Of the fiddler girl's last stand against the spirit-tempest. He smothered the impulse to run toward Signe, pull her back, and blast away with the banisher until its battery ran dry.

Trust me, she'd told him.

"Your sister says it's all in her eyeballs," Paige whispered. "Those goggles are supposed to boost her spookifying powers. Though we never had the chance to test them . . ."

"As the seventh child of a seventh child," Signe continued, "chosen by the universe to maintain harmony, I command you to depart from here." She raised her voice. "Return to whence you came!"

Quinn blinked at the dark mountainside. The spirits had vanished. Every single one of them.

Paige whooped. "Fairy Eyes," she said, "that was the most stupendous thing I've ever seen."

"Thank you." Signe smiled. "Just so you know, it's more than my retinas. Or these." She pulled off her goggles and then stumbled. Quinn caught her before she fell.

"Can you do the same thing to the harbinger?" he asked.

"Only one way to find out," said Signe.

"Are you able to walk?"

"Don't worry about me. We need to keep going." She reclaimed her glasses and fixed her eyes on Lurana. "Precisely where did you see Zora?"

The Spiritist shied away from Signe. "Over by that bend."

"You'd best not be lying," Paige warned.

Quinn tromped ahead through the murk. "Come on, Zora," he called out. "Show me a sign."

The sensors pinged. Not quite what he'd had in mind. "I miss my old banisher," he said under his breath as he swept the device away from the outcrop. When it pinged again, he followed it like a compass needle toward the source of the spirit-energy. The others stuck close to him.

"I see it." Signe brushed her hair back from her glasses. "Whatever it is, it's gigantic, but it isn't moving. An earthbound spirit, I think."

"Zora and I never ran across one of those the other time we were here," said Quinn.

"There aren't any earthbounds on the mountain." Lurana gnawed her lip. "Or at least there didn't used to be."

He advanced more warily now. Every ten paces, another orange bulb came to life on the banisher.

Whispers rose up all around them. Paige lifted her hand to her brow with a befuddled expression as Lurana quailed beside her.

Signe's eyes widened behind her blue lenses. "What's that?" she asked.

Humming filled the air, and a cry of triumph rang through Quinn's skull.

The stars draw into alignment.

"The Voice of the Spirits." Lurana cast herself onto the

ground. Off to their right, a spiral of green took shape among the trees. It spun like a shining wheel—slowly at first, then swifter and swifter until its outline blurred.

The worlds weave together.

A hole appeared in the sky. It was the size of the moon. Ragged as a wound. Beyond it lay an impenetrable haze.

Signe cried out and grabbed Quinn's elbow. Paige cursed, softly this time. "Spare me," Lurana chanted to herself. "Spare me."

My kindred come.

The rip in the heavens widened. The fog on the other side parted to unveil an endless plane of churning green shapes.

Now.

The banisher's sensor panel sparked, and its bulbs exploded into orange shards. Signe crumpled to the ground. As Quinn knelt beside her, she covered her face with her hands. "Can't make them disappear," she mumbled. "Too strong. I can still see them, even with my eyes shut." Her voice turned harsh. "Destroy it, before it lets those nightmares through."

Lurana started sobbing for her mother.

"Quinn!" Paige hit his arm. "I'll take care of Signe. You go and snuff that oversized corpse candle."

"Right." A tap on the banisher's trigger brought a reassuring crackle. He looked at his companions one more time and set off toward the harbinger. A midnight dawn lit his way.

The air rippled, and emerald rays threw bizarre shadows against the mountainside. A wave of dizziness brought Quinn to his knees.

Paige shouted his name.

He stood again and lurched onward through the forest. The

gash in the sky blotted out the stars as it spread. The harbinger was a disk of brilliant green. It had mesmerized him back in Comet Tail Hollow, but tonight he could—

I sense you.

The spirit twisted itself into a pattern that muddled Quinn's thoughts. He swayed on his feet, then raised the banisher's scope to his eye and lined up his target in the crosshairs.

You are helpless to prevent what will be.

He closed his finger on the trigger. Violet light flowed down the weapon's barrel to its silver muzzle.

Behold, and perish.

Foxfire danced along the banisher. The barrel shattered, and glass splinters cut Quinn's hands.

Just like the little one of your kind, whose burning light has failed and died.

As the rift stretched across the horizon, monstrous forms surged toward the opening. They were vaster than mountains, brighter than suns.

Quinn dropped the remains of the banisher and bowed his head in despair.

The new Wakening had begun.

20

ZORA HUNKERED DOWN BEHIND A STUMP. THE MOUNTAINSIDE was still dark, but any moment now the harbinger would sense her.

She pulled off her backpack. Her fingers trembled as she unclasped the fasteners. When the patchwork lure tumbled out, she jammed it into one of her pockets.

A bang surprised her into dropping the pack, and an object whizzed past her. She rubbed her head, fighting to regain her equilibrium while she listened for sounds beneath the ringing in her eardrums. Scarlet light shone from the undergrowth nearby. A flare, she thought, until it began pulsing.

"Stay right there," called out an unfamiliar voice. A gold-robed man with a rabid expression was standing behind her, holding a pistol shaped like a trumpet.

No, not a pistol. A lure-gun.

"Stop shouting," Zora hissed. "It'll figure out we're here." She gripped her crutches and made for the flashing beacon.

Before she could reach it, the man shoved her to the ground. "I'm counting on that," he said. She started to get up again, but he put a boot on her back. "I need to speak to it."

"It wants to kill us all." She spat out dirt. "Including you. No matter what your priest might've told you."

The man snorted. "I'm well aware she's a fraud." He pressed harder with his foot. "That antlered witch shut me out here to die, so I need to cut my own deal with the harbinger."

Zora puzzled over that, and then she understood. "You're the other Spotter who worked with my dad and Mr. McBrain." Otis something-or-other. "Go burn in the Wastes, you back-stabber." She clawed at his ankle and got a heel in the shoulder blades for her trouble.

"Not when I can trade your hide for mine." He reloaded his lure-gun and fired it into the air. "Voice of the Spirits! I caught the gadgeteer kid for you."

The droning intensified as a green glow spread across the ground in front of Zora's face. She pummeled the earth in helpless rage. She'd come so close, only for this sack of buzzard droppings to doom everyone in the Hollows.

The little one I sought.

"She's yours." The turncoat Spotter took his boot off her back. "All I ask for is enough time to find my way back under the mountain. There's plenty of night left for you to—um—lay waste."

You have served me well.

"Yes, mighty one." The man's fawning carried an undercurrent of fear. "Do we have a bargain?"

I no longer require the aid of creatures such as you.

"Wait—"

Nor your master who pretends to worship me.

Zora slithered on her belly toward her backpack, over roots that tore at her overalls, through thorns that scratched her face. She didn't look back at the harbinger.

My kindred will find that one, no matter how deep they must dig.

What's-his-name gabbled desperately. "I'll show you the woman's hiding places," he said, when he found his words. "Let me be your—your foxhound for tracking her down."

I go now to open the way from my world to yours.

A rumble sounded from below. The Spotter dropped his lure-gun and reeled backward.

A devourer has answered my summons, and neither of you can escape it.

Feedback shrilled from Zora's wrist-watcher as she clutched her pack and choked down panic. The harbinger had called forth another elemental, a giant the likes of which the Hollows had never seen.

She didn't stand a chance of outrunning it.

The reverberations grew stronger. All at once, every tooth in her mouth began hurting. She reached into her pack, then cranked a dial on the device she'd completed three days ago. A miniature generator sputtered. She coaxed it to life with a string of pleas and curses.

Phosphorescence snaked toward the Spotter, and green embers appeared by Zora's feet. "Hurry," she whispered. "Hurry, or—"

The generator settled into a steady thrum. A violet halo formed around her, as wide as the wingspan of her crutches, and the pain in her teeth disappeared. She gulped down oxygen. Her new invention was working, even against the granddaddy of all elementals.

Fluorescent vapors rose beyond Zora's spirit-shield to wither the ferns and sear the moss from the rocks. Thunder crashed across the slope as vines of energy encircled the Spotter. He cried out and raised his hands in a gesture of supplication. Pity welled up inside her, but she couldn't do anything to help him.

The man's skin bubbled. With one final gurgle, he dissolved into blood and bone. His bare skull landed on the charred earth and crumbled to powder.

The trees creaked as the elemental leeched their lives away. Bark peeled from trunks, and leaves rained down. Within the space of a dozen breaths, the largest oaks were gone, leaving no vestiges except the pits where their roots had lain.

A landscape of ash stretched away from Zora in every direction.

She steeled herself. The shield's power wouldn't last forever, and if she stuck around here she'd suffer the same fate as that double-crossing Spotter. She put one foot forward. The amethyst globe moved with her.

Bit by bit, she walked across the blight. Perspiration drenched her forehead, but the generator on her back chugged away, and the miasma from the elemental parted before her.

When she came to the limit of the spirit's sway, she pushed onward another twenty paces just to be safe. Then she flopped down and switched off the generator.

Zora smiled to herself. She was still alive. Things were finally going her way. Now all she had to do was find the harbinger again, catch it unawares, and hit it with a perfect shot.

A charge in the air made the hairs on the back of her neck stand up. The night split asunder, and an emerald nebula bled into the sky. Holding out her thumb, she did a quick calculation in her head.

She could make it there before the rift stabilized. Before whatever lay in wait on the other side came through it.

Spectral radiation poured onto the mountainside, turning it a lurid green. Zora set off toward the point directly below the heart of the rupture. Ahead of her, a humming rose and fell in diminishing intervals.

The atmosphere wavered as preternatural forces bent the laws of physics. Time was running out. She quickened her pace, even as her braces jabbed her shins.

At last, she glimpsed the harbinger. It was a whirlpool in a lake of black water, a galaxy in a starless void. She looked away before the thing could hypnotize her and summon some new behemoth to kill her.

It wouldn't see her coming this time.

Zora turned the knob on the generator to cloak herself with the shield again. The droning transformed into a series of nerve-jarring harmonics. She edged forward, keeping her target in the corner of her eye.

The generator coughed. She'd burnt too much power escaping from the elemental.

Plumes of energy from the spirit universe grazed the hilltops along the boundary of the Wastes. The shield winked off and then rematerialized. Stifling a growl of frustration, Zora twisted the dial partway back. The sphere dimmed enough to keep the shield alive, but not enough to let the harbinger spot her.

In theory.

Her heart leaped when she saw a figure approaching from the other direction. It was Quinn, all tousle-haired and scruffy-faced, limping forward with a banisher in his hands.

The harbinger's voice slurred inside her head, its words garbled by interference from the shield.

Sense you.

Zora froze until she realized the spirit meant Quinn, not her. She scurried closer to it, trying to keep her mind as blank as possible.

Helpless.

Her brother drew a bead on the harbinger.

Perish.

A wormy form appeared from nowhere: a tangle, like the one they'd hunted in Saltpeter Hollow. It wrapped itself around Quinn's banisher, smashed the barrel, and darted away.

He looked up. Zora instinctively followed his gaze to the spirits gathering beyond the breach. If those titans made it through the gateway, their fiery green coronas would consume every living thing in the Hollows—starting with her and her brother.

She averted her eyes and stepped into range.

Little one—burning light—failed.

As the shield waned away, the distortion vanished from the harbinger's voice.

Not like the other one from so long ago, who barred my way with vibrations in the ether.

Zora's breath caught. The fiddler girl from those old ballads had been real, and she'd ended the first Wakening with her music.

Nothing will stop me tonight.

The mountainside echoed with booming noises, but Zora drowned them out with a half-remembered refrain from one of Quinn's favorite songs. Only seconds to spare now.

She knelt and lifted her new crutch, the replacement she'd made for the one at the bottom of the Big Lake. Then she pulled off the tip of the metal tube to uncover the device inside. The product of her own wits, the work of her own hands. Her instrument for defeating the harbinger.

A shriek of fury blasted through her brain.

You.

She aimed the brass crutch at the thing that had baited her seven-year-old self into the dark forest outside her home. That had frightened her into wetting herself. That had driven away her dad and haunted her childhood dreams.

Still alive.

She slid back a panel in the crutch's handle to reveal a button.

Impossible.

"Nope," Zora whispered. You should've left me alone, she added to herself as she pushed the button. A rocket shot from the end of the crutch and flew toward the bullseye of the revolving spirit.

How—

The rocket erupted in a bloom of violet energy. The harbinger tilted wildly on its axis. It was a broken gyroscope, a toy top gone wobbling out of control.

Everything around her seemed to warp. She was weightless. Breathless. Disembodied.

I leave you with a vision of your future.

The hills melted and reformed into a ring of dark mountains taller than any range in the Hollows. The zodiac spun across the heavens, and the planets wandered in their orbits.

Time is nothing to me.

Zora shivered from the cold of a winter's night as a gale flung sleet at her face.

The stars will align again.

The spirit-aurora blanketed the sky, from end to end.

I will be waiting.

She was alone in the Wastes.

I will return.

Something stalked toward her through the mountains, hints of its outline shimmering behind the peaks.

You will be no more.

"I don't believe in premonitions," she said.

The harbinger spiraled inward, and then it was gone back to its own realm, like water draining through a sinkhole into the depths of the earth.

The world went black. She lost her balance and fell.

Once her pupils dilated, she saw trees, and limestone monoliths, and the fused end of her crutch. High above her, the portal to the other universe had sealed itself shut; the constellations had returned to their rightful places in the night sky. The Wakening was over, and Quinn was looking down at her with a huge grin on his face.

"You did it!" he shouted. "I'm not sure exactly what you did, but you did it."

Zora lay there, letting the tension flow out of her body. She felt a strange lightness in her chest where she'd carried her hate for so long. Eventually, she managed to nod.

Her brother cocked his head at her ruined crutch. "What was that, anyhow?"

"A rocket-powered spirit-bomb." She sat up and brushed twigs from her hair. "Good work playing decoy for me. I never would've caught it off guard without you."

"That was my plan all along, you know." Quinn ruffled her pigtails. "In my role as your trusty assistant."

She laughed, then stopped short. "Have you seen Paige and Signe?"

"They're not far from here," he said. "They rescued me."

"Let's get back to them." She tried to wedge the tip of the damaged crutch into place, but it wouldn't cooperate, so she handed both pieces to Quinn and stood with just the old crutch.

"This way." He took a step, and a pained expression crossed his face.

"Your knee's hurt." Zora put her free arm around him. "We should help each other there."

"Good idea, little sis. What were you saying about premonitions?"

"There's no such thing as them. Only the brain replaying things it's already seen and heard, connecting them in random ways."

Quinn looked thoughtful. "Funny. I seem to recollect you telling me that, another time."

Together, the two of them hobbled across the slope until a pair of voices called out to them—one loud and excited, one soft and languid.

"I knew you could do it, Foxtails," Paige shouted, dashing over to thump Zora on the back.

Signe came over more slowly and gave Quinn a peck on the lips. "See," she said. "Destiny *did* choose you to help preserve harmony in the Hollows." She held up her goggles to Zora. "Thank you for these. They worked beautifully."

"Is the harbinger gone forever?" asked Paige, who had the beginnings of a black eye.

Zora shook her head. "Just trapped in its own world. But it can't come calling again till the next celestial alignment."

"No telling what's still wandering hereabouts on account of those lures from the ceremony." Quinn glanced in the direction of the Wastes. "We should lay low, unless you have other tricks up your sleeve."

"I've used my one rocket," said Zora. "And my spirit-shield is out of power." She brandished her damaged crutch at a gold-robed figure lurking in the shadows. "Watch out!"

Signe touched Zora's arm. "That's Lurana. She's with us."

It was the bartender from Comet Tail Hollow, looking woebegone—doubtless from contemplating the trouble in store for her when the Rangers found her sorry behind. "So, spirit-lover," said Zora, "got any bright ideas about where to hide till the sun comes up?"

Lurana made an angry face, then lowered her eyes. "There's another entrance to the mine, near the foot of the mountain. They'll have blocked the tunnel, but we might be able to take shelter in the mouth of it."

"Do you trust her?" Zora asked the others.

Quinn sized up the young Spiritist. "I don't think she's any more eager to die than we are. Right?" Lurana nodded fervently.

Paige gave her a push. "Move, then."

The five of them plodded downhill past rocks that loomed like chimneys and turrets. Paige lent Zora a shoulder, while Quinn and Signe leaned on one another. Lurana whined about her ribs a few times until Paige told her to knock it off. Apart from that, the night stayed eerily silent.

"There," said Lurana, pointing to a maw on the starlit mountainside.

Signe squinted at it. "No sign of any spirits."

"Here goes nothing," said Paige, taking a step forward.

The click of a shotgun resonated from the tunnel, and they all backed away.

Two figures emerged from the mine. The burly man from the Big Lake led with the twin barrels of his weapon.

The second figure held a banisher. Zora seethed at the sight of her.

Evelyn Fontaine smiled without showing any teeth. "Happy All Hollows, my young friends. I'm so pleased to find you on my doorstep."

21

QUINN HELD UP HIS EMPTY HANDS AND GLARED AT THE PHONY priest. Ms. Fontaine had traded her robe for a tweed cloak, her crown for a riding hat. Her shotgun-toting companion was wearing a pea coat over dungarees instead of his gold gown.

The woman flourished the banisher toward the aurora-fringed hills of the Wastes. "That way, if you don't mind."

"Shouldn't you be in your burrow?" Quinn asked, as they trudged away from the mine.

"It so happens that a pack of Rangers has infested my sanctum," said Ms. Fontaine. "I'm presently seeking new accommodations."

He consoled himself with the notion of Emerson Tate and his friends smashing through one of the mine's hidden entrances. "Your plan failed."

"Oh, I know that." She waved a hand at the star-filled sky. "My periscope gave me a spectacular view of the Wakening's advent—along with its unexpected ending." Her gaze fell on Zora. "I suppose you had something to do with that."

"That's right," said Zora. "We even saved your good-for-nothing lives. If not for us, the harbinger's playmates would've rooted you out like the rats you are."

The big man shifted his shotgun, and Quinn gave his sister a cautioning look.

"Surely we can resolve this situation peacefully," said Signe.

Ms. Fontaine raised her eyebrows. "You're looking livelier than when I last saw you. And still stuffed full of pollyannaish notions, bless your heart."

"You just keep on walking, kid," said the big man. "Unless you want to test your luck at recovering from a hole in your chest."

Quinn pressed his lips together and tried to think of a way to outfox their captors. Addie the Urchin would've created a diversion or used her opponents' weapons against them, but what could he do?

Lurana turned to her priest with an air of wounded bewilderment. "You left me behind."

"True." Ms. Fontaine shrugged. "I knew your faith would protect you."

"That woman's gall," Paige muttered to Quinn, "is starting to stick in my craw."

His too, but they were safe as long as Ms. Fontaine kept talking. And she might even slip up if given a chance. "So, Lady of the Spirits," he said. "Where's the rest of your flock?"

The woman brushed aside his sarcasm. "When the Rangers found the mine, they began rounding up my followers. The ensuing chaos gave me the opportunity to make a strategic retreat."

He'd guessed as much. "You abandoned them."

"Responsibility sometimes necessitates difficult choices." Ms. Fontaine stopped in front of a house-sized rock. "Speaking of which, I believe this is as far as our uninvited callers can come without hindering our escape."

The big man gestured with his shotgun. "Sit down, all of you."

"What if we don't?" Quinn asked. "You've only got two barrels." He stepped away from Signe so the man couldn't hit them both with a single shell. To his left, Paige slunk into the shadow of the rock.

"I shoot you, and the tomboy trying to outflank me, and then I use the stock of this thing to club your sister and your possum-playing girlfriend upside their skulls. How would you like that?"

Quinn sat on the ground, with his back to the rock. Zora, Paige, and Signe did the same, though Paige's expression was mutinous. "You, too," Ms. Fontaine told Lurana.

As the young Spiritist started weeping again, Zora slipped a small object into Quinn's hand. *A lure,* she mouthed. He closed his fingers around the device to conceal it.

"Mind your elder," said the big man, aiming his shotgun at Lurana. She clammed up and cowered in the dirt.

Ms. Fontaine snapped her fingers. "I'm curious to see what's in your backpack, Ms. Coldiron."

Zora removed the pack and gave it to Quinn. "Only my latest, most brilliant invention," she said. "I bet you'd never figure out on your own how it works."

While all eyes were on his sister, Quinn activated the lure and slid it into the pack. Turnabout's fair play, he told himself as he stood and approached their captors.

"It's a stink-ray," Zora went on, with an innocent smile. "It runs on methane from cow flatulence. It's out of fuel now, but you could try sticking it up your—"

"Hush, you vulgar child." Ms. Fontaine raised her palm. "I'm certain I can reverse-engineer anything you've built, just as I did with this." She flaunted the banisher in her other hand, and Quinn snuck a look at the weapon: one orange light, for Signe.

Ms. Fontaine took the pack from him. "You may resume a sitting position, young man." She inspected her hostages, passing right on by Paige and Lurana to linger in front of Quinn, Zora, and Signe. "Whatever shall we do with these nuisances?"

The big man's eyes glinted. "I say we kill them as a goodbye message to the Rangers, the Spotters, and anyone else who might think to cross us again."

Ice trickled down Quinn's spine. Paige scrunched like a panther about to spring, but Zora caught her by the wrist and shook her head. Signe was watching a point in the distance, seemingly entranced by a scene visible only to her.

"It might be wise to eliminate my competition in subduing the spirits," said Ms. Fontaine. "Then again, it would be a shame to extinguish such talents. An engineering prodigy. A natural-born seer. And the boy reminds me a bit of my own" — she left the sentence unfinished. "Quite the dilemma."

A second orange dot silently lit up on the banisher, but she didn't so much as glance at it. No beeps, Quinn thought. Not since the dunking in the lake. The woman hadn't fixed that.

A crash came from the direction of the Wastes, as if a hundred-year-old tree had fallen in the forest.

"More Rangers, you suppose?" asked the big man.

Ms. Fontaine looked across the spur of the mountain. "Perhaps." She handed Zora's pack to him and gripped the banisher with both hands. "Go spy out what that was."

"If you try to run," the big man warned his captives, "I'll

have no qualms about shooting you in the back." He slung the pack over his shoulder, holstered his shotgun, and set to climbing the limestone monolith.

When another bulb came to life on the banisher, as soundlessly as the last one had, Quinn began doubting the wisdom of his and Zora's gambit with the lure.

"Can you tell what it is?" Ms. Fontaine called up to the big man.

"Not yet," he shouted.

A roar rolled across the mountainside. Quinn looked at his sister, and she looked at him. The two of them knew that sound all too well.

Ms. Fontaine finally noticed the cluster of orange lights on the banisher. One of her eyes twitched, almost imperceptibly. "That's a complication," she said to herself.

The roar came again, but closer. Signe stared into the darkness through her broken glasses. "I see it," she whispered.

"To perceive reality clearly," Ms. Fontaine mused, "is a gift, but also a curse." She took a few steps back from the monolith.

As Quinn's blood pumped faster, he imagined the spirit-lure pulsing inside the pack. "Get ready to run," he said in a low voice. Zora, Paige, and Signe all nodded. Lurana wiped her nose, then nodded, too.

When a glow appeared above the rim of the slope, Ms. Fontaine turned her back on them and stole away into the woods.

At the third roar, Quinn grabbed Zora's hand and pulled her to her feet while Paige helped Signe up. They set off for the mine as fast as they could stagger, with Lurana tagging along at their heels.

The shotgun boomed from the top of the rock. Quinn flinched, but it was Paige and Signe who went sprawling into the underbrush. His heart stuttered as he hunched down beside them. Not now, after they'd made it through so much together.

"We're okay." Paige gasped and tucked her injured hand under her armpit. "I tripped, is all."

Behind them, the Spiritist's hulking silhouette stood out against a green-lit background. That man had wanted to kill them, Quinn reminded himself.

Branches snapped from the trees, and the shotgun boomed again. A shining avalanche swept toward the limestone monolith, flattening everything in its path. The big man let out a terrified bellow, and then the hount rammed him.

Quinn ran, ignoring the agony coursing through his knee. His sister's breaths came in ragged sobs.

"Look," Signe called out.

He turned his head, expecting to see the hount bearing down on them, but it had curved around the rock to flow back the way it had come. The body of the big man hung limply from one of its frayed tentacles.

Paige clutched her side with her left arm and inhaled. "I reckon he was enough of a meal for it."

With one last roar, the spirit vanished into the forest. When the sound died away, Zora swore and pointed down the slope. "There she is."

Quinn scanned the mountainside until he spotted a tall, graceful figure: Evelyn Fontaine, striding northward by the light of the aurora. She saluted them with the banisher and then continued on her way.

Did the woman have another lair somewhere beyond the Hollows? *The spirits killed my brother and my fiancé on one of our expeditions to the Wastes*, she'd said.

"Her fate will find her out there," said Signe. "Let's get back to the mine."

They retraced their steps to the dark mouth of the tunnel. As Paige drew near it, two short whistles split the night. A ribbon of light undulated across the slope, and a moldy smell reached Quinn's nostrils.

You again, he thought.

"Tangle," Zora shouted. Signe grabbed at her indigo goggles, but the spirit was already cannonballing toward them.

Violet exploded in front of Quinn's face, and a trail of smoke wafted past Zora on a gust of foul wind. Their father rushed out of the mine with a banisher-pistol raised high, its muzzle still crackling with energy. Captain Flores was beside him, holding a grenade in each hand.

Zora flapped her free arm. "The other half—"

A loud bam over Quinn's shoulder interrupted her.

"Howdy," drawled Emerson Tate, from the crook of a tree. "Good thing I listened to Ms. Zora's tale about how y'all beat the one in Saltpeter Hollow."

"Quinn. Zora." Their father drew up short of them. "I'm so glad you're all right." His expression turned grave. "The Wakening . . ."

"Hey, Dad." Quinn limped into the mine and sat on the rocky floor. "It's already come and gone. Zora stopped it."

His sister joined him on the ground. "Quinn helped me. Paige and Signe, too."

Captain Flores bowed her head and whispered a few words

of an old hex-chant to herself. Then she smiled. "Everyone, stand back from the entrance." At her signal, Ranger Tate pulled a lever on the wall, and a metal door slid down to seal them inside the mine.

"That should keep out any more roamers," said the captain. "As for the Spiritists, we've caught them all except half a dozen or so." She narrowed her eyes at Lurana. "And there's one of the missing ones."

"Two died out on the mountain tonight," Quinn told her. "The last we saw of their leader, she was headed for the Wastes."

"And an elemental got the Spotter who was helping them," said Zora, with a shudder.

"Otis?" asked their father. She nodded, and he fell silent again.

"Ms. Zora." Ranger Tate put on a stern face. "Shouldn't you and your friends be in Lightning Bug Hollow?"

"We snuck out to save Quinn," said Paige. "And the Hollows. Sorry about that."

The Ranger laughed. "I'm not exactly complaining right now, though your boss and Ms. Zora's mother may feel differently."

"As far as I'm concerned," said Captain Flores, "you four deserve some songs written about you."

"I know a banjoist who can play them," added Ranger Tate. "Once everything's squared away here, I may pay him a visit."

"I think you should." Zora grinned, and Quinn wondered whether she'd finally taken a liking to music.

"Y'all rest here for a spell," said Captain Flores. "Ranger Tate can help with anything you need." She took Lurana by the elbow. "I've got a cell waiting for you right this way." The young Spiritist went with her meekly.

"What'll happen to her?" asked Quinn. "She did help us tonight. After conspiring to murder us, but still."

Ranger Tate rubbed his chin. "Y'all reckon the Judges should give her a second chance?"

"Maybe," said Zora.

"I can't rightly say," put in Paige.

"Yes," said Signe. "If she keeps working to earn it."

Quinn looked at his father's haggard face, and then he nodded.

Once they'd caught their breath, Ranger Tate picked up a lantern and led them through the labyrinth of the mine. A winding tunnel brought them up to Evelyn Fontaine's mansion and into her gallery of spirit photographs.

"Secret passageways," said Zora, in a tone of grudging admiration. "So that's how she hid from you."

"Feel free to take a look around," the Ranger told them.

Paige found the bourbon in the grand study. "This ought to take the edge off my broken hand," she said, and swigged straight from the bottle.

"I can bring you to our medic to get that fixed up," offered the Ranger.

"Peachy." She held up the bottle. "Anybody else want to try this?"

Quinn took it and drank a sip that burned his tongue on its way down. "Before you go," he said. "I wanted to tell you something."

"What's that?" asked Paige.

"Thank you for risking your life to save me." He looked her

in the eyes. The left one had swollen partway shut. "You're a good friend."

She gave him a half-hug. "I missed you, Pine-Box." Her voice dropped. "For what it's worth, I think your new honey might just be a good match for you." On her way out of the room, she gave Zora the bourbon and a poke on the shoulder. "You deserve a shot of this, Foxtails."

Ranger Tate shook his head as he trailed after Paige. "Didn't count on all this when I busted a pair of teenagers chasing after spirits."

Signe came over and took Quinn's hands. By the electric candlelight, he could see the flakes of dead skin peeling from the blisters on her face. He squeezed her fingers. The revenants in his grandma's tales always disappeared back to their graves at the end, but Signe stayed right where she was.

"You know," she said, "Paige and I had plenty of time to talk on the journey here. She has lots of stories about you."

"Flattering ones, I hope." He felt shy now that the danger was over.

"Diverting ones," said Signe. "I'm off to look for a shower. You three are due for a family reunion." She let go of his hands and set out on her search.

Zora plopped onto one of the couches, folding her legs beneath herself so that her boots rested on the velvet cushions. Quinn sat beside her, while their father took the couch across from them.

"You followed me," Quinn said to him. "After I left your house. And you found Signe."

"Yes." Their father looked even wearier—or maybe older—than he had back in Sassafras Hollow. "If I hadn't run off all those years ago, instead of facing my troubles head on, maybe things would've worked out better."

"They worked out okay tonight," said Zora.

"Because of you two." Their father pulled out his pipe. "I'll understand if you don't want to see any more of me come tomorrow, but if you do"—he tapped the pipe against his palm— "I'd like to try to start over."

A watchful stillness filled the room, and the antlered woman in the stained glass window seemed to stare down at them.

Quinn let all his old anger build up in his chest before he breathed out. When he looked at his sister, she motioned for him to go first.

"I'll think on it," he said.

"Same here," said Zora.

"I appreciate that." Their father stood. "In the meantime, can I do anything for the two of you?"

"Could you get our horses and wagon?" Zora asked. "I mean, your horses and wagon. Paige stashed them at the bottom of the mountain."

"I'll fetch them here. And they're still yours." Their father put his pipe back in his pocket and left them alone with one another.

Zora leaned on Quinn's shoulder. "Didn't you tell me you'd 'think on it' when I first asked you to go spirit-hunting with me?"

"You have a good memory." He patted her head. "Nifty bit of misdirection while I planted the lure in the pack."

"You were quick on the uptake there, big brother. And for someone who didn't know an etherscope from an ectospectrometer a few moons ago, you're awfully clever with spirit-tech." She pushed herself up with her good crutch. "Now that I'm inside this mansion, I can't resist trying to find that woman's workshop. If she hadn't been so underhanded, she might've made for a fine lab partner. Not on my level, but who is?"

"Nobody, little sis."

Zora picked up her ruined crutch from where Quinn had stowed it. "I'll fix this, too."

He shut his eyes until Signe returned. Her hair was wet, and she'd cleaned the dirt from her spiderweb-patterned dress. "The shower upstairs is sublime," she announced.

A gold-plated clock chimed out twelve notes. "Midnight," she said. "What are your plans now that All Hollows is over?"

"I figure Zora and I should track down all the roamers the harbinger and the Spiritists riled up this summer." He hesitated. "Would you like to join us? You could use your spirit-gaze to herd them toward the Wastes, and then Zora and I could banish any stubborn ones."

Signe snuggled up against him. "I foresee us working together to restore balance in the Hollows."

"First, though, I need a breather," Quinn said. "What with being locked away under a mountain, getting offered up as a sacrifice, and . . . well, I've handled my share of corpses at my mom's funeral home, but until a few days ago I'd never actually seen anybody die." He ran his fingers through Signe's hair. "I thought I'd watched you die, too, and that was the worst of all."

"Perhaps we could take a vacation to recuperate," she said. "I've never been to Hot Springs Hollow."

"Me neither." He kissed her gently on her sunburnt lips.

Quinn awoke to a green-tinged sunbeam on his face. He grumbled and tried to roll over, but he wasn't in his bed, or any other bed. Also, something—someone—had pinned him against the couch: Signe, asleep on his shoulder.

"Good morning," said a voice he hadn't heard since leaving Cascade Hollow—was that thirteen days ago?—with Zora.

"Mom?" He goggled at her. "What are you doing here?" She was sitting on the opposite couch with an amused expression. Judging by the light shining through the stained glass window behind her, the sun had risen a good while ago.

"I got your letter." His mother said it as though that explained everything.

"But how'd you find me?"

"I drove the hearse to Lightning Bug Hollow expecting to find you there. Instead, I ran into Zora's mother and Mr. Epps leaving for Clack Mountain. They invited me to help them search for you, your sister, and your friends."

Signe yawned. "Quinn, who's—oh!" She sat bolt upright, put on her glasses, and hastily smoothed the folds of her dress. "Ms. Prosser?"

His mother nodded, then carried on speaking as unflustered as ever. "When we reached Comet Tail Hollow yesterday evening, we met a woman and her daughter who said they knew you, and a tattooed man who'd talked to Zora and her friends. He used one of your sister's inventions to drive away a swarm of spirits that came from the north, and afterwards we watched the strange light show in the sky."

"That was the Wakening," Quinn said. "Or would've been, at any rate."

"I know. Your father told us the whole story when we arrived here a few hours ago. I gather I underestimated Zora."

She leaned forward and smiled. "And I'm proud of what you've done."

His face went warm.

"I could tell you never really wanted to be an undertaker," his mother continued. "This new family venture you've launched with Zora seems to fit you better. I'm sure I can find an apprentice to help around the funeral home. As a matter of fact, Paige's little sister seems rather keen on the job." She coughed. "Now, shouldn't you introduce me to your friend here?"

"Mom, this is Signe Janasdottir," said Quinn. "She helped rescue me from a sinister cult and the horde of spirits they summoned from the Wastes."

Signe stopped straightening her hair and bobbed her head.

"It's a pleasure to meet you," his mother said. "And I love your dress. You should visit Cascade Hollow, so I can make you dinner."

"I'd like that, ma'am," said Signe. When she reached for Quinn's hand, he entwined his fingers with hers.

22

ZORA LOOKED AT THE SCORCH MARKS ON THE CRUTCH SHE'D mended last night. At the splint on Paige's hand. At the copper pipes and brass cogs laid out in perfect rows along the shelves of Evelyn Fontaine's workshop. Anywhere but straight ahead.

"You lied to my face," said her mom. "And ran off as soon as I turned my back." Her voice reminded Zora of the Big Lake: calm, but only on the surface.

Paige fidgeted with an etherscope she'd picked up from one of the tables, a chrome model that would've sold for a hundred bits at the Spring Fair Exposition. Mr. Epps watched her with his hands held behind his back.

"You're coming straight home with me," Zora's mom went on. "First thing tomorrow morning. To stay." She paused, as if expecting an argument, and then sighed. "At least till you turn sixteen."

Zora slumped onto a bench. Half a year, but she could spend it tinkering in the barn and testing the effects of fiddle string vibrations on the wisps in the sinkhole. Maybe she'd even write to Mr. Slocum about his business proposition.

Her mom sat next to her. "I was so worried about you," she whispered. "I kept thinking of how Vern and I came home that night eight years ago to find you under your bed, hiding from spirits in the woods." Her voice broke. "Of how I wasn't there to keep you safe."

"I'm sorry." Zora hugged her mom tighter than she had in years—tighter than when she'd quit school, or when they'd buried Static—and then turned to Mr. Epps. "You can blame me for dragging Paige here. Please go easy on her."

At the sound of her name, Paige stopped playing with the etherscope. The bruise around her eye had gone from purple to greenish-gray.

"Ms. Zhu." The Spotter stared down at her with a severe expression. "You flouted my injunction to remain in Lightning Bug Hollow."

"Yes." Paige lowered her head. "And I won't kick up a fuss if you—"

He silenced her with an upraised finger. "I have devised a suitable sanction for your transgression, my pixilated apprentice." The corners of his lips turned upward. "You shall spend this autumn at the athenaeum, proofreading and indexing the second edition of my *Taxonomy*. If you fulfill this task to my satisfaction, I will consider your return to fieldwork."

"Thank you, sir. I'll get right on—I mean, I shall endeavor to complete my assigned duties in an expeditious manner."

"With that out of the way," said Mr. Epps, "allow me to express my profound gratitude to both of you for delivering us from a new Wakening." He surveyed Ms. Fontaine's assortment of argon electrodes, spark-gap transmitters, and multi-wave oscillators. "I must say, the owner of this domicile possessed an impressive laboratory."

"I prefer mine," Zora said. "Even if it's full of hay and drafty in the wintertime."

Her mom pointed to a thick glass tube that spanned the length of one table. "This looks like a barrel for a cannon-sized banisher."

"I'm bringing it home, along with everything else in here." Zora had staked claim to the lab's contents as her fee for the dahoo-hunt, plus expenses. "Captain Flores said I could."

"If that'll help keep you occupied." Her mom peered through her bifocals. "I see you're wearing your hair down."

"I decided the pigtails were obsolete."

"I like it this way. You know, I really do have the smartest, prettiest, bravest daughter in the whole wide Hollows." She touched the tip of Zora's nose. "My grown-up fox kit."

"Oh, Mom," said Zora, but her heart swelled like a puffball.

A pair of familiar neighs outside drew Zora to the front hallway. She met Quinn at the threshold, and they walked to the stable together.

Their dad was stroking Undine's mane. "I missed these two," he said, as he fed Ursula an apple. Then he glanced out the window at Signe's wagon and Ms. Prosser's hearse. "Now that your mothers are here, I should be on my way. But you can come see me anytime, if you want. Or write, and I'll visit."

Zora nodded, and Quinn did, too.

"One more thing." Their dad handed her the banisher-pistol he'd used to shoot the tangle. "You can have this back."

"Take it with you," she said. "Who knows if you'll need it someday."

That evening, the seven of them plundered a rack of venison from the mansion's refrigerator, cooked themselves a feast, and ate in the same dining room where Ms. Fontaine had laid her trap for Zora and Quinn. Paige spent the meal pumping Ms. Prosser for the latest gossip from Cascade Hollow, while Signe talked optometry with Zora's mom and Mr. Epps quizzed Quinn about all the spirits he'd seen.

Zora sat mum, feeling restless and oddly detached from the conversations going on around her. She watched Quinn and Paige laugh at stories from their old schooldays. She watched her mom and the Spotter sneak looks at one another across the table. She watched Signe blink and stammer when Ms. Prosser asked about her plans for the fall. The twin candelabras shone gold light on all their faces.

Outside the bay window, the sun was sinking toward the hills on the horizon.

As everyone dug into bowls of berries with cream, Zora's mom waved her spoon at Quinn. "So, young man, didn't you promise to keep my daughter out of trouble?"

"I promised to *try*, ma'am."

"Knowing Zora, I might as well have asked you to build a perpetual motion machine out of sticks, or fly to the moon on a black powder rocket, or scry the future through a geode."

"I wouldn't know about machines or rockets," said Signe, "but I do believe in precognition."

"An intriguing concept," said Mr. Epps. "One of my

colleagues has theorized that exposure to certain rare types of spirits can induce a form of psychic temporal displacement resulting in vivid sensory experiences."

Zora closed her eyes and called up the memory of a place she'd never visited in her waking life. The Wastes lay all around her, covered in greenish snow. Thunderous footfalls approached through the mountains.

She opened her eyes again and took a bite of berries.

Ms. Prosser frowned. "Next you'll be telling us folks can speak to ghosts through a planchette and talking board, like my mother used to swear."

"That's not so preposterous," said Paige. "After all, Foxtails here has figured out a way to raise the dead."

"I'm walking proof," agreed Signe, before Zora could protest.

The Spotter adjusted his round-lensed glasses. "By the way, Ms. Janasdottir, we owe you an apology for commandeering your wagon to journey here. The direness of the circumstances compelled us to do so."

"You've chosen a charming color scheme for the interior," said Zora's mom. "And you own quite the collection of novels. I took the liberty of browsing through a few on the way here."

"Which ones . . ." Signe blushed. "I'd be happy to loan you any of them."

After dinner, Zora's mom poured glasses of hard cider for Mr. Epps and Ms. Prosser. "I'm sure you kids have lots to talk about," she said, shooing the four teenagers toward the study. As Zora walked past the bookshelves, she looked up at the antlered figure in the stained glass window, but sunset had left it dark and dull.

"So," Quinn said, "Signe and I had a notion to track down the stray roamers left over from all the recent spirit weather. Can we count you in, little sis?"

His face fell when Zora shook her head. "I'm going back home for the next six moons," she said. "Mom's orders. But I'm sure you two can handle the job without me." She felt wistful already. "Come visit me, though. The goats in my lab aren't the best conversationalists."

"We will. And we'll be waiting for you to join us, seeing as how you're our team's brilliant inventor."

"What does that make me?" asked Signe.

"The fey young woman with mystical powers?" he said.

She beamed at him. "I rather like the sound of that."

"Which reminds me," Zora told Signe. "When you and my pulp-drunk brother drop by my neck of the woods, I'd like to run some experiments on your eyes to figure out how you—um—spookify spirits."

"*Signe*-fy them," corrected Paige. Then she giggled at her own pun.

Zora rolled her eyes. "While I'm at it, I'll build you a parasol with some special features. A compass, spirit-sensors, retractable blades for self-defense—you name it, and I'll add it."

"That would be lovely," said Signe.

"What about you?" Quinn asked Paige. "If you can wrangle a break from your training, your Spotter know-how sure would come in handy."

"We'd love for you to accompany us," Signe added.

"Sorry, but I'm off to Three Mounds to spend the fall blue-penciling my boss's doorstopper of a manuscript." Paige smirked. "Y'all will have to get by without a chaperone."

Signe crossed her legs and put on a prim face. "I suppose we'll manage."

As the others forged plans to reunite for the winter solstice, Zora slipped away to wander the mansion. The wainscoted hallways led her to a bathroom with marble floors, silver fixtures, and green trellised wallpaper. She stared into the mirror, then washed her face and dried it with the softest towel she'd ever used. The briar scratches on her chin had scabbed over, and the acne on her forehead had faded to a smattering of pink dots.

By the time she returned to the study, Quinn and Signe had cozied up on one of the couches. His arm was around her waist; her hand was resting on his knee. She'd taken off her cracked blue glasses, and he was reading a book to her: *Addie the Urchin versus the Enchantress of Electricity.*

Paige was fast asleep on the opposite couch.

Zora stood quietly, lost in thought. Maybe this year she'd talk her mom into bringing her to the Harvest Festival for once. Maybe she'd meet someone to dance with while the band played, or to hold hands with by the bonfire.

Or maybe she'd just stay home and listen to the radio while she worked in her lab.

Her brother closed the book, using his finger to mark his place. "We wondered where you went," he said. "Want to stay for the next chapter?"

"It's quite enthralling so far," said Signe.

"You two keep reading," Zora said. "I think I'll duck outside to clear my head."

Quinn corrugated his brow, which still bore a faint imprint where her crutch had struck it during their first spirit-hunt. "Are you sure you're all right?"

She nodded. "I'll see you tomorrow morning before I leave. No need to wait up for me, big brother."

"Good night, then, little sis."

Zora passed through the foyer, on into the crisp autumn evening. Crickets filled the air with chirps, and a fountain bubbled in the garden.

A stroll across the front yard brought her to the wagon that had been her home for the summer. When she climbed inside and turned on the light, she found the banisher-pistol. Her father had left it behind with two sealed envelopes. One had *Quinn* written on it; the other, *Zora*.

She picked up the letter for her and slid it into one of her pockets. She took the banisher-pistol, too, just in case.

Her braces chafed against her ankles as she walked to the edge of the summit. The sky had turned from deep blue to purple.

She sat on the grass and studied the darkening range of hills to the north. A breeze blew her hair across her face. The last of the sunlight faded, and the aurora rippled to life above the Wastes.

Evelyn Fontaine was still out there, and so were untold millions of spirits.

Far below, a glowing scar on the mountainside marked the grave of the man who'd sold out Nevan McBrain to the Spiritists. Zora silently composed her own epitaph for the hermit resting beneath the lake: *Here lies the greatest Spotter in the history of the Hollows. A leviathan slew him, but an elemental avenged him.*

A lone orange light appeared on her wrist-watcher, and a tiny green star winked from the woods. A boge. Probably a straggler drawn here last night by the lures.

As Zora raised the banisher-pistol, the boge floated toward her and then stopped, almost within spitting distance. She lined up her aim for an easy shot and tensed her finger on the trigger.

An owl hooted from a distant tree.

She let out her breath and relaxed her grip on the pistol. The boge drifted away into the night.

Vanquishing the spirits could wait, at least until next spring.

Zora took one last look at the Wastes and turned toward the mansion. Toward her friends, and her brother, and her mom. Toward the road that ended back at her own doorstep in Lightning Bug Hollow.

ZORA AND QUINN WILL RETURN IN

THE
SPIRIT WASTES

ACKNOWLEDGMENTS

I'm deeply grateful to my family for their support during the writing of this novel. My wife, parents, and brother gave me tough feedback along with constant encouragement, while my children spent countless hours with me searching for inspiration in graphic novels, animated television shows, goth rock, and heavy metal. I'm thankful to my beta readers—including Adrienne, Brian, Chris, Josh, Lydia, and Tricia—for their help in bringing Zora and Quinn's world to life. I'm also thankful to Nichole Bennett for her copyediting work, LeslieAnn Khoury of Lizard Ink Maps for capturing the spirit of the Hollows with her cartography, Bodie Dykstra for typesetting the book, and Stephanie Garcia for designing the Lockegee Books logo. Finally, I'm indebted to the makers of the original *Ghostbusters* movie for sparking my lifelong interest in paranormal investigations.

ABOUT THE AUTHOR

P. R. Brewer grew up on a fish farm in Rowan County, Kentucky, a short hike away from Cave Run Lake and a winding drive away from Clack Mountain (the site of sinister rituals, according to local legend). He currently lives in Delaware with his wife Barbara and their two children. In his day job, he teaches and writes about science and the media. His nonfiction work has appeared in *National Geographic*, *Skeptical Inquirer*, and various arcane journals. *The Spirit Hollows* is his first novel.

To learn more about Zora, Quinn, and the Hollows, visit www.prbrewer.com.